DAISY CHAINS

Daisy Chains

Samantha Evergreen

EST.   2019
BLKDOG

Thank you to Crystal Stanle, Del and Phill

CHAPTER 1

1975, Watkinsville, Georgia.

March 25th.

"**C**ome on Rose, we don't have all night you know," Lily called, sounding bored. Rose rolled her eyes and looked at herself one last time in the mirror. She had curled her brown hair to perfection so it sat high atop her head, looking just like the models in one of Daisy's magazines. Even her make-up had worked out tonight, her lips a deep red going with her dark blue eyeshadow.

"Rose, come on, we're going to be late!"

"Lily, chil. Daisy and Violet will wait for us," Rose replied, coming out of the bathroom and stepping into her bedroom. Her bare feet warmed by the white shag carpet Lily still sat on, painting her nails a bright yellow.

Rose wandered over to her closet and looked at the line of dresses. She let out a sigh and picked out a light blue one and slipped it on, the skirt going down to her knees. She stared down at her row of kitten heels and stepped into a black pair before turning around.

"Do I look ready?" she asked.

Lily glanced up, her pageboy hairstyle swaying around her head in a blonde halo. "Looks like it to me, thank god," she said, getting up to grab her backpack.

Rose did the same, picking up her bag just in time as they heard her mother's footsteps on the stairs. "Damn," Rose swore under her breath as her mother opened the door, her lavender perfume filling the room.

"Lily, Rose, there you are. I believe Daisy and Violet are waiting for you outside in that blue thing you call a truck."

"Thanks, Mrs. Waters," Lily said, making a break for the stairs. Rose moved to follow but was stopped by a hand catching her arm. She was spun around so she faced her mother, her blue eyes looking Rose up and down.

"Well, at least you look better than last time," her mother said, most likely referring to last month when she'd tried wearing a pair of jeans and a simple top. An outfit her mother made her throw away afterwards because it wasn't something she'd gotten her.

"Thank you, mother," Rose said, looking down feeling her cheeks pinken.

"Have some fun tonight Rosalina, but don't drink too much or you'll get a beer belly," her mother said with a smile.

"Yes, mother," Rose said making a break for the stairs, not daring to breathe until she was out in the darkening night.

Once outside, Rose stopped and took a deep breath of the night air, looking up to see Daisy already watching her from the front seat. Her green eyes and strawberry colored hair were alight with the last bits of sunshine as it blew around her small, pale face.

"There you are! Hurry up and jump in the back, we need to book it to Mark's if we want the good drinks," Daisy said, a bright smile on her pink lips.

Rose ran over to Violet's old baby blue truck and hopped into the back along with Lily who was already busy rifling through her bag, most likely looking for her cigarettes. As the engine started and they pulled away, she found what she was searching for and lit one up, the smoke swirling around them as they drove.

"You want one?" Lily said, offering one to Rose.

"You know I can't stand those things," Rose replied, wrinkling her nose at the smell. "They'll end up killing you someday."

"Oh, please. My mom smoked when she was pregnant with me and I'm fine." She breathed out the words with a puff of smoke.

"Are you sure about that?" Rose poked at her forehead. "Sometimes I'm not so sure there's anything up there."

Lily smacked her hand away with a smile and blew smoke at her. "Gross," Rose laughed, waving a hand around her face and Lily couldn't keep a little chuckle oh her own from escaping as she put her cigarette out on the bed of the truck.

* * *

They pulled up to Mark's house ten minutes later, but had to park a few blocks away, seeing as he was hosting the last party of spring break. Everyone knew it was the one to be at, because tomorrow would be the first day of school. It looked like everyone had gotten that message. It seemed everyone Rose had ever met was there.

She hopped down along with Lily and joined Daisy and Violet as they started heading for the two-story house that was blasting rock music. Teens of every age were coming and going, all with cups in hand.

"Oh, yeah, almost forgot I made these for you." Daisy handed Rose a crown made of chained daisies. Taking it, she placed it atop her head. Daisy handed one to Lily and Violet as well. Finally, she put on one herself, beaming like a child.

"They're beautiful," Violet said, tipping her's sideways, making Lily smile knowing it would piss off Daisy. Daisy just shook her head. The girl acted as if she were the mature one, always tired of playing childish games, when in reality she was the youngest, sixteen when the rest of them were seventeen.

Suddenly, Lily grabbed her hand, as Daisy did with Violet's, and they all dragging each other down the sidewalk until they were on the front path leading to the party's wide open door. The people around the entrance were all either talking or making out, so they had to dodge and weave just to make it inside.

When they finally did make it in, they found it wasn't much better. A large crowd, thirty or more, danced in the middle of the room. Even more lined the walls talking or doing so much worse.

"Welcome to Mark's Big Spring Break Blow Out Party! And, yes, you can take that however you want," Mark Hollow announced as he appeared before them. His hair was almost as long as Lily's, going down to his shoulders.

"Hello, Mark," Daisy said, carefully taking the drink he held out to her, "Love the outfit."

Mark glanced down at his light blue bell-bottoms and deep yellow V-neck, showingoff the little chest hair he had. Then, his gaze flicked back to her, checking her out. "Well, I could say the same of you Daisy doll. Love the oversized overalls."

"Thanks," Daisy continued to smile as she handed the cup off to Lily, not taking her eyes off him.

"If you don't like the drinks," Mark offered, "We have soda in the kitchen." Rose knowingly lowered her gaze, recognizing the reason for the growing tension in the room, until Mark turned his attention to her.

"Oh, Rose, I just remembered. I saw your brother somewhere around here."

She blinked, surprised that he would even speak to her, given that he hadn't in over a year. Still, the fact her brother was unexpectedly there took priority.

"What do you mean? He shouldn't be home from college until October."

"Well, go tell him that. Maybe then he'll stop drinking all my damn beer."

"Where is he?" she asked, her voice small.

"In the kitchen," Mark said, taking a long drink from his own cup.

Rose bit her lip and turned to her friends. They all looked uncomfortable just standing there.

"Go have some fun," Rose waved them away.

"You don't have to tell me twice, girl," Lily said and quickly moved deeper into the house with Violet and Daisy following after her. Daisy was the only one to look back at her, a hint of worry showing on her face as the group made their way into the crowd of dancing bodies.

Rose turned, heading for the kitchen, slowly making her way through the waves of people. She stopped as she reached the doorway. She found her brother immediately even if he hadn't noticed her yet, too busy making out with one of the cheerleaders at her school.

"Hey, what the hell are you doing here?" She called to him watching as Jason pulled back from the woman with a smile on his lips. He met her gaze, his blue eyes as dark as his hair.

"Hey there, little sis. Miss me?"

Rose tried to give him a hard look, but she couldn't help the grin that broke out across her face. "You didn't answer me. And weren't you dating a girl named Linda Cross?" Rose asked.

Jason pushed the girl away at the mention of the name. The cheerleader gave an indignant huff, stomping away, leaving them alone.

"And you didn't answer me, Rosey. Did you miss me?"

"Of course I did, loser, but why are you home so early? You've only been gone three months."

"What? A brother can't come and check up on his kid sister just because?"

She raised an eyebrow at him and he let out a loud laugh. "I just have some business to take care of with dad, but I heard Mark was throwing his famous spring break party and just had to come and see his last one."

Jason was right. Mark became locally famous for his parties these last five years. His parents always left him on his own for the week before school started, going on their yearly anniversary trip. But that would all be over after this party, since he would be starting his first day as a police officer this week.

"How is mother by the way?" Jason asked, taking a drink from one of the open cans that sat, abandoned, on the yellow countertop.

"She's been worse since you left," Rose said honestly, her gaze dropping to the floor.

"I'm sorry Rosey, maybe I can talk to her. For some reason she'll listen to me," A pained look crossed over his face.

"There's no point. She'll just go right back to it after you leave." Rose sighed, tipping her head up to stare into the kitchen's overhead light.

For a moment neither of them said anything, both knowing it was no use rehashing the same issue they had gone over too many times to count. The silence was finally broken by Lily who came running in, beer in hand. From the looks of her, it was her second.

"Rose, there you are. You have to come and see this! Tommy is doing body shots off of May," Lily words were slurred and, before Rose knew what was happening, she was being pulled away from her brother into the TV room. Immediately she was handed a beer and found that yes, Tommy Johnson was in fact, doing body shots off of May Jacobson, surrounded by about five other men who were all lining up to take their turns.

Rose could only shake her head at them, eyes pinned to her drink, before she downed it. The taste was bitter but she grabbed another one anyway, and another after that. She drank until she couldn't stand up without rocking from side to side. The next thing she knew there were people chanting her name as well as Jeff Marlow's. Then somehow the two of them were kissing hard and fast, touching each other, as Rose wondered what happened to get her to that point. But as she kept drinking and dancing, with men she wouldn't remember the names of in the morning, she found that she cared less and less as the hours passed them by.

The whole night felt unreal to her because, in reality, she would never let herself do this . . . kiss random men, drink until she could barely see straight. But her mother's words kept playing back in her head and maybe her mother was right . . . act like a normal teenager who hadn't been missing for six months for once.

Well, maybe coming home drunk would make her mother happy. Unlikely, but the thought of her mother being happy for once almost made her want to laugh.

"Hey, Rose, are you spaced out or what, girl?" Violet asked, bringing her back down to earth. She looked away from where she had been diligently counting the boards of dark wooden paneling hanging on the wall only to see a mostly sober Violet. "Did you seen where Daisy went?"Violet questioned her as Lily came over to stand next to them, her hair a mess and make-up now ruined.

"Wasn't she with you?" Lily asked, sucking on another cigarette.

"No, she went to go get me another drink but never came back," Violet said, looking at them with worried eyes.

"I'm sure she's just getting it on with someone," Lily offered.

"She most likely went outside to pick some daisies or just got tired and had to go home," Rose added, knowing how tired Daisy got at times.

"Yeah," Violet said, looking tired as well.

"Want to look around, and if we can't find her after fifteen minutes we go home?" Rose asked.

"Why not?" Lily gave a shrug a little off balance.

"I'll take the upstairs," Rose said, and with that, they broke away. Violet headed for the basement turned smoking room for whatever you wanted and Lily went to go check the kitchen and backyard.

Rose made her way through the crowd of people who sat on the steps, halfway-conscious, until she reached the first bedroom. She opened the door and found two bodies on one of the beds doing...well, what you do on a bed besides sleep, before quickly closing it as quietly as she could, her cheeks heating.

She moved on to the next room, finally only an empty guest bedroom decked in bright green wallpaper and an orange carpet that hurt her eyes. She shut that door and moved to open the next one in the long hallway, but stopped when she heard her brother's voice.

"What do you want me to tell you, Mark?" Jason hissed, his voice rising, "What do you want me to say? 'Sorry?' Is that it?"

"No, I want you to tell me why. Why are you here?" Mark asked, sounding angrier than Rose had ever heard him, "You left without a word after months of hating me."

"All I can tell you is that my plans changed and you don't want to know the reasons."

Suddenly the door swung open and Rose came face-to-face with her brother, looking disheveled. "Rosey, what are you doing?" Jason asked looking down at her, anger washing away in seconds.

"I -- I was just looking for Daisy. We want to go home but we need to find her," Rose stammered, her words coming out too loud.

"How much have you been drinking?" He suddenly asked, with eyebrows raised.

"A beer or two," Rose lied, and it was a pretty bad one at that given how poorly she was doing at walking at the moment. She'd almost tripped over her own feet as she tried taking a step back, and would have fallen on her face if it weren't for Mark catching her arm to keep her upright.

"I'm taking you home," Jason said, taking her from Mark. "I -- I still need to find Daisy," Rose tried to argue with her brother, looking up into a pair of blue eyes that matched her own.

He began pulling her downstairs, "If your friends haven't found her by now she most likely went home, Rosey."

She didn't respond, too preoccupied with trying to make sure that she didn't fall over.

As they reached the bottom step, Lily and Violet approached them, "Rose, did you find her?"

"No, she didn't, and now I'm taking all of you home," Jason announced to the group.

"But-" Violet started, but he cut her off.

"Like I told Rosey, if you haven't found her by now someone most likely took her home already."

Jason took Violet's car keys and started for the door.

"She wouldn't do that," Lily sounded defensive, "Daisy would tell us if she wanted to leave early."

He shoved people out of his way as they made their way outside, "What can I tell you? Maybe she hooked up with someone and they went somewhere more private."

Rose made a face, but the world had started to rock and she felt as if she was going to vomit, so she stayed silent. The two of them made it outside into the night air, Violet and Lily following close behind. Her friends quickly moved out of the way, however, as Rose pushed past them and emptied her stomach into the grass at their feet.

She heard a few people laugh, along with a few other nasty comments, but her brother's voice rang out, clear as day telling her to meet them at the truck when she was done.

Rose was left alone. After a few more minutes of clearing out her system, she looked up with blurry eyes to see one of the daisy chains Daisy had made just lying there in the middle of the yard, broken and stepped on.

She looked around, half-expecting to spot those familiar green eyes. See that familiar smile on lips telling her how happy her mother will be to learn her daughter was coughing her guts up like a normal teen. But she saw nothing, and her headache kept her from wanting to check things out further.

So she didn't. Rose turned away, and oh god how she would hate herself for that. Because no matter how much pain she was in, she should have looked for Daisy. Daisy had been there for her through so much, and what did she do when she was missing? Nothing.

The drive home was quiet as she sat in the front seat next to her brother, the soberest one out of everyone. They had already dropped off Lily and Violet, Jason telling the latter that he would drive out tomorrow morning and return her truck.

"I knew I shouldn't have left for college," he said, breaking the silence, "I knew you wouldn't be able to handle that big of a change, not so soon after-"

"Stop," Rose cut him off. "Jason. I'm fine."

"Really? You call drinking until you throw up 'fine?'"

"I was just doing what mother has been wanting me to do. Act like the last year didn't happen."

"I'll talk with her." Jason said, his voice softer.

"Go ahead and try, but like I said before. She'll never get over it. I'll always be the crazy girl that made her mother look bad."

Before Jason could reply they pulled into their driveway and she jumped out of the truck, running into the house and up the stairs.

She heard their parents call up after her, but she slammed her door and fell into bed. Rose knew if Jason hadn't been there, their mother would have barged in and demanded to know what happened.

But Jason was there. She fell asleep to the sound of her mother's excitement over just how surprised and happy she was to see him, her golden boy.

* * *

The next morning, Rose awoke to a headache that only seemed to get worse as she got up and showered, the too bright sun hurting her eyes.

She could barely think as she dressed, throwing on her new lime green dress and red heels, a pair of rounded sunglasses perched high on her nose.

"There's my angel," she heard her father coo as she walked into the kitchen and sat down at their old oak table, a piece of furniture far too big for her family of four.

"Good morning, dad. How was work last night?"

"Don't try and change the subject, Rosalina," her mother snapped, sliding a plate of eggs in front of her before moving to sit down across from her father at the end of the table. Mother immediately started picking at her own food, her blue house dress fanning out around over her knees, blonde hair curled up in waves that looked perfect as always.

"Tell us what happened last night."

Rose took a breath and turned to her mother with a smile, "It was everything you could have asked for in a spring break party, Mother. Drinking and dancing to music you couldn't stand. I was the perfect little party girl. I drank until I couldn't stand."

"That's good to hear. And did anyone ask about last year?" her mother asked coolly.

"Of course not mother, You did amazing work telling everyone I was just seeing our aunt." Rose looked down at her food, her face warm.

"Don't act as if I did it for myself, Rosalina. I did what I needed to for this family." As her mother took a sip of coffee, Rose noticed the dark bags under her eyes for the first time. Rose opened her mouth to reply, but decided it was better to not start things all over again. Daisy was right, it wasn't worth her time. And her mother always seemed to get so much joy out of it.

"I need to get going," Rose announced and got up, only having eaten half of her eggs. She really didn't care, though, as she grabbed her book bag and headed outside so she could spend the ten minutes it took Violet to pick her up in peace and quiet. Sitting on the steps, and away from her mother's eyes, the early spring air could freeze her to the bone, but it still felt better than listening to her mother's voice go around and around in her head.

Rose stood as Violet pulled up, jumping into the old brown passenger seat and glancing over to see her friend was looking as bad as Rose felt. Her normally high waves were down and didn't look to have been washed. Her brown eyes had deep bags under them, standing out even against her olive skin.

"You look awake," Rose joked, passing Violet her sunglasses. She took them and yawned as they pulled away, heading for Daisy's house.

"I was up all last night. My dad wasn't too happy about Jason taking my truck."

"I'm sorry Violet. He wasn't drinking, was he?"

"No, luckily, but he wasn't . . . happy." Rose looked at her, all humor gone, "You know my offer still stands right?"

Violet said nothing and, Rose knew why. Violet couldn't stand charity. Couldn't stand the thought of being given things for free. She worked a part-time job at a bookshop six days a week to buy her own clothes, school supplies, sometimes even food, when her dad didn't remember.

But the day Violet came to school covered in fist-sized bruises, Rose had offered to take her in.

She didn't care that her mother wouldn't like it, they had more than enough money to help. But Violet had given her a flat out "no." Her father hadn't meant to hurt her, she insisted. And she wouldn't leave him. Not after her mother had just passed away a few years back.

"You already know my answer," Violet said with finality as they pulled up to Daisy's house. Rose didn't argue, looking out of the yellowing window at the bright green grass of their friends yard. The one filled with the wild white daisies that Daisy used to make her chains.

The memory of another spring day in second grade came to her . . . the time when Daisy had tried teaching Rose how to make them. Unfortunately, she had never gotten the hang of it. They would always fall apart at the lightest breeze, but Daisy would always try to make it all better by throwing her own chain away. It would just lay there as they stayed together in the grass, Daisy braiding her hair in the grass, making her smile.

"Why the hell isn't she coming out? We can't be late on the first day back," Violet grumbled, eyeing the large house with frustration.

"I don't know," Rose answered, confused herself, Daisy was almost always on time.

"Let's go knock." Violet started getting out and Rose quickly followed after her.

They ran up the grassy path and stopped on the doorstep. Rose gave the doorbell a few quick rings, but heard only Mrs. Young's gray, husky barking to go away.

"Her mother probably took her to school this morning," Violet offered with a shrug, turning back for the truck.

No, Rose thought, No, she would have called and told me she was going to school with her mother. She had a bad feeling, and it had been growing since last night. Still, she couldn't say that now, could she? It sounded crazy, and that was the last thing she needed.

"Come on, Rose, let's get going," Violet called out to her. Rose gave one last look at the door before she turned and ran for the truck.

They rode to school in silence, as Violet was too busy driving and Rose was lost in her own thoughts. She was unsure of why she had such a bad feeling in the pit of her stomach, but hoped it was just some lingering effects of her actions last night.

She was brought back to reality as they pulled into the school's parking lot, hopping out to make their way towards their high school's wide open doors and into the main hallway.

Suddenly, Rose was jumped on from behind. She made a sound and found Lily standing there, a lively smile on her face as if they hadn't gotten drunk the night before.

"Morning. Sunshine," Violet said opening her locker to put her books away. Rose proceeded to do the same.

"Oh lighten up the both of you. It's not like it's your first time with a hangover. Remember last Halloween?"

"Barely, " Violet admitted, tired, and Lily laughed like a little kid. Rose smiled a bit to herself before that sick feeling hit her again, making her stop and look around.

Teens passed them by, going to class or their own lockers, but she didn't see who she was looking for.

"Have you seen Daisy today?" Rose asked, glancing over at Lily who was now leanimg against her yellow locker looking down at her nails. She looked up and gave Rose a confused look.

"What do you mean? She came with you guys, right?"

"No," Rose saif feeling worry take hold of her, "We went to her house, but she wasn't there."

Lily frowned. "That's weird. Do you think she's staying in with a hangover?"

"No way," Violet argued. "Her mother would kill her if she tried skipping on the first day."

"More like she would hate herself if she missed a day of school. Remember that time she almost passed out in math when she had a high fever?" Lily asked.

"Not helping," Rose commented, turning away from her friends to walk over to a familiar figure down the hall. It was May, one of the cheerleaders Daisy had helped with homework a few years back after the girl broke her arm, at practice. Afterward that she made sure that no one messed with Daisy.

"Hey, May," Rose asked, crossing her arms as she leaned against one of the lockers, "Did you hear if Daisy left with anyone last night?"

May looked down at Rose, her lips a bloody red and eye shadow an apple green. "I didn't see it myself, but I heard she was talking with an older guy last night on the phone. They made plans to go somewhere, though it could just be a rumor. But my congratulations if it isn't. She's really stepping up her game."

Rose opened her mouth to ask when this had happened, but May continued, "There's no need to worry, of course. If anyone's stupid enough to try and say anything about it to her, I'll make sure to stop them." There was truth in her words.

All Rose could do was nod, knowing Daisy has this ability to make everyone love and want to protect her, no matter what. Because she did everything in her power to help them in return. She did so for the simple reason of being able to see them smile.

"Come on Rose. We need to get to English before the bell rings." Lily said, grabbing her arm and pulling her away as May left to find her own class.

Rose had no choice but to race down the hall with her friends, making it to their seats just as the bell rang.

They sat down right as Ms. Ball started roll call for the first day of class, but Rose wasn't as relieved as she should have been. She felt her heart freeze as she saw Daisy's desk was empty no books, no backpack, no smiling girl . . . nothing.

She looked over at Violet, who normally sat next to Daisy. For the first time today, her friend looked worried. It would have to take something very bad for Daisy Young to not to show up to class.

Rose was forced to sit as their teacher called her own last name, and in a hoarse voice she answered. Then the whole room went quiet as everyone's eyes turned to Daisy's seat, a sea of raised eyebrows.

"I see Miss Young is running late today," Ms. Ball said, and after a moment of silence she moved on to Violet, but Rose could hear the whispering all around her. Questions about sicknesses or worse, and she couldn't do anything about it because she didn't know why Daisy wasn't there. Even when she knew how much Rose needed her.

Halfway through the class, she got her answer. Rose looked up as a knock came from the frosted glass door, hopeful that it would be Daisy. But a second later it opened to reveal Police Chief Thompson, and behind him an uncomfortable Mark Hollow who was fidgeting in his new black uniform, refusing to look any one of them in the eye.

"Ms. Ball, may I talk with you a moment? " the grayed-haired chief asked. "Of course, sir," Ms. Ball complied, leaving the classroom and closing the door.

The room didn't stay quiet for long.

"What the fuck?" someone exclaimed from the back of the class, and suddenly the room was filled with excited chatter. All Rose could do was look at her friends, both of whom looked freaked out.

"Do you think this is about last night?" Violet hissed, getting up and coming over to Rose.

"I have no idea," She admitted. Lily came over as well, seeming equally scared, "You don't think Daisy is hurt, do you?"

Rose felt the blood drain from her face and opened her mouth to reply when the door opened once more. Their teacher returned looking pale, and the whole room went silent.

"Rose, Violet, Lily. Chief Thompson would like to talk with you in the principal's office."

Rose felt everyone's eyes on them as the three slowly got up and made their way toward the door, stepping out into the hall to find Mark looking paler then they had ever seen him, along with Mrs. Young's tear-stained face.

CHAPTER 2

Rose stopped in her tracks at the sight of Mrs. Young standing there, looking as if she hadn't slept the entire night before. Her makeup was a mess, her red hair in tangles, and in her long white dress she looked out of place.

"Mrs. Young?" Rose choked out in question, but the police chief intervened.

"Miss Waters, Miss Luiz, Miss Andrews please follow me. I need to ask you a few questions about last night," He said, leading them into the main office where Rose found Principal Lewis behind dais workstation, looking grim in a way Rose had never seen before. It was as if someone had died.

"Please take a seat, ladies," the chief gestured toward the three seats set up in front of the large desk, "Officer

Hollow, take Mrs. Young somewhere else until we're done here. I'll have a few more things to ask her later."

Rose turned to look at the door and saw Mark place a hand onto Mrs. Young's shoulder, guiding her away as he closed the dark wooden door. This left Rose and her friend's with nothing else to do but sit down.

They watched Chief Thompson take his position next to Principal Lewis, expression serious as he spoke.

"First thing first," he said, crossing his arms, "I need to confirm that all of you and Miss Young went to a party last night."

Rose looked down at the floor, feeling sick, and knew her friends were the same.

"It's alright," Their principal chimed. "You girls aren't in any trouble. We just need to know the truth, is all."

For a moment no one spoke, but eventually Rose broke the silence. "Yes, we were at..." She paused a second, not wanting to get Mark in trouble on the first day on the job.

"I know the party was at Officer Hollow's residence, and I know there was alcohol served to minors there. That's not the part I care about, trust me," Chief Thompson explained, "So, please, tell us everything you girls can remember."

Rose swallowed hard before launching into the events of last night, telling the men everything. She told them about, how they went to the party and ended up drinking too much, and how after hours of dancing they had wanted to go home. She told them about how they had looked for Daisy, but never found her. And after she had started feeling sick, her brother had taken them home without her.

"Did your brother go back to the party to look for her?" he asked. Rose felt surprise at not having thought about it before. "I honestly don't know," Rose admitted, and the older man nodded.

"Did you see her talking to anyone unusual?" Principal Lewis asked.

"No, but someone said they saw her talking on the phone. It could just be a rumor, though, "Rose biting at her lip, thinking, then spoke again, "Sir...you still haven't told us why you're asking us these things. Did something happen last night? Is Daisy hurt?" Her voice small.

The two men shared a look between each other, perhaps thinking of not telling them, or to lie, but Rose knew there was no point in that. In this small town news spread like wildfire.

So, after a moment, Chief Thompson let out a breath, then looked them in the eye, "Daisy Young didn't come home last night. She hasn't been seen by anyone for almost half a day now, and in this small of a town that's not normal."

Rose felt as if someone had just punched her in the stomach, her world tilting and falling off its edge. Her mind went blank because there was no way in hell that her best friend, who she'd known since she was three, was missing.

No, the girl who taught her how to ride a bike when her father couldn't due to all of his business trips, the girl who had helped her learn to speak without stuttering, the girl who had visited her every day when she had been hospitalized. Daisy wouldn't just disappear.

"What the hell are you doing here, then!" Rose yelled, surprising both of the older men and her friends, who all looked at her as if she'd just grown another head, "You need to be getting a search party together, be out there looking for her. She could be hurt. Or worse."

Rose got up and moved for the door, unsure what she was going to do. But at least it was something. Before she could, someone grabbed her arm, and she looked back up to see Chief Thompson staring at her just like he had almost a year ago. As if she really was crazy.

"Rosalina Waters, I need you to calm down and take a seat. We are working on forming a search party at this very moment, but we need your help. We need information on Daisy's actions last night, and you and your friends are the best hope we have of being able to find her. You were likely the last ones to see her."

For a moment the room was quiet, everyone looking between the two of them. "Fine," Rose concerned, "But I want to help with the search."

"Of course." he moved to sit down, and for the next hour her and her friends they were grilled about last night. What Daisy had been wearing, if she drank anything suspicious, and so on. They asked question after question until the three of them were finally told that they could leave.

* * *

Lily stepped out of the office and into the yellow and blue hallway, her heart feeling as though someone had just drop-kicked it. She was little dizzy as she looked around, almost as if this day was all a dream. But, No, it was all too real.

"I need some air," Violet's voice was shaky as she started for a side door that led outside. Lily and Rose followed after her, unable to think of anything else they could do. They had been told that the teachers were to be informed about Daisy's situation, and that school would be canceled for the rest of the day. Maybe even until they found Daisy.

The three of them walked out into the far too sunny day for the news they just received words that still rang in their ears. Violet sat down on one of the warm steps that led up to the school and Lily did the same, sitting next to her and slowly reaching into her own back pocket. She took out one of her cigarettes, lighting it with shaky hands and took a deep drag.

She breathed out, her eyes closing and letting the familiar, bitter taste roll over her tongue. It relaxed her far too easily.

Then she reopened them and watched Rose pace nearly. Her friend seemingly unable to stand still. "Rosey, try to calm down. You're not going to be of any help to her if you're worked up," Lily said, a breath of smoke escaping from her lips.

Rose didn't say anything in reply, just kept waking back and forth until Violet got up and grabbed her arm, annoyance clear in her voice now, "Rose, just damn well stop."

And she did then, turning her deep blue eyes on them, "How the hell am I supposed to just sit here when my best friend is missing? I need to go look for her. She needs me and I need her."

"Hey, no smoking on school property," Someone called out from behind them, and they all looked up to see Mark coming down the steps. He looked just like his old self, if not a little paler than normal in his dark uniform.

"Don't you dare start," Violet hissed, "You used to sell them after first period."

"Maybe, but I'm a cop now. Meaning I have to do my job," he said even as he took the cigarette that Lily held out and lit it, breathing in and blowing out a puff of smoke.

"Where's Mrs. Young?" Rose asked, still looking like a wild animal antsy and ready to jump at the slightest sound. "Chief Thompson is taking her back home so she can get something to use for the tracking dogs that will be brought in if she's not found by tomorrow."

"God," Lily breathed, "This is really happening."
"I'm afraid so," Mark let his cigarette fall to the ground and stepped on it, "But we're going to do everything we can to find her." He looked at Rose as she did the same to him, her eyes sharp. Lily could feel the tension in the air, something that had been growing for over a year now.

"Now come on," Mark said, turning to head for the parking lot. "Where are we going?" Lily asked, letting her own cigarette fall to the sidewalk as she got up and they all followed after him. "You said you wanted to help with the search right?" Mark said as he unlocked his police car that stood out starkly in black and white next to Violet's truck.

"Of course," Rose said, stopping next to her friends. "Then follow me, the search party is starting at my house since she was last seen there." Mark got into his car and without another question Rose hopped into Violet's truck. Violet sooned followed, but Lily just stood there in shock. Not two hours ago, she had been thinking of asking Jake Reed to watch the football game with her and wondering if her new yellow and red top would look good with her white boots.

But now she was going to go look for her friend, who could be badly hurt or even worse.... No, Lily thought to herself. No, Daisy would be fine, and alive, and worried about everyone who had gone out looking for her. After all, she was Daisy Young the girl everyone loved no matter what.

She jumped into the bed of the truck and they followed after Mark. As they drove, Lily was taken aback to see people talking. Talking to their neighbors, to their family. Everywhere you looked people were talking, and Lily could feel it in the air they knew about Daisy. Because people don't go missing here everyone knows where everyone is, no matter who you were. So the idea that one of the most beloved people around could go missing sent a shockwave through everyone. After ten minutes, Lily noticed car after car joining them in a line so long she didn't know where it ended, and the knowledge that everyone she knew with them in this horror show gave her a little hope.

* * *

They pulled up in front of Mark's house to see his parents, now returned from their vacation, looking pale and a little sick as ten other cars pulled up to the sidewalk alongside them. Many more parking across the road.

Rose jumped out of the truck before Violet even had the chance to pull the key out of the ignition and handed for Chief Thompson, who was busy talking to three other officers. But before she could make it to him, though, she was stopped by a gentle hand on her arm. She looked up to find Mark.

"Don't bother him right now, Rose. Go with your friends and sign in. I'll try and get you on my team, okay?"

"Your team?" Rose repeated. "Yeah, I'm the one who knows the tree line around here like the back of my hand. And she's your best friend, so if anyone has a chance of finding her it's us, working together."

She opened her mouth to say something, she didn't know what. Maybe to ask if he thought they were friends now after everything he had done to her, but she was stopped as she heard her name.

They all turned to see Jason running up to them, and before she could say a word she was wrapped in his embrace. "God damn, Rosey, I just heard from mother that Daisy is missing. I'm so sorry this is all my fault, I shouldn't have just left without her, but I-"

"Stop," Rose said, cutting his rambling off, "it's not your fault."

It's mine, she thought but didn't say. "Alright, everyone, I need you all to listen up," Chief Thompson suddenly shouted, and everyone turned to face the older man, listening as he went on, "First, I would like to thank all of you who have come to help with the search on such short notice. The first twenty-four hours are the most important in missing person cases like this, especially when it's a child."

"Daisy would kill him if she heard him say she was a child," Violet whispered so only Rose could hear her. "She will when I tell her," Rose said back, not leaving any room for doubt in her words.

"Chief Thompson continued, "Now, we need to get going so we can use as much daylight as we have. We will be assigning every volunteer a group to work in."

Everyone listened as their names were called out, as they were paired with one of the officers. Like Mark had said, he had gotten her and her friend's names on his team, along with Jason and a few others.

Next, Chief Thompson gave the teams the directions for the areas they would be searching in, and Rose was happy to hear they would be going into the east side of the deeply wooded area that sat just off of Mark's house she had played there too many times to count as a kid.

"So, we have until sundown to find her before we're supposed to come back and regroup, right?" Lily asked, and Rose nodded as they walked behind the group. "It's not that long, but we just have to make it count," Rose replied, then looked up as Mark spoke.

"Come on," he egged them on, leading them into the trees and moving branches aside for them to pass, "Stay close to me, no more than six feet. Just in case you need or find anything. Got it?"

"Fine by me," Jason said coolly as he looked around at the tall thick pine trees. Rose did the same, searching for anything that could help her a golden bracelet, an earring, anything that could be Daisy's.

"Daisy!" Lily called, her small voice ringing out, and Rose could hear other voices in the distance doing the same. Rose stopped as she daw movement at the corner of her eye, turning to find...nothing. Nothing was there but trees.

The world seemed to disappear then, as she moved to look for what it could have been. Further away from the voices and people. She walked forward in a daze until she stopped suddenly, her heart freezing as she knelt down to get a closer look at the small white petals.

"He loves me. He loves me not. He loves me. He loves me not. He loves me," a small voice sung. Rose bit her lip hard and closed her eyes, waiting a moment, letting it fade away, then stood and continued following the flowers that seemed to be going somewhere.

For who knows she followed them, she didn't know, but the sound of other people was far off now as she finally reached where they led. And when she got there she couldn't help but gasp. Rose looked around at the clean, clear river running through a rocky river-bank that was so perfect, it could have been a dream. But Rose had learned a long time ago how to tell a delusion from what was real.

She walked down to the river's edge, until her boots almost touched the water, and scanned the surrounding areas. If Daisy had run from something, or someone, she would have run for somewhere dark. And where better than a tree-covered bank? She could have hidden down in the rocks if someone had gone looking for her, then maybe have crossed to the other side when the coast was clear.

Rose started to take a step forward, but yelped in surprise as someone grabbed her arm and pulled her back so hard it felt as if her skin would bruise.

She turned and found her own blue eyes staring back. "What the hell are you doing, Rosey? Jason said, "I've been looking for you."

"I'm searching for Daisy. What does it look like?" Rose asked.

"Why would she go down here?"

"There's a lot of trees where she could hide, and I saw white petals from the daisies she always used to make her chains. "What are you talking about? he shook his head, confused, "What white petals?"

"The ones right th-"

Rose cut herself off as she looked back and saw he was right the petal trail she'd followed was gone.

"Rosey, are you okay? Do we need to go home? Because this is hard on everyone, but I can't imagine what you're going through right now."

"Quit trying to sound like the doctors," Rose hissed, "I'm fine, and I don't need you trying to-"

"Rose, Jason what are you doing down here?" Mark asked, coming out of the woods behind them to stand beside her. "Nothing," her said, "Rose just had to relieve herself and I got worried when she didn't come back, is all."

Rose felt her cheeks heat up a bright pink, and she hoped it could be written of as it just being sunny. Mark stared at Jason for moment, and Rose could see he was thinking, but of what she couldn't tell. Then he turned to her. "If that's all, then you could have told me, Rosey, and I would have-."

"Don't call her that," her bother snapped, cutting him off, and both Mark and Rose just stared at him, "You don't deserve to use her nickname after what you did."

Mark took a step back, eyes-down-cast, "How many more times do I have to say that I'm sorry?"

For a moment, Rose believed that Jason would try something, but he simply shook his head. "Sorry. I think everything has just caught up with me, is all. Thinking about how Daisy really could be hurt somewhere out here."

Mark paused a second at Jason's sudden change, then nodded in agreement, "I know, man. This is one messed up day, but all we can do is hope she's okay and keep looking."

They were quiet for a moment as his words of surprising comfort filled the air around them. "We had better hurry back I know the other girls will be missing me," Mark said, breaking the tension. "Like any woman would miss you," Jason muttered the words under his breath and followed after him.

Rose moved to leave as well, but stopped and looked back at the path where the white petals had been. She still found nothing. Taking a deep breath, she followed behind her brother until they met up with her friends, who had gone on with calling out for Daisy to no avail.

It went on like that for hours, until it had gotten dark, and Rose was almost forcibly carried away by Jason as night fell because she didn't want to stop. She didn't want to lose the hours that it would take them to go home and sleep.

Day after day, Rose, her friends, Jason, and Mark went into those trees, looking from first light to sunset. After two weeks they were branched out to search areas that were further away from Mark's house, then even further. Police officers with bloodhounds were called in from other towns, and over four-hundred volunteers helped with the search over the next week. But as weeks turned into a month people started to lose hope. The Youngs broke down more and more as people started to talk about Daisy in the past tense.

Rose knew that it was normal for people to want to give up, and as another month passed, and a war that had been going on for nineteen years finally ended, almost everyone wanted to start anew. Not forget, no, people loved Daisy after all. She was a light in the lives of so many. But she had been missing for over two months now with no leads, and the police were slowly starting to admit that it was likely she wouldn't be found. At least, not alive. But Rose knew better. She wasn't one to give up so easily.

CHAPTER 3

1975, Watkinsville, Georgia.

June 15.

Rose

Rose sat up straight as her mother talked to their dinner guests one of father's business partners and his wife from the bank. Two people who somehow looked positively delighted to talk about the soup that her mother prepared, and her father looked far too busy enjoying it too, the point that Rose guessed he would have his ear talked off later for not listening by his wife.

She turned her tired eyes away and found Jason sitting across from her, she was struck by how much he took after their father. He was almost a clone from his younger years black hair and blue-eyed, with a smile that made a room fall in love with him. He looked up at her then and he raised his eyebrows a little.

To anyone but her it would mean nothing but when you're a kid in the Waters household you learn quickly to keep quiet when the grown-ups are talking. So, a raised eyebrow could mean many things but she could tell it was a question being asked now. Most likely he was asking if she was okay a question he had been asking regularly since that day.

She gave a small nod he had been worried about her for the last two months, to the point he had decided to stay in Georgia to make sure she was fine. And, of course to make sure she kept taking her meds. Because, unlike her parents, he actually cared if she was still seeing and hearing things when all her mother wanted was to make sure no one knew about it.

Suddenly, there was a lull in the conversation, and she took her chance, "Mother, may I be excused? I have homework to look over," Rose asked with so much sweetness it could give you a cavity.

She looked annoyed for an instant, but covered it with a bright, white smile. "Of course, darling. I'm so happy you're finally feeling up to it."

Rose kept her own smile on as she got up and took her dinner plate to the kitchen, her dark red dress swaying around her ankles. As she turned her back towards, the stairs,the smile fell.

She slowly made her way up to her room, and as soon as the door was closed she almost ripped her dress in her haste to get off. It felt too tight tonight.

Taking a deep breath, she looked over at her closed door. Pinned to it was a map of Georgia, with testimonies from people who had been at that party, who had seen

Daisy, who knew if she had been drinking or talking with anyone. There wasn't much there barely anyone could remember anything from that night. Still, it was better than nothing.

Rose turned to her closet and looked at all of the dresses hanging inside, her old jeans and t-shirts gone after she had been hospitalized.

Her mother had thought it better for her to just start all over again, but with her mother's style dresses that looked to have been made in the 50s and heels.

She closed the door and went over to her bed, dropping to her knees and looking under until she pulled out a small, brown box. Sitting up, she opened the lid and took out a pink jumpsuit that Lily had given her, along with a pair of old brown boots that were still caked with mud from camping.

Rose got up and looked out of her bedroom window that showed her dark backyard. A white picket fence lined it, but behind that was a road with a baby blue truck waiting for her.

She quickly pulled on her new outfit before opening her window, staring down at the ground a story below. She took a breath and grabbed the windowsill, pulling herself out into the cool, June night.

Her hair blew around her face as she stood on the edge of the sill, and Rose looked up at the old maple tree Daisy had taught her to climb when she was nine. The leaves were as green as ever.

Rose slowly turned her body around to face the tree, a voice repeating over and over again to not look down.

She took a breath and closed her eyes for a moment even if she had been doing this every day for the last month, the knowledge that she wasn't immortal hit her again. After all, she found out the hard way that she wasn't last year. She opened her eyes and, letting out a breath, she jumped.

For the brief moments that she was soaring through the air, it always took her breath away. But the feeling of being alive pumped through her veins. She hit the tree a second later, catching herself on one of the branches, and immediately, grabbed the one next to it to keep herself upright as she moved to stand on a thick branch.

Rose turned back to her window one last time, then hopped down to land on to the branch below. Then she jumped to the next lowest branch, and the next, until she was able to grab hold of the tree trunk and finally make it down to the green grass of her yard.

She looked up then and saw her family through the larger first floor window they just kept smiling like they really were the perfect little family. Like, dolls in their own little playhouse. Rose turned from them a second later and didn't look back as she met her friends.

* * *

Violet

Violet could smell the smoke from Lily's cigarette as they walked, the darkness around them lit only by their flashlights. The only sounds were their boots breaking the damp branches and leaves under their feet.

She looked back at her friends who were looking around, just like they had been every night for the past two months, and she knew just like all of those other nights they would find nothing. But she didn't dare say that, not to Lily, because she would get angry at her for not believing. Nor would she say it to Rose, because she had been there last year when everything had gone down she couldn't stand to see her like that again. And, if she was being honest she liked being out of the house and away from her dad. From his sorry eyes that hadn't looked happy in over four years.

Not since her mother's death, a week after becoming a U.S citizen from Portugal. After a man had shot her, for no reason other than being different. But that was a long time ago, and that man was in jail, and she was here making sure that no one else would ever have to see so much red again.

"Why are we going to the river again?" Lily asked, putting her cigarette out under her boot. "Because," Rose was leading them through the woods, "I know what I saw that day. Daisy ran through there, I know it. And the heavy rains lately may have unearthed something that could help with the investigation."

Both Lily and Violet shared identical looks with one another, Lily biting her lip hard and staring at Rose's back with pity. But Violet couldn't just let her keep doing this keep thinking something would happen. That they, a bunch of stupid teenage girls, could do anything to find a girl who had been missing for two months. Who had disappeared without a trace.

"Rose, stop," Violet stopped walking, as did Lily, who was looking nervous. Rose kept going for a moment more before turning back to her friends, her eyes wet and shining. She already knew what Violet was going to say.

"Please," Rose said, almost in a whisper, "I can't keep doing this living on when she's gone. She's somewhere out there and needs our help I'm not just going to leave her I know what I saw."

"I know," Violet words were soft, "But Rose you have to admit that your medicine may not have been working well that day. And with the stress-"

"Please," Rose cut her off, anger hardening her voice now, "Don't start with my fucking meds being off and that this is all just in my head. Because it's not, it was real."

Violet took a step forward, wanting to comfort her friend but Rose just shook her head and a moment later she was running.

****

Rose

Rose didn't want to hear it again couldn't. Her mother had said the same thing not two weeks ago, when she had been studying a map of Watkinsville at the kitchen table. Her mother had walked in and snatched the paper, balling it up in her fist.

"What the hell?" Rose said in surprise as she looked up into her mother's unkind eyes, blonde hair tied back in a tight bun that always made Rose think of a witch. "This is quite enough Rosalina. You need to get over Daisy already. She ran away and you shouldn't be so worried."

"Who told you she ran away?" Rose asked narrowing her eyes. "Oh, please, Rosalina, don't you listen to anyone besides your chain-smoking friend or that spic?"

Rose looked away at the slur but said nothing to defend her friends, knowing what would happen if she talked back. "Everyone believes that she ran away at this point, likely with an older man."

"Not Mrs. and Mr. Young," Rose muttered under her breath, but of course her mother heard her. "Don't act dumb, Rosalina. You're an intelligent girl of course her mother doesn't want to think of her daughter being with an older man at the age of sixteen But everyone knows it's the truth that's why the police are the search parties next week."

"They can't," Rose snapped jumping up from her seat, her heart was racing, "They can't just stop now, after only a few months."

"People are tired, and the police can't just keep putting money into something so worthless anymore. Not when there is no evidence of foul play. And it would be best for you to do the same. Your brother is only staying here because he loves you, and, of course, your father is worried sick."

"I'm sure he is when he actually remembers he has a family," Rose shot back without thinking, her anger taking over for a moment. Seconds later it finally hit her, what she had just said, and regret rushed through her. But that regret did not hurt nearly as much as her mother's hand when it connected with her cheek, the slap so hard that it sent her careening into the table, her ribs taking the brunt of impact. It knocked the wind out of her as her mother loomed.

"Don't you ever talk about your father that way again, /h/6young lady. He's done more then you will ever..." Her mother paused, and Rose looked up to see an expression she couldn't read. It almost seemed like worry.

Her mother let out a breath, calming down, "Rosalina, it's time to stop this obsession. I don't want to see you go back to your aunt's after all."

Rose looked away, not wanting to think about that place again, and kept her eyes on the floor until her mother's footsteps faded away. She held her cheek, knowing it was likely bright red.

But she felt nothing as the fact that the police would stop looking for Daisy settled within her. Fine, let them give up. But that didn't mean she was going to.

Rose was brought back to the world as she heard her name called over and over again, but she didn't stop. How could she when her friends would say the same thing as her mother had. When they would give up on Daisy just like everyone else.

She kept running, not caring if her boots were getting muddy. Hell, if she ran far enough then, maybe, she would disappear just like Daisy. Then what would her mother do?

The question actually left her lost in thought. That was, until she ran into something hard and heavy. The next thing Rose knew she was on her back.

She cried out as she hit the ground hard, her flashlight sent flying somewhere into the tree line, but she didn't need it, the moon-light bright enough to see by. She looked up to see Mark Hollow laying on the ground with her.

* * *

Rose

Rose could only blink at him for a moment, he looked disheveled in his plain jeans and old t-shirt, dressed like the 21-year-old he really was.

"Rose?" he asked, pointing his own flashlight at her, blinding her.

She put a hand up to shield her eyes, "What the hell, Mark? Get that out of my face."

"Right. Sorry," Mark apologized and lowering the beam. Rose got to her feet and wiped at the first in her clothes, "Are you alright?"

"I should be asking you that," Mark said, getting to his feet as well, "Actually, no, what I should be asking you is why the hell you're out here this late at night?"

"Why are you here?" Rose knew he wasn't on duty at this time of night. "I'm an officer, and I have self-defense training, so I'm doing a little over time by looking for Miss Young. And you shouldn't be out here by yourself. Have you ever heard of the phrase the criminals always return to the scene of the crime?"

"Do you know how hard Daisy would laugh at you for calling her Miss Young?"

"Well, I think she would be laughing at that outfit. Why are you wearing that?" He asked, gesturing to her clothes. Rose looked away, "I didn't think a dress and heels would be that suitable for jumping into a tree."

Mark opened his mouth to say something, maybe to ask why she only had dresses when a year ago she always wore jeans and tops like a normal teenager, but the sound of rushing footsteps made them both turn around. Lily and Violet raced into the small clearing behind them.

"Oh, come on," Mark groane, tired, "You brought your friends with you?"

She didn't answer, too busy wondering if Lily was going to kill her from the dangerous look her friend was sending her way. "Why the hell did you run away from us?" Violet yelled, the anger thick in her voice, and Mark turned to look at Rose, confused.

"I couldn't just stand there as you told me to give up on my best friend. I've known her since I was three."

"I wasn't saying that, but we have school tomorrow. My dad ..." Violet stopped and snuck a glance at Mark, "isn't too happy with me going out so much at night."

Rose stared at her for what felt like the first time in two months, taking not of the new bruises that looped her olive wrists and forearms.

She felt as if she had just been kicked in the chest. Daisy would be pissed at her for doing this, for putting Daisy above the rest of her friends and her own safety.

Daisy worked so hard to make everyone smile, had stopped Kerry Lews from hurting herself when they were seven by just talking her down. She had been the one to make friends with Lily on their first day of middle school, telling her that she liked her tie-dyed t-shirt they would later learn was her father's. Daisy who had let Violet sit with them on her first day at their school when everyone just looked at her as if she was a zoo animal just because she was Latina, Daisy had never thought about treating her differently. All she ever cared about was what people were like on the inside, as cheesy as Rose thought that sounded.

And that same Daisy would hate Rose for all of this, but because she was Daisy she would still understand and, like an idiot, forgive her.

"I'm sorry," Rose finally said, backing away to look at her friends, "This was my fault, my idea I should have known better."

"It's okay," Lily said, "We'll get through this together."

"You really think so?" Sky

"Of course," Lily said.

Rose smiled, because maybe it would be okay. Someday, maybe she would be, too. But seconds later her world turned upside down again, as she took a step and felt her foot slip off of the earth to and meet only air.

The next thing Rose knew she was falling backwards. She only heard her name called once before her body hit the cold water of the river.

She had been too close to the bank, and in the dark, she hadn't seen the edge. Even when she had visited it every day for the last two months, she hadn't seen it.

Rose opened her eyes to see a world of swirling darkness above her head, the cold water freezing her in place a moment before she sat up and sucked in a deep breath. She coughed luckily, it was only a few feet deep at this spot, the water just barely going up to her chest.

"Rosey, Jesus Christ," Mark yelled, starting to climb down into the bed, his flashlight bright on the water offering her a hand, "Are you alright?"

She took it and he pulled her to her feet, "I'm okay. Just wet and-" her voice died as she turned her head to the right, and then someone's voice was screaming. But it wasn't out loud, no, it was only in her head. She couldn't move, couldn't think, couldn't stop seeing the thing that couldn't be there, because this was a hallucination. Violet had been right that her meds had stopped working.

"What is it?" Mark asked, confused, then turned his flashlight over toward where she was staring. She watched his own face go pale.

"Are you guys okay?" Lily's voice drifted over from where she and Violet still stood atop the bank, the two of them looked down at where Mark's light had stopped. Violet's scream was the only sound that broke the silence as their attention was captured by the yellowing skull, eternally smiling up at them from a hole rocks had been covering just minutes ago.

CHAPTER 4

Rose

Rose just sat on the of the hood of the police car, deaf to the world as someone wrapped an orange blanket around her shoulders. She couldn't have told you who it was too many people were milling around the scene now after Mark had called into the station.

When she hadn't been able to stand,too shocked to move, he had picked her up and carried her out of the river. Setting her down on the fallen trunk of a tree a little ways from the bank. Her friends waited with her to talk with Chief Thompson, who had been the first to make it to the scene. The coroner soon followed.

Rose had zoned out at some point slowly coming out of it as she felt someone loop a warm arm around her. Looked up, she saw Lily and Violet, both red-eyed and puffy from crying for some time now, and Rose briefly wondered what was so wrong with her that she hadn't felt a tear in her eyes this whole time.

"The chief called our parents," Lily said, rubbing her eye.

Violet grumbled, drawing her gaze to the night sky, "That's just great."

Rose, on the other hand, looked out blankly at the world of red and blue lights as one of the coroners wheeled a stretcher out of the ambulance and started down towards the bank. She turned away sharply and instead watched Lily, who's hands were shaking so violently that she couldn't even steady them enough to light her cigarette.

"Here. Let me," Mark said softly, taking the lighter and flicking the fire to life. Lily held her cigarette over it until it was smoking, taking a deep drag as Mark handed it back. As he turned to go, Rose grabbed his hand, stopping him in his tracks.

"Is it her? Is it really Daisy?" she asked, her voice breaking like thin ice. He looked back at her with pained filled brown eyes, young and hurting just as much as her. Daisy had been like a little sister to him once.

"I don't know, Rosey. I wish I could tell you no, I wish I could tell you it was someone you'd never even met, but I can't. At least not until the coroner is finished."

"Who would want to hurt her?" Violet growled, anger rising now as the initial shock had faded, "Why her?"

Mark shook his head, "I couldn't tell you that if I tried."

"Where is she? Where's my daughter!"

Everyone turned to see The Youngs charging out through the trees. Mr. Young looked exhausted, his cheeks were sunken, his clothes disheveled, and he seemed to be on the verge of crying as he tried holding on to his wife's hand to pull her alone. Still, his stress was nothing compared to what Rose saw in Mrs. Young's eyes alone. The woman looked like she hadn't slept in weeks maybe months her eyes were rimmed with red, her graying hair unkempt, as if she hadn't combed it in all of that time. She had the of like a wild animal, ready to kill, which Rose guessed was what any mother would do if she was in this situation. If it was their child in the riverbed.

"Where is my baby?" She almost screamed as she threw herself at Chief Thompson. The chief looked genuinely sorry for this broken woman.

"Honey, please," Mr. Young cooed at her side, "the girls are here."

Mrs. Young glanced around before spotting them, her face crumbling as tears fell from her cheeks. It was that sight, of her best friends mother breaking down, that lifted the spell keeping her own emotions in. The tears from a woman who, for the longest time, Rose thought of as a second mother, made the dam break within her and her own tears fell free.

"I'm sorry," Chief Thompson said honesty as he walking off to manage the scene far away from the woman sobbing hysterically in her husband's arms.

"Lily?"

Rose turned her head and saw Mrs. Andrews, Lily's mother, walking over to them with Mark in tow.

"Mom," Lily said, her own voice cracking through her tears.

Her mother grabbed her then, pulling her into a tight hug without even mentioning the glowing cigarette that fell from her child's hand and into the grass. grass

"Violet, are you alright?" Mr. Luiz asked next, coming to stand by the group. His daughter let her gaze fall to the ground but still shook her head, and Rose watched as he took the girl into his arms paternally, if not a little awkwardly.

Then it was her turn as her own mother walked up the women's light blue 50s styled dress, with its bullish skirt and cropped sleeves, looked dirtied now from her brief trek through the forest. Her normally-pristine teardrop pumps were grass-stained and muddy as she watched where she stepped with the keen awareness of something who'd already made that mistake once that night. Somehow, in the midst of this hurricane of mournful tears, hysterics, and numb shock, her mother still managed to look more annoyed than anything else. Pain shot through Rose's entire body then, starting from her heart, at the knowledge that her mother would never hold her like Mrs. Andrews held her child. She would not take on her pain.

"Hello, mother," Rose acknowledged the woman, meeting her hard gaze.

"Why must you always do this to the family? Are you trying to make us look bad? Ruin us?" her mother hissed once she was close enough to not be overhead, her arms crossed.

Rose opened her mouth to answer, but was stopped by a cry that pierced the night. She turned and saw that the coroners had returned, this time with a black bag laid out on the stretcher.

It was Mrs. Young who had let out that ear-splitting cry and made a move to approach them until Mr. Young and Chief Thompson intervened. Both men comforted her in their own ways her husband wrapping her back up in his arms and the chief removing his hat. Instead of being reassured, she sank helplessly to the ground, the crunch of long-fallen leaves muted by her screaming. It was such a pained sound that Rose had to look away, for if she didn't she knew she would run to her and join with the one already roaring in her chest.

"Come, Rosalina. We need to get home before morning." Her mother drew her attention with an impatient tone, urging her daughter away from the haunting scene.

"Don't I still need to talk with Chief Thompson?" Rose asked not to her mother but to Mark, who was staring at the two of them with wet eyes. "No, I'll take care of it," he told her, turning away. Rose pinned Mark with her gaze, her ears filled with the sound of Mrs. Young's sobbing as she knelt on the ground, begging for answers. But no one could help.

When she didn't start moving right away her mother grabbed her arm, pulling her out of the clearing and weaving in between the trees in forced silence until they were bucked into the seats of her red Corvair and driving away much faster than what's legal. Rose's nails dug into the upholstery.

"Do you even care?" The words were so quiet as the world outside the windows passed by in a blur, "My best friend was just found dead, mother. Is all you care about that our family name is going to be on the news tomorrow?"

She made a wide left turn at the stop light, jostling Rose in her seat as she switched gears. "Of course I care about Daisy. She was one of the best influences you ever had kind and sweet good at cooking, too. It's a shame she'll never find a man, now. Whoever he was going to be, he will be missing out now, but we all manage."

Rose had to turn away then, silent tears leaving tracks down her cheeks to stain her callar, and for a moment when she saw her own reflection she wished she had been the one to die. Daisy was good at heart, excelled in whatever she did, and she loved you no matter what.

But what was she? Rose was nothing but a broken girl, crazy. Her prescriptions of antipsychotics proved it better than her actions ever could. No matter what she did right, he was just a disappointing daughter who only got her family's name in the newspaper in a bad to drag it through the mud. If anyone deserved to be dead, it was her.

She closed her eyes and leaned her head against the glass until they pulled into their driveway, the frame of the car shuddering around her as the engine died. Rose got out in a daze, following her mother up the front path on unsteady legs. As they reached the door, her mother opening it for her, she was greeted with a view of her father and brother sitting at the kitchen table, looking just as out of it as she felt. Daisy had been like a second daughter to her father, and a little sister to Jason. They had all gone on family trips together, planned birthday parties so that they could celebrate the occasion on the same day. They had been there of Daisy the second she had woken up to the sound of her own heartbeat.

"Rosey," Jason started to get up, but her mother put her hand on his shoulder and pushed him back down into his seat.

"Rosalina is going to her room for tonight as punishment for sneaking out. And for managing to drag our name, once again, into the news-paper."

"Deborah," her father tried to reason with her, the surprise clear in his eyes at her actions even if it wasn't shocking at all to Rose at this point.

"Mother, Daisy was just found dead. Don't you think Rosey needs to be around people right now."

Her brother was treating her like fine china, ready to shatter if you so much as breathed too hard near her.

"Don't kid yourself, Jason dear. Your sister was the one to find her, so it must have been what she wanted. After all, she went out tonight when I had told her to stay home, so as punishment for breaking the rules she will be sent to her room for the rest of the night. And she will be going to school tomorrow."

There was no sympathy in her words, and both men looked at her mother, knowing she was being unreasonable. Still, neither argue with the decision, because her word was law in this house. Just like every good little housewife's was.

Rose turned away from her family and took to the stairs, the living room television already announcing the news. The words echoed through the house, following her to her bedroom with a sadistic clarity. "It seems that the missing sixteen-year-old from Watkinsville, Daisy Young. The girl people of the community have been searching for over two months now, has had her investigation come to a heartbreaking end this evening. It is believed that the body of Daisy was found, buried in the bank of a remote river, by three young women walking the ground this evening, reports say. Chief Thompson has not yet given our crew his statement on if he believes this is a terrible accident or if foul play was involved, but for now, until we know more, it is with a heavy heart that this community waits for more answers as they make the necessary preparations to lay such a this bright light to rest."

Rose closed the bathroom door and grabbed onto the sink as she tried to keep herself upright, her tears blinding her now as she fought to keep her sobs in. Her hand came up to cover her mouth, clamping over it as her fingers were soaked by her own tears. She looked up into the mirror and saw her own stupid face, red as a tomato, and at that moment the sadness drained until she was only filled with rage. How dare she cry when someone had hurt Daisy when someone had, killed her. Was it quick or did they drew it out? She must have been so scared and maybe in her last moment, she had thought of Rose. Maybe she had, wondered why her best friend wasn't there for her when she needed her most. When Daisy had always been there for her.

She stood up straight then and opened the medication cabinet. Grabbing her pill bottle, Rose popped open the lid with barely a second thought, emptied the contents into the toilet, watching them sink for a moment before finally flushing them. She was tired of not being allowed to think clearly of being treated like she was crazy just because she heard and saw things other people couldn't. Rose knew that needed to focus if she was going to find the person who had done this to her best friend. They weren't getting away with this.

***

Violet

Violet awoke to the sounds of pan-scraping and metal clinking against metal coming from downstairs, and for a blissful moment she thought of her mom. She could almost see her mother, brown hair put up in a loose ponytail that brushed the straps of her old yellow apron, singing along to the radio and flipping a half cooked pancake in their kitchen back in Portugal.

But reality checked in a second later when she heard her dad's angry curse at the clatter of something hitting the kitchen tile. She didn't react to his outburst,only closed her eyes and rubbed at her arm, knowing it would be covered in small dark marks by now. Bruised by the beer bottle that her dad thrown the night before in his stupor. It had hit her by accident, or at least that's what she told herself.

She slowly made her way out into the hall to the bathroom opposite her bedroom, the walls inside painted a soothing mint green, and took a quick shower. With the hot water on her back, Violet let her own brown wavy hair down and washed it, a few missed crystals of glass finally dislodging themselves before disappearing down. As she stood under the stream, the water beating down on her shoulders, she inspected her forearm touching the thin cuts along the soft inner skin and finding that the damage really wasn't as bad as it looked. It didn't hurt all that much.

Maybe she was just numb, like she had been when her mother had died not able to feel a thing not pain, not happiness nothing. And it had only been when she'd met Daisy, when Daisy had smiled down at her as she sat alone and told her she could sit with them, that Violet had actually started to heal. But now she was back at square one, just like four years ago. And this time she didn't know if anyone could help.

She stepped out of the shower, dried off, and got dressed in her light blue bell bottoms, picking a plain pink shirt with sleeves long enough to cover most of the damaged, then took up a brush to tackle her hair. With each run of the bristle through her waves, Violet watched as the hair got higher and higher until they were like a cloud around her head. Once it was how she liked it, she quickly painted her lips a dark pink and brushed on some dark green eyeshadow, looking to the world like a young Raquel Welch.

"Violet get down here and eat. You've got school today."

She looked up at the stucco roof and took a deep, centering breath, resigning herself to whatever horrors this day would bring before heading down. When she got to the foot of the stairs and walked down the hall to the kitchen, she knew that it was one of those days for her dad he already had a beer open on the table next to his plate of eggs as he read the paper.

Violet had to take a second to remind herself how to breathe when she saw the photo of Daisy on the front page it was a discolored photo taken last year on school picture picture day of her smiling as brightly as ever. It hit her then, as she stared at the headline, that she would never see that sweet smile again. Daisy was dead.

"Sit down. Your eggs are getting cold," her dad said as he flipped to the next page, oblivious to her pain. She sat down without responding and dug into her overdone eggs. It stayed silent between them until she had finished her breakfast and washed both of their plates, which was fine by her. Anything was better than screaming.

She went to grab her bag off of the back of her chair, ready to walk out the door when she heard her dad call out to her. "I'm sorry about last night. I didn't mean to hurt you."

Violet looked down at her hand as it rested on the knob of their front door, eyeing the fresh nicks and old bruises that poked out of her sleeve. She thought back to the ones she knew ran down her arms from when he got mad at the people from work, or at someone who looked at him wrong, at her mother for leaving him alone when she had promised to stay by his side forever.

He would always lash out, sending cans of beer or whatever was in arm's reach at the moment flying across the room. And she was normally around when it happened, trying to calm him down and ending up the way that she was.

He was always sorry afterward, and for the past two years she had tried her best to understand that it wasn't his fault. He was just never taught how to control his strong emotions and so they controlled him. But as the cuts and bruises got deeper and deeper, and as time went on without anything getting better, she wondered how much longer "sorry" would be enough.

She didn't look back to him as she opened the door, simply telling him, "It's fine. I'll see you later," before walking out of the house.

He didn't reply as she closed the door behind her and made her way to the truck her mom had driven for over ten years before Violet had finally gotten her license. Having it meant that she no longer had to ask her dad for a ride and risk getting barked at.

She hopped into the driver's seat and swung the door shut or at least she tried. It would always pop back open, refusing to fit into her truck's dented frame, and it took her a few tries this time to get it to finally click. A few more frustrated seconds of trying to get the engine to wake up, and finally she was on her way to Rose's house.

Passing the lines of rundown houses of her neighborhood in a blur of faded siding and thirsty lawns, she reached picturesque grasses and rooved awnings of the peaceful suburbs, idling in front of a house she could only dream of being able to live in. After a few minutes of waiting, Rose stepped out into the front walk in one of her uncomfortable, starchy dresses and kitty heels that Violet knew hurt like hell.

How Rose could stand wearing thper terrible things for almost sixteen hours a day without dying from the pain, Violet didn't know.

But, to be fair, her friend did look like she was dying today, anyway, so they probably were a good fit. Rose brown hair was a mess, knotted locks brushing her shoulders. She wasn't wearing any, makeup, something her mother must love, and was sporting a look that said she wanted to hurt someone, but just didn't know who it would be yet.

"Hey," Rose said as she got into the passenger seat. Her voice was small and Violet understood why her friends was breathing apart in every corner of her soul, but neither of them had any idea how to fix it. Violet felt the same way, but she knew that there was no way to make the hurt go away, at least not this soon.

Once Rose was buckled in next to her, they took off for Lily's house. No words passed between them, their unspoken thoughts keeping them trapped in a heavy, constricting silence. Once Lily was in the car, having jumped into the back seat looking as if she had been stabbed in the gut, the air seemed to ache with their shared pain. They drove the endless ten minutes to their school, but their commute was stopped about suddenly two blocks away from their destination when Lily signaled for them to pull over to the side of the road.

Violet felt her heart pounding as she put the truck in park and stole a glance at Rose, worried, and found her friend wore the same look.

They waited a moment for Lily to come out and explain why they'd stopped, but she didn't move to get closer to them. Their friends just stayed tucked away behind the headrest of Ross's seat, and they didn't need to look to know what she was doing back there. Violet shot Rose a knowing look, and not a second later they were both jumping out and circling the outside of the truck to reach the door on Lily's side. Opening it, they found Lily curled up in the backseat, sobbing quietly as she buried her face in her crossed arms.

Violet felt as if someone had kicked her in the chest. She could barely stand to look at her friend as Lily made herself small, her legs pulled up to her chest and breath hitching in her throat.

"Lily?" Violet called to her, her tone soft.

"Why?" Lily eventually choked out, "Why was it her? What did she do to anyone? She was good, and kind, and I loved her so damn much. And now I have to go to school, to her classes, the day after finding her bones?"

Rose had to look away the pain clear in her eyes. It was Violet who had to answer, then, so she swallowed hard and told her, "I have no idea why, Lily. I have no idea why someone killed her."

She heard Rose take a sharp breath, but she didn't care. It was something they would need to get used to, because they would all be hearing it for the rest of their lives. The "sorry for your losses," the "tell me if you need anythings," the sympathetic looks shot at you that you never asked for. But behind your back they'll whisper words that were never meant to be quiet, "Poor thing."

"Such a shame she had to die so young."

Violet grimaced at her friends react, slapping her hand against her truck's cool metal frame, "I don't know what to tell you both. The only reason I'm going to school today is because I don't know what else to do. I can't just sit at home and not know what happened to her. I need to move and keep going or I'll shut down."

Rose was the first to react, nodding as her eyes glazed over with tears, "My mother is making me go as punishment for sneaking out last night."

Hearing that, Violet reached out without much thought and took her friend's hand, then Lily's. She gave them both a knowing squeeze. "I'm going to school because I want to be in a place that she loved," Lily finally said.

At that Violet let out a warm chuckel, "She was the only kid I've ever met who cared about school that much."

"She loved learning," Rose added as she stared off toward the side of the road, "She wanted to be an art teacher."

This made Lily's half-smile of remembrance drop back into a frown. Their friend looked up at the clear blue sky, tears dripping down her cheeks into her blonde hair, "She'll never graduate now."

Violet felt Lily's hushed words hit her hard the thought of never seeing where their lost friend would have gone in life. Who she'd have fallen in love with, how many kids she'd have. At a sleepover they'd had when they were fourteen, Violet remember them joking about all the children Robby Benson would give them. Daisy, of course, was the one among them that had her whole life planned out she had wanted two kids a girl and a boy the perfect little family.

"Then we will just have to make sure to live the life she can't."

Rose met her gaze as Violet offered her own resolve, and Lily's red and puffy eyes rose to look at them both. "Let's go, then," Rose straightened up and started walking back to her seat, "Daisy would be pissed if we were late because we were crying over her."

"You're right," Violet said, feeling more determined as she shut Lily's door and moved to get back into the truck.

They drove the rest of the way a bit faster than necessary, pulling into their school's parking lot only five minutes late. Almost everyone else was already there by the time Violet killed the engine and hopped out, only the rare delinquent or over-sleeper rushing in with them. After helping Lily get down, their friend having cried herself out, Rose let out a long breath as they approached the building, looking over to Violet.

"How bad do you think it will be?"

Violet knew why she was asking her she was the only one among them that had been through all of this before.

"To be honest?" she started to replay, linking arms with Lily to keep her friend steady. It's going to be a living nightmare. Everyone will be looking at us, staring, but the whispering will be the worst part. The things said behind our backs will be pretty bad, and a lot of it will be rumors and made-up stories to explain what may have happened that night. It's still a mystery, after all."

Rose nodded, looking a little pale,

"Are you ready for that?" Violet asked.

"I don't have another choice but to be do I?"

"I'm afraid not," and with that Violet took her first steps into the building, her old sneakers connecting with the floor of the bustling hallway and carrying her inside. A second later, Rose and Lily followed suit and they all headed for their classes.

***

Lily

Lily hadn't looked up as they walked through the parking lot a place that had been all but abandoned now their classmates were already inside. Instead, she had clung to Violet, crossing the threshold into the school arm-in-arm. She had been unsure of what halls full of people would be like. Still she couldn't help but glance around as they entered the building before being left breathless as everyone's eyes turned on them the second they opened the door. The whispers reached her ears next.

"Why are they here?"
"Weren't they the ones who found her?"

"Do you think she was murdered? It could have been an accident."

Lily did her best to shut them out, ignore them, but their words were like water, they seeped in at the corners of her mind. They tried to outrun the voices, but someone blocked their path by stepping out in front of them, making them come to a sudden stop in the middle of the hall. Everyone was looking at them now, like animals in a zoo.

"Morning," Violet greeted Tommy Johnson as he stood before them. Instead of replying with a "hello" of his own, he simply said, "I'm sorry."

For a moment they didn't know how to respond, but Violet eventually found her words.

"What are you talking about?"

He didn't look them in the eyes, barely elaborating with a vague, "You'll see."

Lily felt the air grow colder, then the air in the hall suddenly feeling too thick to breathe. Her throat felt as if someone had poured acid down it, the pain eating away at her insides, and before she knew what she was doing, she'd torn herself out of Violet's supportive grasp to run for the nearest bathroom.

People threw themselves out of her way without question, and the instant she was locked in one of those ugly green stalls, she knelt by the toilet and dry heaved, Nothing came out and soon she was left sitting there, shaking and barely able to anything but gasp for air. Unconsciously her hand moved to her back pocket, searching for her cigarettes and pink lighter, and she pulled herself into a sitting position on the lid as she slowly lit one.

She sat there for what felt like hours, smoking one cigarette after another, letting the ashes fall onto the floor Lily knew it was wrong, but right now she just couldn't bring herself to care. She thought of what Daisy would have said, if she knew that her friend was skipping class to sit in the school bathroom and smoke. But the truth was that Daisy was the reason she had picked up smoking cigarettes in the first place.

After Lily's dad had left her and her mom, years ago, she had used food to cope with his absence baking sheet after sheet of his favorite cookies, hoping he would come home for them. For her. But that never happened.

It got to a point where she didn't want to do anything else. All she would do was bake, sleep around, and some out in the back of classes, never really talking to anyone.

But Daisy wouldn't let that happen, not even if to the school slut. Daisy would make Lily sit with her and Rose at lunch every day, all but begged her to come out to shop with them on weekends. Daisy was the one who dragged her to the party where Lily tried her first cigarette.

It hadn't been something she had even thought about Daisy had been talking with an older guy. Rose and her in tow. She had been a wallflower, just happy to be there, when the guy offered Daisy a drag of his lit cigarette. She had taken it from his fingers and put it to her lips, sucking in and, after a moment letting out a cloud of smoke and a little cough.

"Hell, Jared, you were cheap tonight. I see," Daisy had said with a laugh, her voice sounding warm as a spring day.

Upon finishing her drag, Daisy had passed the cigarette over to Rose, who looked at the smoldering but as if it had just drowned a basket of puppies. When the cigarette was then passed to Lily, she turned it over in her hand and looked to Daisy for pointers on what to even do with it.

"Go on," Daisy encouraged her with a kind smile, "It's easy just hold it to your lips breathe in deep, and wait a few seconds before you blow out."

Lily stared down at the half-burned cigarette for a moment before bringing it up to her pink lips and taking a long drag. She couldn't tell if it had been that night that she had become dependent on them as a stress reliever, or if it had been gradual, but as she breathed out now and watched that familiar billow of smoke disappear into the air, she could feel her panic slip away.

She knew why it was so hard for people to quit, why would you want to give up your access to something that helped you? A cigarette could calm you down so quickly that it happened in a single breath. When she went to take another drag, Lily heard the bathroom door open. Holding her breath, she hoped that whoever it was would just do their business and leave, but she wasn't that lucky. Someone called out for her.

"Lily, "I know you're in here." It was Rose

"Go away," Lily called back looking up at the ceiling and praying that all of her problems would turn to smoke.

"Daisy would be pissed at me if I didn't make you go to class," Rose's voice was voice was strong, determined, from beyond the still door, and Lily wondered how her friend could sound so sure at a time like this. They had just found their best friend's bones last night, for god's sake.

"I can't face them." Lily told her, swallowing hard, "I can't just go and take notes and answer questions like nothing happened."

"You said you wanted to be in a place where Daisy was happy. That's what you said, right?" Rose asked, sounding like she was standing just outside the stall door.

Lily's gaze dropped to the floor, taking in the mess she'd made with her cigarette ashes.

"Yes."

"Well, Daisy wouldn't want you to just be here. She would want you to go out there and do your work. She would want you to learn, just like she did."

Lily closed her eyes, feeling the warmth of hot tears that streaked down her cheeks that never seem to stop falling nowadays. "Come on," Rose pressed, her words soft, "Don't make me start quoting Daisy at you now."

When Lily didn't respond, her friend knocked on the door and called out to her, trying and failing to imitate Daisy's sweet, small video. "Lily Andrews, if you don't come out of there in the next minute. I will never let you have the last orange creamsicle again!"

Lily couldn't help but laugh at that Daisy loved those things to the point of obsession.

"Come on, Lily, you didn't miss much. It's only the first bell."

At that, Lily opened her eyes and stood up, letting her cigarette fall into the water of the toilet bowl, and unlocked the door. Rose was standing just outside, looking far too tired.

"Let's get this over with then," Lily said and started for the door that led back out into the hallway, only to stop when she noticed that her friend hadn't moved. Rose seemed to be distracted, eyes staring intently at something in the next stall over.

"Rose are you okay?"

She seemed to snap out of her trance, then, and turning to face Lily with a little smile. "I'm fine. You go on without me I need to use the restroom."

Lily just nodded, not thinking much of it, and left her to it, and left her friend to her business.

* * *

Rose

Rose waited until the outer door squeaked shut completely before turning to the old, stained mirror that hung above the sink. She walked over to it watching the reflection of the mirror as Daisy occupied the open stall, reading the graffiti scrawled across the wall.

"Did I do good?" Rose asked and her friend nodded.

"You did. And thanks, I can't stand the thought of her just sitting in here smoking her life away because of me."

"I know I wish she would stop smoking altogether but that won't happen, will it?" Rose sighed, her questions handing around in the air between them. This time, though, Daisy didn't answer. And the next time Rose blinked, her friend was gone.

CHAPTER 5

Rose

Rose leaned against the back of Mark's house, the world swaying back and forth as, her stomach felt much the same. She pushed off the wall to get a refill of whatever she had just spilled on the ground, but something-maybe a stray beer can or an empty wine bottle that someone had blindly tossed into the cease-fire her up. The lack of support from her kitten heels meant that she would have fallen flat on her face it someone hadn't grabbed her hand to keep her upright. When she looked to see who had saved, she was met with the familiar green eyes of Daisy.

"It looks like I'm falling for you," Rose words slurred, her eyes taking a moment too long to focus, but when they did she saw that Daisy's flower crown was crooked. She reached up to fix it for her, but stopped when Daisy grabbed her wrist.

"It's okay, Rosey, I like it this way."

"But it'll fall off if you leave it like that," Rose argued, a little confused. "It's fine if it falls off, Rosey I'll just make another one."

"Will you make me another one?" Rose plucked her own crown off of her head and examined the small, white flower, the blooms already starting to wilt.

Daisy shrugged, "Maybe, if I have a little more time I'll make as many as you want. Hell maybe I can finally teach you how to make them yourself."

"Why do you always act like you're older than me?" The question was sudden,unexpected. "Why are you the one everyone looks up too?"

Her friend gave her a sad look, "I don't know why, Rosey. I wish I know, so I could fix it but that's just the way it is. And now I-I need to act older, more than I ever have before."

"What do you mean?" Rose started to ask as Jason came over. He was doling out more booze without saying a word, and somehow Daisy ended up with a red solo cup in her hand. For a moment she was quite just stared at the contents of her cup as if it had the world's answers. Then, she looked back up at Rose with a smile.

"It's nothing, Rosey. Just try and enjoy the party okay?" Daisy told her, handing her the cup and wandering off into the dense crowd.

Rose watched her go before looking down at the cup and chugging it in one go, not caring what it was. Almost instantly she spit it out, the awful taste of something metallic coating her tongue, but as her backwash splattered across the white shag carpet she saw something else mixed in with it the distinctive dark red of blood.

Panic hit her a second later then it should have as she stared at it, and upon realizing what she was looking at she wiped at her mouth with her hand her fingertips came back stained red. Rose looked around herself, her breathing too fast and head pounding to the point that she wanted to scream. Her pain list it's importance when she found that the room, once full of people, now was completely empty apart from for a body lying on its back in the middle of the floor, unmoving.

Rose tentatively stepped closer for a better look, unable to stop her own feet as she noted the person's strawberry-colored hair that she had loved to run her fingers through as a kid. She had been taken aback by the color at the time, such a vibrant shade unheard of in her youth.

Blood coated the floor around Daisy, her loose overalls and yellow t-shirt now a deep red. Rose could feel the stinging tears in her eyes before they even started to fall.

She kept approaching her heels painted red, blood seeping into her soles, until she finally found herself standing above the body.

"Daisy?" Rose whispered, her name spoken just loud enough to escape her lips, but it just echoed back in the now-dark room. The only light came from above a rainbow of colors that made her head spin more so than it already was.

"Daisy, please wake up," she pleased as she fell to her knees in front of her best friend, the blood now soaking through her clothing, costing her skin. It was still warm, but the air was cool near freezing.

"Why didn't you look for me that night?" her friend asked, her lips the only part of her body that moved.

The words hung in the air around Rose, the endless echo beating down on her from every side, "I'm sorry. It was the first big party I'd gone to since I was hospitalized. I was tired," Rose could feel her tears dripping off her chin as she spoke, each one rippling the ever-growing pool of red.

"Excuses, excuses, excuses, excuses, excuses! You always have a damn excuse for everything, don't you, Rose? Well, I died by myself, in the dark, in pain. I then i was buried in a cold, dirty riverbank. And why? Because you were 'tired'!"

Her friend's words cut deep opening countless old wounds left by her mother and, making her cry even harder, like the stupid child she was. "I-I i'm so sorry Daisy! Please, please don't leave! I need you, please, I need you to keep me sane, because I can't think straight without you!" Rose cried out, reaching to take Daisy's pale, lifeless hand. The golden bracelet of daisies that Rose had gotten her was now dripping blood, but to her horror, when Rose touched the skin it melted away, leaving only white bone.

All Rose could think to do was scream. If it was a scream of pain, of anger, or of longing, she didn't know. She screamed and screamed as the Daisy she knew disappeared, turning into the bones they'd found at the river before her eyes until she could taste her own blood in the back of her throat.

"Rose! Rosey, wake up! It's just a nightmare!"

Rose's eyes shot open to a world of harsh light. A figure standing over her, strong hands shaking her violently. She tried to shove them away, her voice dry as she mumbled, "S-stop it."

"Thank god. Rosey, you had me scared," Jason let out a long sigh, letting her go as he sat down on the edge of her bed.

All Rose could do for a minute was blink as her eyes adjusted to the sunlight shining through her open window. When her eyes refocused she noted that Jason was fully dressed, his normal work outfit of a blue button-down shirt and black suit pants a staple now that he was temporarily employed at her father's bank. She was surprised to find that he looked so pale, though.

"What are you talking about?" Rose asked, wondering what I'm earth he had to be afraid of. Her brother just looked at her for a moment, biting his lip and seemingly wondering if he should say anything.

"Rosey, you were screaming like someone was killing you up here."

She looked away, her cheeks heating up, "Sorry, but it was just a nightmare. I hope I didn't wake mother."

"Rose, you can tell me what the nightmare was about. I am your big brother, after all."

"I-I can't remember what it was about now," Rose brushed off his concern, her words a clear lie, but she knew Jason wouldn't press her for more details. Not after that day.

"If you're sure," he finally conceded, standing up and heading for the door. Before he left he stopped and turned to face her. "Today is the funeral, isn't it?"

Rose dropped her gaze to her hands and, for the first time, felt the cold air of the room hit her face. Her cheeks were wet, she realized she had been crying in her sleep.

"It is," Rose was slow to answer. "Do you need a ride?"

"No, Violet is taking us this afternoon. After that, we're going to Mrs. Young's house."

"Alright, I was told to let you know that mother has been making tuna and noodle casserole for Daisy's family. She wants you to take it with you."

"Sounds great," Rose wasn't paying attention, her eyes drifting over to her closet where a new black knee-high dress hung from a hanger her mother had gotten it for her just a few days ago.

"Rose, how has school been? I mean, in the past week. After.. " he paused, "After she was found?"

"People have been kind. Daisy helped so many no matter who you were. The school is holding a memorial service this morning."

Jason nodded,his eyes downcast, "Rose, if you need someone to talk to, you know you can come to me."

Rose gave no reply, and after a moment Jason just sighed and left her to the horrors that this day would bring. After a second of hoping that this new nightmare would end and she would wake up to see those green eyes again, she gave up and moved to stand before her closet.

She wouldn't have to wear that god awful black dress until she came home this afternoon, but this day felt as if dark clothing was needed. So, instead, she picked out the royal blue dress her mother had fallen in love with, throwing it on. Next, she found the darkest shade of red lipstick she owned the ruby red of drying blood, and put it on along with some deep blue eyeshadow to make her own blue eyes look off as deep as the darkest parts of the ocean.

"You look like you're preparing for battle," Daisy commented, "And s bloody one, at that."

"Aren't I, in a way? I'm having to say goodbye to you, after all," Rose retorted and glanced around, but this time it was just her friend's voice that filled her room, not her. "You're stupid for flushing your pills, Rosey," Daisy whispered into her ear.

"I needed to hear something other than my own voice for a little bit," Rose answered as she walked over to where she'd stored her dark blue heels, slipping them on before heading for the bedroom door.

"Oh, but Rosey, you have no idea what you're doing to yourself."

Instead of answering her, Rose just opened the door and shut it behind her in the hopes that Daisy would take the hint. Instead, she found her friend waiting for her, now fully visible, at the bottom of the stairs. Her eyebrows were high on her face, as if asking if Rose had really thought closing a door would help.

"Rosalina, you're finally ready, I see," her mother chided as Rose sat down across from her father and brother, "I, on the other hand, have been up since four o'clock this morning making Mr. And Mrs. Young a tuna and noodle casserole that you will be taking over after the funeral along with a poke cake."

"Of course, mother," Rose said, taking a long drink from her coffee cup.

"Well, I'll be heading out for work now," her father set down his paper and got up, with Jason following suit. "I'm sorry I can't go to the funeral today, Rose, but it wouldn't feel right. I didn't know her parents all that well."

"It's okay, Father," Rose didn't look at him as he planted a kiss atop her head. Instead, her gave stayed fixed on Daisy, who was currently dancing to a commercial's song that was playing on their living room TV.

"I'll see you tonight, then, darlings," her mother wished them well, flashing a smile as she handed them their lunches and saw them to the door. It fell from her face the moment the front door closed behind them.

"Don't you need to get going Rosalina? Violet will be here soon."

"Yes, thank you, mother," Rose rolled her eyes as she got up to leave happy to have left uneaten food on her plate for her mother to clean up like the perfect little housewife she was.

As she stepped outside into the warm spring air, her brown hair whipping around her face as she walked down to the sidewalk, she let the quiet consume her. Had it really only been a year since the night she'd been sent away? She's been shipped off to silence the voices that had become too loud to handle. Though of course, Daisy had been there at the time to help heal her, what was stopping her now? What was keeping her here, keeping her from running away to find a permanent solution to the problem a way to end the pain forever. But I still need to find the person who killed my light, she thought.

"Rose."

She snapped out of her thoughts to see Violet and Lily staring at her from their seat in Ol Baby Blue, and she put on a little smile for them.

"Hey."

Rose walked up to Lily's window and. Violet nodded, her friend looking as if she hadn't slept in the last week, "How are you holding up?" Rose asked, and even though she already knew the answer it felt as if she had to, maybe because her mother had thoroughly beaten the formality into her after all these years.

Violet almost smiled, but the upward curl quickly died on her lips, "Shouldn't I be the one asking you that?"

"That's not an answer," Looking over at Lily, Rose found that her other friend looked half asleep as she sucked on a cigarette, th

e smoke filling the small, poor-vented truck.

"I still don't know honestly," Violet said and Rose nodded understanding as she hopped into the back seat.

"Same."

They pulled into the road a moment later, Rose turning in her seat to watch her house begin to shrink in the distance. She saw the mailman drive up, her mother coming out onto their lawn with a lovely smile on her face, looking just as eye-catching as she had been in her teens. Her youth was something she would never tire of talking about, it seemed.

"I was so beautiful in my teens and early twenties that men came from all over town to ask if I would go dancing out with them. Now look at yourself, Rosealina. Even with my good genes, no one wants a girl who's crazy."

Rose let her gaze fall on her wrists, at the white scars that marked her skin. The sharp image of red flashed across her vision, and the next thing she knew Daisy was there, sitting next to her.

"Why are you thinking of that day so much, Rosey?" Daisy asked, her hair blowing around her face in the nonexistent breeze.

"You already know don't you?"

"Well, of course I do. I'm in your head aren't I?" Daisy said, closing her eyes and tipped her head back against the seat.

"Why am I only seeing you this time?" Rose asked.

Before she had started taking her antipsychotics last year, she had seen so many people, all whom were people she had never met. Rose had heard their voices, every one foreign and oppressive, but now the only person she heard and saw was Daisy.

"I have no idea why, Rosey. Remember I'm just in your silly, little head."

Rose looked away from her friends to watch the world pass her by, and the next thing she knew Daisy was gone again.

* * *

Lily

Lily let her cigarette fall to the ground as they approached the school, once again being the last ones here. They had been late for school everyday the last week, which was totally fine with her anything was better than being stopped by their classmates and asked what Daisy's bones had looked like interrogation on if their friends remains had been bloody or broken when they's been pulled from the river. Just the other day, a teacher had come up to ask if it was true that Daisy had been dating an older man, and all Lily could do was look at the woman in pure disbelief.

Things like that had been happening multiple times a day, people would come, expecting the three of them to help verify the rumors and lies being tossed around to explain why someone would have wanted to hurt Daisy it was as if people had totally forgotten the kind girl that had helped them when they needed it, caring more about the mystery than the beautiful life that was the lost to fuel their entertainment. But things looked to be getting worse instead of better, it seemed the worst theorie yet had only just began to circulate and as they walked over to their lockers Lily felt her heart stop. Her eyes went wide with shock as they saw what had become of their friend's memorial.

Scrawled in red paint across Daisy's old locker were the words "Manther Lover!" the flowers and photos they'd stick to the locker door now laying in tatters on the floor below. To Lily's surprise, none of their classmates were sparing a glance at the defacement as they passed only Mark, currently in-uniform, and Principal Lewis took any notice of the damaged. The two of them were talking as they hovered around the crime scene, Mark taking notes as their principal inspected the red writing.

That was, they did so until Mark noticed them storming toward the lockers and his eyes filled with pity.

"Who?" Rose growled, her voice booming, and for a moment the hall went quiet, "Who the hell did this?"

Mark met her hard gaze, his eyes going soft, "Rosey, calm down, we are-"

"No," Rose cut him off, "Do you know who did this to Daisy's locker?"

"We don't know anything at the moment. Don't make a scene," Mark tried to pacify her, his words soft in the hopes that she'd calm down. It wasn't working and Lily knew why she wanted to scream just as much, just as loud.

"Okay, Mark, I'll stop making a scene when you find Daisy's killer, because we all know she didn't just fall and hit her head that night. I don't care what Chief Thompson says!"

Mark couldn't even look at them, because what could be said? It was true that Chief Thompson wanted this all to be an accident, because that meant that the people in the community would feel safe letting their kids ride their bikes around the neighborhood. He wanted them to be able to walk to and from the school without the fear of getting murdered en route.

But Mark had known Daisy Young since she was three years old, him being just give years older, and he knew that she was a native to those woods.

She knew them too well to have just fallen down and died he knew that the only way she could have ended up in that riverbed was if someone had killed her.

"Rosalina Waters," Principal Lewis started to address her, his voice trying to sound assertive, but Lily could tell that Rose wasn't going to hear another word from someone who thought they knew better on this matter.

"Shut up!" Rose barked, her tone low and serious as she glared at her principal, meeting his stern gaze head on. Lily felt her jaw drop at her friend's words no one had ever yelled at their principal like that, and it wasn't long before Rose went pale at the realization of what she'd just done.

A collective breath was drawn throughout the hall as everyone looked to Rose with wide eyes, sharing Lily's shock. Rose glanced around herself, fear obvious in her eyes, and Lily reached out a hand to comfort her. Her friend turned away in sudden panic, however, and Lily guessed it was at the thought of what her mother would do when she heard about this outburst. Without another word, Rose took off running for the school's entrance no one made a move to stop her as she shoved the doors open and disappeared into the bright daylight.

"Well damn," Lily mumbled under her breath.

"God damn it," Mark swore as he eventually gave chase, jogging to the entrance and letting the doors swing shut behind him.

Lily turned back to check Principal Lewis reaction, but he was only shaking his head he looked more disappointed than anything as he started to head back toward his office. She felt her heart drop into her stomach, knowing all too well what Mrs. Waters would do to Rose if she heard that she had been so disrespect. It was the mental image of Rose locked away in her room, alone, for the rest of the week or worse, sent away again that pushed Lily to her run after him. Violet followed right on her heels as they moved to stop him.

"Please, wait," Lily called after him as they turned down a mostly empty hallway, away from the onlookers "Please, sir, just give us a minute to explain."

Their principal slowed to a stop and turned to face the two of them, his voice even as he said, "I know what you're going to say, ladies but I can't just let this disrespect slide. The other students might get the idea to bad-mouth their teachers, or me, in the future."

"We understand that, sir, but please just don't call Rose's mom okay," Violet begged.

"And why is that Miss Luiz?"

Her friend opened her mouth to respond, but Lily could see Violet didn't know how to answer him, she couldn't tell him about the things Mrs. Waters did to Rose. If she did, their friend would only get into more trouble than she was in now.

"May I talk to you in your office, sir? Alone?" Lily asked, chewing the inside of her lip.

"Alone?" Violet let all of the questions she had slip into her voice, but Lily didn't have time to discuss this with her. "Please. Mr. Lewis," she urged him to give her his time without checking Violet's reaction, and after a moment their principal nodded, opening the door to his office for her. She followed him in, leaving Violet to gawk at her beyond the doorway, mouth hanging open.

"Sit," Principal Lewis gestured to one of the available chairs as he circled around his desk and sat down, absently adjusting the blue tie around his neck. Lily did as she was told, crossing her legs as she took her seat. Once she was settled, she leveled a look at him that she hoped showed him how serious she was.

"You're not going to call Mrs. Waters."

"Now Lily, you know I can't-"

"My name is Miss Andrews to you, Mr. Lewis," Lily corrected him, calmly meeting his gaze. After a moment of awkwardness, he looked away and she continued. "Do you know what they would do to you if I told everyone what we did last month?"

She knew full well that he did, but she wanted to hear him say it.

"Of course I do, Lil- Miss Andrews, bu-"

"And you remember what happened to Rose last year right?"

Her principal nodded, briefly dropping his gaze to his desk.

"Good, because I don't want something like to happen that again, so this is what you are going to do. First, you're going to cut her some slack after losing her best friend, especially when it's only been a year since she tried to-"

She paused for a moment, unwilling to speak the words into reality, before going on, "after everything that happened last year," Lily got up and walked around to where her principal still sat, wary of what, exactly, she was planning to do once she reached him. Using a finger, she tipped his chin up to meet her eyes, "And if you don't lay off of my friend, I may just have to tell Officer Hollow and the chief of police about those late nights you spent at my mom's house when the two of you were still dating. And how you somehow ended up in my bed instead."

Lily couldn't hold in the feeling of satisfaction as the esteemed Mr. Lewis couldn't look her in the eye. Just like all those nights, he was powerless to fight her.

"I'll forget what Miss Waters said today, so long as it doesn't happen again."

"That's what I thought," Lily said with a smug smile as she turned and opened the door, for once being the one with the last word, "See you at the memorial service."

* * *

Rose

Rose had to take a deep breath to keep from screaming, as she rushed around the outer perimeter of the school to sit on the steps they had sat on the day that Daisy had gone missing. Had that really only been two months ago?

Two months spent putting up missing posters. Two months spent watching The Youngs fall apart. Two months of watching herself fall apart and, at that moment, she began to wonder how much more she could fall. Maybe until there was nothing left of the person she had been a year ago.

"Rosey, are you okay?" Mark asked walking over to her, his hands stuffed into his pockets as if he was in his blue jeans and not a police uniform.

"Of course I am," Rose replied, sarcasm clear in her voice as she looked up at him. "What a silly question, Mark or should I call you Officer Hollow, now?"

"You think I don't know how you're feeling right now, Rose? She was like a little sister to me," he told her, his hands combing through his mess of brown hair.

"And what was I then?" she asked plainly, and when, he didn't answer she went on, "Don't act like you know what I'm feeling right now."

"It feels like you're broken, and you feel it in every cell in your body," Mark's voice was soft as he sat down next to her, looking out over the green grass of the school's lawn, "It's as if the grief could drown you in its depths in the dead of night, or when you're left alone, and all you want is to make things right, but you can't."

"Jokes on you I guess you can't break if you're already broken."

Rose watched him as he continued to look across the field, sitting next to her seeming to be a million miles away.

"You know I loved her, right?" Mark asked, finally turning to meet her gaze and Rose raised an eyebrow at him.

"Not like that," he waved away what he knew she was thinking, shaking his head, "I loved her because, in a way, I wanted to be her. I wanted to be able to smile when it was raining, to help people like she did. I wanted to be able to know what was wrong with someone without them telling me and then work to make it right," his eyes shined with such a knowing that Rose had to look away.

"Everyone wanted to be like Daisy, Mark," she said, closing her eyes for a moment just to see that kind smile again, "We can't let whoever did this just walk away."

"And I'm trying my best to keep this investigation going, I really am Rose. There just isn't that much evidence besides the body at this point."

"But how did the coroners know it was her then? There wasn't any clothing or anything."

"I can't tell you that. For now, it's still an ongoing investigation, Rosey."

"How did she die?" she asked, looking up at him once more only to find that he was already watching her.

"Rose. I can't-"

"Please," her words came out as little more than a whisper, "I need to know if it-" she took a breath, "If it was fast. That she didn't suffer."

Mark let his eyes drift up to the sky, biting his lip and shaking his head, but eventually answered, "Daisy died from blunt force trauma to the back of the head, so she would have been out of it for the most part when…" he stopped himself, unsure if he should continue.

"When what?" Rose pressed, her heart beating against her ribs so hard that it felt as if they would bruise.

"I shouldn't be telling you this!" Mark groaned, rubbing at his face with his hands, "I could go to jail for god's sake!"

"Then don't," she started to back off, the realization of what they were doing finally hitting her, "I couldn't live with myself if I got you in trouble, Mark."

At that he let out a pained breath and, for a moment, everything was quiet. When he spoke again it was far too fast, with a voice that sounded strained.

"She was strangled to death, Rosey. After the blow to her head."

"Sounds like it hurt," Daisy was quick to comment, walking over to loom over Mark's hunched form, and all Rose could do was gawk at her, eyes wide with horror. He must have thought that she was looking at him that way as his next few words were ones of comfort. "I'm sorry, I shouldn't have said anything."

"No," she replied, trying to keep her tone even. "Thank you for telling me. Really, Mark I mean it. And you said that she most likely out of it when it happened, right?"

"Yes, she would have most likely been only half-conscious when she died. With the size of the crack in her skull, she likely wouldn't have felt much of anything at that point."

"That's good," Rose said, nodding as she stood up.

"Well, I died in quite a horrible way, didn't I?" Daisy quipped, circling around Mark to dance playfully next to him, "But you haven't asked if he knows who did that to my locker, Rosey."

"Right. And who do you think wrote that junk on Daisy's locker?" Rose asked turning her attention back to him.

"I have no proof, but I think it's someone that just wanted attention. There wasn't any, serious intent at play here, and I'm sure Chief Thompson will agree."

As they started heading back inside, Rose slowed to a stop on the sidewalk.

"Will you come to the memorial service with me?" she asked, "It should be starting soon."

He seemed to hesitate, suddenly unsure, "Are you sure you want me to be there? I mean, after what happened last year? I know you and your friends don't have the highest opinion of me."

"Oh boy, is he right about that," her friend joked as she walked up to stand beside her.

"You're not wrong," Rose said, "But what can I do? You're trying to find the person who hurt Daisy, so you're my best bet for the moment."

"Well, I'm glad I can be useful, then," he said opening the door for the three of them.

"Damn, girl! Are the two of you going to start making out?" Daisy asked walking behind Mark.

"Shut it," Rose hissed under her breath, but Daisy just laughed. As their little group made their way down the now-abandoned hallways, Mark seemed to be a bit unsure of where exactly they were headed. After a few moments, he brought the group to a stop at the crossroads of two hallways.

"Which way was the gym?"

"Shouldn't you know that at least?" Rose asked, "You used to play on the basketball them with my brother right?"

Mark Inn nooked away then, scratching the back of his head awkwardly. "Yeah, I guess I did. That doesn't mean that I remember where the gym is."

"Really?" Daisy circled around to get up in his face, but he just kept passing through her, "What were the those two doing if they weren't at the gym then?" Her question was punctuated with the mischievous smile on her face as she proceeded to look him up and down.

"The gym is this way," Rose said and started down the left hall, hearing both Mark and Daisy follow after her.

As they walked, she noted that there was almost no one out and about, the school's hallways being just as empty as the bottle of antipsychotics that lay under her bed at home.

"So, everyone must be at the memorial service for me, then? I wonder if there will be cake?" her friend asked, running up to walk beside her.

"Cake?" Rose repeated looking at her. "Why not?" and with that, Daisy was giving her one of her small half smiles, "It could be a dark chocolate one, you know? Dark to fit with the dreary the mood and all."

"God, Daisy, that's messed up."

"What?" Mark chimed in, leaning in to catch what she was saying, "What did you say just now?"

"Nothing. I was just thinking out loud," she gave Daisy a sideways look, but her friend just shrugged in return.

Rose stopped them before they reached the doors leading into the gym, reaching out for the handles only to pause when she found that her hands were shaking.

"Are you sure you can do this?" Daisy asked Rose, her eyes filled with pity. "I have to," Rose said, and pushed open the door, Mark coming in right behind.

Luckily for them, there were still people up and about trying to find their seats on the school bleachers those that were already seated were too busy

talking amongst themselves to notice the two of them as they made their way over to Lily and Violet. She could already tell that they were uncomfortable sitting in this endless wave of people.

"Lily! Violet!" Rose called out as she finally got close enough for them to hear her and her friends looked up, eyes going wide and, for a moment, Rose thought that maybe it was because of Daisy. Maybe they could see her too. But then she remembered that Mark Hollow was with her, all six foot four of him.

"Why is he here?" Violet hissed, turning away from Rose to glare at Mark as they took their seats next to her friends.

"Because, at one time, he Jason's friend. And he knew Daisy," Rose said simply.

"And you're just going to forgive him for what he said to you?" Lily sounded dumbstruck, to the point that Rose couldn't match her gaze her eyes as she answered.

Her words were a hushed whisper, just low enough that Mark wouldn't hear her, "I need him to help me find out who killed Daisy, okay? So just be cool."

Lily snuck a glance at Mark, who was busy surveying the room as everyone settled down.

"I still don't like it," Violet crossing her arms.

"I'm with Violet on this one," Daisy seconded their friend as she sat down beside Mark, giving him a sour look, "What he said to you that night is unforgivable in my eyes. You're lucky I'm dead or he would be."

Rose just rolled her eyes, "Thanks."

"Thanks for what?" Lily gave her a confused look, leaning closer, and Rose felt her cheeks pinken.

"Um, I-I-" Luckily, Rose wasn't forced to explain herself, as her stuttering was cut off by Violet.

"You should be thanking Lily, you know. She stopped Principal Lewis from calling your mother earlier, somehow."

Rose immediately turned to Lily, who was now looking down at her book bag with a sudden blush burning her cheeks.

"How did you manage that?"

"Bet you that she told him she'd make his life a living hell. Especially since he's dating her mom," Daisy flashed a wicked smile.

"It doesn't matter how I did it," Lily to her friend with a thoughtful expression, "Just that I did, and that you're safe, Rose."

"Thank you," Rose held her gaze, refusing to look away until Daisy felt the need to comment.

"Should I be worried that the two of you will start making out?"

A blast of ear-splitting static rang out across the gym floor, making everyone wince as the microphone was turned on Principal Lewis voice echoed around them as he stood in the middle of the gym, surrounded on all sides by students.

"Good afternoon. I know that this is a day that none of us would have ever wanted to see. We have all felt the loss of a bright, young star, taken from us far too soon. Daisy Young was an integral part of our community smart, kind in so many ways she was a beacon of hope that lit up the halls of this school with her smile. She was dedicated to helping other, such as with her volunteer work with her church, reading to the children. But, most importantly, she was a dear friend to every person that she met, in this school and beyond. This is why I wanted to start off this memorial in her honor by offering the stage to any of those people who feel that she helped improve their lives. I invite you to come and talk with us about her to paint us a picture of what kind of girl she truly was."

Rose was taken aback as people all around her stood up and made their way down the bleachers people that Rose had never talked to, or even recognize but could believably have been impacted by Daisy in some way.

They all lined up quietly before the principal, and Rose was surprised to see Tommy Johnson at the front of the line. He was at the party, something that felt so long ago now, but he looked much worse for wear his hair was much longer than it had been back then, his skin pale as a ghost. But what caught Rose's attention in particular was that his hands were shaking violently at his sides, and for a moment Rose thought it was another hallucination. That was, until he took the microphone from Principal Lewis and turned to face the crowd.

"Well, this will be fun," Daisy laughed, laying her head on Mark's shoulder.

The room was once again assaulted by harsh static as Tommy cleared his throat into the mic, and Rose felt her heart skip a beat as his gaze locked in on where Rose and her friends sat. is light brown eyes were clouded, hinting at something she couldn't read, but she didn't linger on that thought for long. A second later, Tommy had already started his speech with four unforgettable words.

"I killed Daisy Young."

CHAPTER 6

Rose

For a second the whole room didn't move, didn't look away, didn't breathe as all eyes turned to Tommy the words ringing around the gym. "Well that's new," Daisy said and like being hit with a bucket of ice water everyone moved at once.

Tommy dropped the mic causing a burst of static to ring out and started for the exit doors before Principal Lewis or anyone else could think of moving, but Mark was already on his feet running down the stairs and Rose knew how fast he could go after years of running after her and Daisy in the woods behind his house when her mother would make Jason take them.

So it wasn't a surprise to her as Mark caught up and slammed Tommy into one of the blue and yellow walls his hands behind his back. Rose stood up eyes wide along with everyone else except Daisy who still sat down laughing as if this was the funniest thing since all in the family.

"Tommy Johnson you're under arrest for the murder of Daisy Young," Mark almost growled as he handcuffed Tommy anger clear in his voice as they started for the door.

Rose stood there a moment before reality hit her and she quickly made her way down the stairs followed by her friends as everyone was still too shocked to move from where they stood.

Rose swung the door opened to find Mark talking into his walkie talkie to the station but she didn't miss the blood running from Tommy's nose.

"You son of a bitch!" Rose said, her voice low as she walked down the hall towards him and she couldn't help the little smile as he paled because she knew how terrifying she could look when she was angry because her mother looked much the same.

Rose balled her hand into a fist and started running for him and was about ready to clock him in the face but was stopped by someone wrapping their arms around her pulling her back was such strength she knew it couldn't be one of her friends.

She looked up to find Jason looking down at her his eyes wide, "Rosey what the hell were you thinking?"

"He killed her! Didn't you hear him!" Rose almost screamed breaking free from his arms. "Of course I did, but you think hitting him in the face will do anything to help anyone?" Jason asked looking down at her worry in his blue eyes.

"Damn," Lily said as she joined them in the hallway along with what looked to be everyone in the school.

"It was Tommy?" Violet said looking confused, "That doesn't make any sense at all."

"Move, move out of my way!"

Rose turned to see Principal Lewis moving through the crowd and stopped next to Lily, "Have you called Chief Thompson Mr. Hollow?"

"Of course sir, I'm going to take him down to the station right now and get a confession in writing."

"Good luck with that," Tommy said from where he stood against the wall his head down not looking at anyone. "What did you just say?" Mark said pushing Tommy against the wall getting into his face.

"Pig," Tommy said and spit hitting Mark in the cheek making him take a step back looking pissed off, but to Rose's surprise he seemed to stay calm as he wiped at his face.

"Go ahead and get it out of your system now Johnson, because the next few hours of your life will be a living hell," Mark said and Rose could see the wicked smile on his lips.

Rose watched along with everyone else as Mark pulled him from the wall and pushed him down the hall towards the front doors where she could hear sirens getting closer.

"Well this is getting interesting at the very least," Daisy said watching Mark walk Tommy down the hall.

"Come on Rosey, let's get out of here," Jason said grabbing her arm and pulled her through the crowd of people and back into the gym. "Where are you guys going?" Lily asked following after them along with Violet who looked to be dazed, and of course Daisy.

"Did you forget about the funeral?" Jason asked opening the exit door for them. "Jesus Christ," Lily said a hand to her head, "This can't be happening right?"

"I said the same thing two months ago," Rose said, "And it's all too real."

"Violet, Lily take your blue truck back home and get ready, I'll drive Rose home, she'll see the two of you there," Jason said and pushed her towards his car and all Rose could think to do was get in looking out of the window and watched Lily and Violet do the same looking just as out of it as she felt.

Jason got in and started the car for home as if nothing at all had happened, as if the man who had killed Daisy hadn't just been arrested in front of her.

"You don't look that good Rosey," Daisy said, but Rose didn't answer her not wanting Jason to hear her and she didn't much feel like talking to anyone in the first place. "You know I'm not one to be ignored right Rose?" Daisy said. But Rose just closed her eyes.

"You're an idiot Rose, I can still talk to you even if you can't see me right? I can keep going and going and going an-"

"Shut it!" Rose snapped looking back at a now empty back passenger seat. "Rose, who are you talking too?" Jason asked looking over at her. "No one of course," Rose answered looking back up. "Rose you're still taking your medication right?"

"Why wouldn't I be?" Rose asked not looking him in the eye. "With everything going on it would be understandable if you forgot to take it."

"I'm not that stupid I wouldn't just forget to take them."

"No you're stupid enough to throw them out is all," Daisy said from the back of the car.

"I know you're not stupid Rosey, "But you can tell me things you can't tell mother."

Rose smiled up at him, "I know Jason, thank you," and for a moment Jason turned to look at her a smile on his own face but as soon as he turned away it fell.

He wasn't wrong, she had told him things she could never tell her parents. When she had first started hearing things that couldn't be there at fourteen, whispers that grew into the screaming, when she thought her mother had tried to poison her morning coffee, then seeing people who weren't there.

She had told him all of it and he hadn't told their mother like she had asked him too. But in the end he would tell her he blamed himself, for what Mark said to her. For not telling their parents sooner, for going off to college when she had just come out of the hospital and she knew he blamed himself for Daisy. Something in his eyes always changed and all she wanted to do was tell him it was going to be alright, that she didn't blame him, but how could she when she didn't believe it herself, she blamed herself along with everyone there, her friends, Mark, every person who could have done something.

They pulled into their driveway then and Rose looked up to see their mother waiting in the doorway for them or more likely Jason.

"Is she wearing another color of lipstick than this morning?" Daisy asked but again Rose didn't answer only got out along with Jason who her mother almost ran too. "Darling I got a call from your father telling me you left work and never came back, what happened?"

"I when to the memorial service at Rosey's school for Daisy mother," Jason said as they walked into the living room, their mother taking his suit jacket and hung it up without even looking Rose's way once. "That was very nice of you Jason to be there for your sister and her friends, but why did it end so early?"

"That's the thing mother..." Jason paused and looked over at Rose maybe unsure if he should make her relive it all so soon after the fact. "Go ahead and tell her Jason she'll hear about it soon enough in this shitty small town," Rose said crossing her arms and started up the stairs towards her room.

"Language Rosalina," her mother called after her but she was already halfway up the stairs and didn't look back as Jason started the story that everyone would be talking about for the next week.

Rose made it to her room before Daisy started up again. "So you learned who my killer is and get to go to my funeral all in the same day…Have to say if it was me I would have made sure to eat my eggs, you must be starving by now and you know how much I hate seeing you not eat, remember when you were in the hospital and I brought you a bag of Bubble Gum Cigarettes?" Daisy asked sitting down on the edge of Rose's yellow comforter watching Rose kick off her heels.

"Lily came and ate them all the next day, I just didn't tell you," Rose answered letting her dress fall around her ankles and stepped out of it going over to the black thing that her mother had gotten, old fashioned in every way just like her mother, with perfect clean cut edge's to the collar and skirt.

"I know," Daisy smiled, "She really needs to stop smoking so much you know. "

"No help from you," Rose said sliding the sleeves down to cover the white lines. "You look so very sad Rosey, do you now that?" Daisy asked sadness laced in her voice. "What else do you want me to look like?" Rose asked sitting beside her and started to brush her own brown hair, "I'm going to your funeral of course I'm sad."

"Please don't be Rosey, you know how much I hated seeing you like this, here let me," Daisy said and reached over and took the hairbrush from Rose's too pale hand and started running it through her hair as she started to sing her voice soft, "Spring has come so smile again, we will get to play in the Roses day after day as the wind makes the world sway and the sun makes everything oh so okay, oh how we will play day after day you and me Rosey because no one can tell the flowers it's time to stop not rain or shine will we stop."

Rose closed her eyes at the old memory of the day Daisy had come up with it. She had been seven at the time and Daisy six when they had been sitting outside Mark's house in the backyard as Jason and Mark played a game of baseball in the cool spring weather, even then Mark had looked younger than the eleven years old he really was with his skinny arms and legs.

"Did you know we are both named after flowers?" Daisy asked the words sounding funny since she had lost her front teeth. "Of course I did Daisy everyone knows that," She said trying to sound older but unlike Mark, Daisy had always acted and talked liked someone older than her age. "Well do you know the meaning behind our names then?"

Rose looked up from where she had been watching a few butterflys dance around the tall grass interested now, "What are you talking about?"

"Well I read white daisies symbolize a lot of things but my favorites are purity, innocence, new beginnings, and healing, but also true love because each daisy flower is really two flowers blended together in harmony. The inside petals are one flower encompassed by the petals of another flower, it means that the person who gives them to you can keep a secret and keeping a secret is a grown-up way to show that you truly love one another, like eating the rest of Mrs. Hollow's cookies and not telling anyone kind of love," Daisy said with a smile as she reached over and picked a few white daisies from the yard that was littered with them and started tying them together.

"And what do Roses mean?" Rose asked watching as Daisy started to make a crown with the little flowers. "Well like mine a lot of things, but everyone in the whole wide world thinks red roses mean love and beauty, doesn't that fit you so well?" Daisy asked looking up from her work with a smile but it fell as she saw the tears forming in Rose's blue eyes.

Daisy felt her eyes go wide in panic, "I'm sorry Rosey, please don't cry. There are a lot of things a rose can mean like a yellow rose can mean friendship, you can be a yellow rose."

"It's not that," Rose sniffed wiping at her eyes with the back of her arm, "My mother doesn't think I'm beautiful, so my name doesn't fit me at all."

Daisy looked at her with as much shock as her little body could handle, "What do you mean? You're mama didn't say that did she?"

"Well not in those words, but I heard her telling Jason he was really pretty With his dark hair and blue eyes, so he can't do bad things, because angels don't hurt people. She's never said something like that to me because I'm so plain, with my dull brown hair," Rose said and looked down at her brown hair that sat around her shoulders.

"Rosey you must have heard wrong because you're so pretty, your mama must need glasses because I think your eyes are beautiful and they're the same as Jason's anyway," Daisy said sounding like the grown-up she always wanted to be.

Rose nodded but didn't look up. "Hey, do you want to know a secret?" Daisy whispered leaning in closer so the boys wouldn't hear them.

"Secret?" Rose said looking up again the tears drying away in the sunny day. "Yeah like what grown-ups do when they love you."

"But I can't love you," Rose said, "Not like grown-ups do."

"It's not like that," Daisy giggled, "We're not going to kiss or anything like that, but like the love of best friends."

"Best friends secrets?" Rose asked her tears now gone. Daisy nodded, "Do you want to hear it?"

Rose nodded excitedly now.

"Okay so the secret is…. i think Mark likes you," Daisy said then giggled at Rose's reaction, her mouth open a little and her cheeks pinkening as she turned around to look at Mark who had just failed to catch the baseball for the fourth time in a row.

"I-i- you can't know that!" Rose said looking back at Daisy who was trying not to laugh. "I know, but he definitely likes you, I see him looking at you when you're not looking."

"But he's four years older than me," Rose said sticking out her tongue. "So?" Daisy said sitting back on her hands looking up at the warm sun, "My daddy is older than my mama by like six years and their happy."

"I guess," Rose said watching the flowers sway in the wind.

"Do you want to know another secret?" Daisy asked looking out at the boys who were now trying to see who could throw the ball the highest up in the air. "Of course," Rose said picking at the hole in her jeans. "I think Jason is cute."

Rose felt her eyes go wide, "You can't be serious Daisy! He looks like my fath-" Rose words were cut off then by a ball landing in front of them.

"What to play a game?" Daisy asked quickly. "Um, I guess," Rose said unsure where she was going. "Then follow after me, " Daisy said and grabbed the ball just as Mark reached down for it.

"Hey, that's mine give it back!" Mark said but Daisy was already backing up now and Rose knew what she was going to do next and got up herself ready to follow.

"If you want it you're going to have to catch me."

And not a second later Daisy was running through the yard and then the trees Rose on her heels as the boys both tried to catch up to them, but it really was no use with Daisy because she could run faster than anyone in their school. And within minutes they had lost the boys in the greenery of trees.

"What are we going to do next?" Rose asked looking down at the ball in her small hand. "Well we need to wait for them to find us, but they are boys so it could take ages, I guess we could come up with songs or something," Daisy said sitting down in a patch of sunlight.

"Songs?" Rose said sitting down next to her trying not to get more dirt on her jeans because unlike Daisy who had ruined her white dress her mother would kill her if she came home muddy.

"Yeah, I came up with a song for you the other day, want to hear it? " "Yes please," Rose said looking up at the trees where a squirrel sat eating some berries. "Okay but you have to promise not to laugh."

"I would never laugh at you Daisy," Rose said looking down into the younger girls green eyes.

For the next two hours, they sat there singing and laughing together, Rose's voice nothing compared to Daisy's sweet one which rang in her ears even now.

"Daisy, do you remember that day?" Rose asked coming back to herself, "When we got lost in the trees?"

"Of course I do," Daisy said putting the brush down and picked up a ponytail and started to put Rose's hair up in a bun. "Did I ever tell you what my mother did to me that night?"

"No, I can't say you did."

"It was the first time she slapped me in the face, because Jason ended up going home without me," Rose said looking at the mirror across the room and touched her cheek with her own cool hand as she looked down a moment at her shaking hands the hair brush sliding from her fingertips to hit the floor.

Rose felt the burning pain in her eyes that meant tears. "You know I don't know what I did to make her hate me so much besides being born a little different in the head," Rose said and looked up to see Daisy in that white dress simply bigger to fit her.

"Oh, Rosey you know I never cared about what those voices said but don't act dumb you know the reason why she hates you."

Rose opened her mouth to speak but was cut off by a knock at her white door.

"Rose are you almost ready?" Jason asked from outside. "Coming," Rose said looking back to see Daisy was once again gone. She quickly stood and did her make-up and stepped into the black heels, looking one last time in the mirror at the pale girl that stood before her.

"Rose we really need to get going," Jason said softly with another knock. Without another word Rose walked over and opened the door to see her brother dressed in a black suit jacket and pants, his black hair combed to the side making him look like a good little choir boy.

"I'm ready," Rose said moving pass Jason and down the stairs finding her mother waiting for them by the front door. "Give this poke cake and Tuna and Noodle Casserole to Mrs. young and tell her I'll have more to bring over later on in the week," her Mother said handing Rose the two pyrex dishes. "Mrs. and Mr. Young will love it mother," Jason said with a small smile and took a dish from Rose's arms. "Thank you Jason," her mother said kissing him on the cheek then turned to Rose and patted her cheek making her flinch away.

"I'll see the both of you tonight at dinner," Their mother said and left them to themselves. "Come on Rosey let's go," Jason said with a sigh as he opened the door for the both of them and she walked out into the late afternoon sun.

They walked towards Jason's black dodge charger and Rose opened the back and placed the food her mother had made for after the funeral, then walked over and got into the passenger side door letting Jason close it for her.

"I bet my mom is going to love the poke cake," Daisy said in her ear, "But my dad can't stand tuna so mom will get to have that all for herself."

"I'm sure mother will bring something better next time," Rose said looking out the window to see a few wild daisies in front of their mailbox. "I'm sure she will," Jason said making Rose jump a little bit not noticing him before as he turned the key and started the engine pulling out of the driveway.

It stayed silent for the ten-minute drive to the funeral home, music from the radio the only sound keeping her from screaming until they pulled up to the sidewalk outside of the small dark little place along with the rest of the cars, Rose was about to open her door when Jason spoke.

"I know this is killing you Rosey, I know Daisy was your best friend and that you did everything together, but today you need to let her go."

Rose stopped and turned her head so quickly to look at him she thought it would break. "How can you say that with a straight face?" Rose asked not believing him, he sounded like their mother.

"Rosey you can't keep counting on her, she's gone and that's it, she isn't here anymore, She's not kit your dog, I can't lie and tell you she'll be back someday," Jason said with such force it made Rose sit back away from him and a moment later he realized his mistake.

"Rose I didn't mean it like that but I can't stand seeing you like this, she was a chapter in your life, a big one and I get that, but you can't keep reading it over and over again in hopes it will change because it won't."

Rose looked away from him, "You think I don't know that? That she isn't coming back? Because I do but I need more than just today to let the one person who loved me for no reason other than I was me!"

Jason opened his mouth to reply but she wouldn't stay around to hear how dumb she was. She threw open the car door and started for the open door that Mr. Young held open for everyone and when he saw her coming he tried to put on a smile, but it didn't reach his eyes.

"Hello Rose, how are you holding up?"

"I should be the one asking you that," Rose said. "I take it you were at school when..." Mr. Young trailed off looking down but she saw the look of anger on his face, "When that boy told the whole school that he killed my baby girl."

"Yes, sir I was," Rose answered. "Did she know him? Were they together in some way?" he asked looking her in the eye hoping for any kind of answer.

"No, I don't think they ever talked much sir, maybe once or twice at best."

The older man nodded and Rose saw the gray hairs that hadn't been there two months ago. "You should head in now Rose, you have a spot at the front along with the other girls."

Rose nodded, "Thank you, sir."

She walked past him wanting to say so much more, how sorry that he had to bury his daughter, that she hadn't done something to stop it from happening and that she still talked to her when he couldn't. But it wasn't really Daisy was it, she would be thrown back into a hospital if anyone knew and this time they would throw away the key.

She looked up and followed a few people she didn't know down a long hallway decked in green carpet and light wooden paneling, the smell of fake vanilla everywhere covering the pain in the air. Rose looked to her side and saw the walls lined with paintings of trees and Autumn frosts.

"Very cheerful," Daisy said from where she stood at the end of the hallway that led into the viewing room and Rose felt her stomach twist as she came closer to see what Daisy had been looking at.

A painting of a sunny green meadow full of white flowers. "Do you think mom will try doing her garden now that I'm not there to help her?" Daisy asked looking over at her.

"I don't know, but I'll make sure to ask her if she needs help with it," Rose said turning to face the open doorway and saw that the room was decked in the same colors as the hall but this one was packed with people and because everyone wore some kind of black it could have been anywhere from twenty to a hundred people in there.

"Keep your head down okay," Daisy said taking her hand, "And remember to breathe."

"But everyone will be looking at me," Rose said panic closing her throat.

"Rose trust me, no one is looking at you today, when you have me in the room."

Rose nodded and swallowed hard as she stepped into the room. The grief was the first thing to hit her, it was thick with sadness and pain no one could see, it was something you felt to your very bone. She kept her head down like Daisy had said until she heard her name.

"Rose over here."

She looked up to see Lily and Violet in a row behind where Mrs. Young sat. They were in all black like her, but Lily wore it in a long sleeved shirt and skirt with a pair of black sandals and Violet wore a dress that went down to her ankles while Rose looked like someone from a good housewife guide.

She sat and looked up to see the casket that sat on a catafalque in the middle of the back wall so everyone could see it. It was a lovely deep dark wood with what looked to be daisies carved into the sides.

It was closed of course and a large photo of Daisy smiling in the park taken last year stood in front on an easel, but what caught Rose off guard was that it was surrounded by flowers. Hundreds and hundreds of flowers all of them red roses.

"Why are there so many roses?" She asked looking over at her friends but got the answer from Mrs. Young who looked back at them then, her eyes red from crying and her make-up looked as if it had been wiped away from the tears. "They were sent over this morning with a card."

"Who was it from?" Violet asked. "It didn't have a name it just had a message to Daisy written on it, do you think it's someone from school?"

"Do you know where the card is?" Lily asked. "Yes, I have it here," Mrs. Young said opening a small black clutch and took out a little white card and handed it to Violet.

"Are all of the flowers from them?" Lily asked trying to look over Violet's shoulder. "No, a few are from family but they are to the side, all of the red roses are from the card's sender."

Rose looked over at Violet and saw her eyebrows come together confused, "I have no idea who could write this," She said handing it too Rose.

Lily tried to grab it but Rose was quicker and looked down reading over it, then had to read it over a few times trying to understand it, but it didn't make any sense.

"Daisy, you and I had a lot of fun all those night's. I'm sorry it had to end so soon. But take these roses as my last gift to you, after all, it's how we found our way together." - Sender.

Rose blinked as she looked up, Lily taking the card from her. "What do you think it means?" Mrs. Young asked looking worried. "I-I have no idea," Rose said and she didn't, it could have been Tommy yes, but why not just sign his name then? he confessed to being the killer after all.

"Do you think it's from that boy?" Mrs. Young asked looking sick to her stomach at the thought.

"No I don't think so, it doesn't feel like something he would do after this morning," Rose answered looking at the room, at all of the people around them and tried to see if anyone from their year hadn't shown up. But as everyone stopped to sit down she saw everyone from school was there, even Susan who had to be the only girl who disliked Daisy in all of history because she had been able to skip a grade and bested her in the art show last winter.

But it also looked as if almost everyone in their town had come, making the room swim with people in black so it was hard to see just one person.

"Wow all these people here to see me and you can't even see my pretty face," Daisy said from where she stood in front of her own casket back facing Rose as she trailed her index finger along the daisies on the side. "Do you think it hurt much when he hit me over the head?" Daisy asked as she turned to face Rose who let out a gasp and covered her mouth to keep from screaming.

Daisy's red hair was dripping blood, staining her white dress a ruby red so deep it matched the roses.

"What's wrong Rosey, is there something on my face?"

All Rose could do was stare at her as Daisy reached up and wiped at her face, more blood starting to flow from a deep cut in the side of her head like something had really hit her.

"Oh dear, what a mess," Daisy said tipping her head to the side before her eyes rolled back into her head and she fell forward hitting the floor, and just like in her dream this morning Rose could only sit there and do nothing watching her best friend bleed out in the middle of the room.

She felt the tears start to fall as she choked back a sob. "Oh Rosey," Lily said seeing her reaction thinking it was because of the funeral, the sorrow of having to bury their friend taking over her and she pulled Rose into her arms. Rose let her, turning her head away from the scene in front of the room.

She stayed that way for the next hour as amazing grace was sung and people stood up talking about memories they had shared with her, from getting help with homework to her listening to their problems. Then about her volunteering to read for the children at the town's church, so on and so on.

Then the priest stepped up telling them all about how she was a bright girl and now she was watching over them along with god himself. But to Rose, his words fell flat. Daisy hadn't been religious, only going because her parents did and the kids she read too, she believed in god yes, but hated how people twisted it in ways to spread hatred at people who loved differently than them or made different choices.

But as he finished up his speech Rose looked up and saw that Mr. and Mrs. Young were nodding along holding onto one another, their own tears dripping to their black clothing and she got it then. Funerals weren't for the dead, no they were for the living. To remember someone they loved one last time in the best light they could, to say goodbye and reinsure themselves that the person they loved was in a better place not just going into a hole in the cold dark ground for a sleep they would never wake up from again.

But it wasn't the same for Rose, after all, she would be the one in a box if it hadn't been for Daisy, and a little piece of her still wished it was.

"We shall go now and lay this beautiful young soul to her final resting place," The Priest said and at that everyone got up making a line to past the casket before exiting.

Rose and her friends ended up being the very first ones next to Daisy's mom and dad, she watched them walk over to it still holding on to one another, hands laced together as they placed them on top of the casket where Daisy's heart would have been.

"Baby I don't know if you're here or not, but I want you to know I loved you so much. I wanted to see who you would have become but that won't happen now, you'll remain the same kind, sweet sixteen-year-old I knew you were," Mr. Young said and Rose could see that he was trying to hold back his own sobs.

Mrs. Young covered his hand with her other and leaned down placing a kiss to the lid of the casket. "Goodbye baby girl."

Rose watched as Mr. Young led Daisy's mom towards the hallway and the line moved up so she stood in front of it and was unsure what to do, she swallowed and placed her own too white hand on the top. "I'm so sorry I wasn't there for you when you needed me, Daisy, I should have been, will you ever forgive me?" Rose whispered and jumped as something warm touched her cold hand.

She looked over and found Violet and Lily standing next to her, hands on top of her own.

"Of course she would forgive you Rosey," Lily said and Violet nodded in agreement tears in her eyes. Rose looked around the room to see if her Daisy was around but found nothing. Just her friend's sorrowful faces trying hard to be strong, but Rose could see through them to their pain, after all Daisy was the reason they had met in the first place.

Rose nodded looking away from them so they wouldn't see the tears filling her own eyes and headed for the hall, her friends right next to her.

* * *

Violet

The blue sky was clear of any clouds or wind, everything seemed to stand still as Violet watched a few of Daisy's cousins and father load the casket into the back of a black hearse.

For a moment she felt as if she was back on that day four years ago, but it had been raining as if the world was crying for her then.

It had been a cold December day as she watched her mother be lowered into the frozen ground, no one there besides her dad and the priest, her breath fogging up in front of her.

She had been only thirteen at the time just integrating into the world that was Watkinsville Georgia, her dad had just started working at a hardware shop in town. Both her and his English had been poor at the time plus it didn't help that she had no one to turn to for comfort but her dad and he never wanted to talk, maybe wishing it had been her instead.

After all, she had been there when her mom had been gunned down outside a shop for no reason other than that she was at the wrong place at the time. Well, that's what she believed until she walked into school and the first thing she learned that day was if you were dark skinned and knew almost no English you better keep yourself out of the way or the next thing you knew it would be you in a grave.

Because in a place where everyone was white you needed to stay out of the way, that was in less you had Daisy Young on your side.

If you had the girl everyone loved next to you she would blind them long enough for them to not care that your accent slipped out or that you still had a hard time understanding why disco music was so big when it gave you a headache. And of course Daisy had tried to help Violet with her dad, telling her she could come and stay at her house anytime she needed never understanding that Violet couldn't just leave her dad, not when he was the last person she had in her small family even if sometimes it ended with a bruise or cut, who else would loved her in this world?

"Violet am I riding with you?" Lily asked snapping her back into reality and she let go of her mother's ring that hung around her neck.

Violet looked over to see the hearse pulling away and Rose following Jason toward his car. "Where did he come from?" Violet asked watching after them.

"I think he was somewhere in the back but I didn't see him, too many people," Lily answered.

Violet looked at them a moment more as Rose got in looking like a ghost herself. Then she turned away and started for her truck, Lily in tow.

The drive to the graveyard was slow in almost a dreamlike way with people pulling over and tipped their heads at them in respect, not only to the family but the girl everyone knew.

Violet had to look away at the blue sky too bright for the kind of day it was as an older man who had called her names behind her back waved.

"Are you okay?" Lily asked worry in her eyes.

"No," Violet answered simply, "I don't think I'll ever be with Daisy gone."

Who's going to save me now? she didn't say.

"I know right," Lily said looking down and placed a hand on top of Violets own maybe hoping it would comfort her. But it only brought tears to her eyes, the ring heavy around her neck.

They pulled up with the rest of the cars outside of the graveyard which was lined with a short black fence, the grass as green as any spring day, new and old stones everywhere looking like a maze.

Violet was about to get out but stopped a thought going through her. "Lily, do you think Daisy was the glue of the group?"

"What do you mean?" Lily asked letting the smoke dance around the car from her half dead cigarette. "I mean what is going to happen to us now that she's gone? Will we break apart and go our own ways without her?"

Lily bit her lip a moment, "I don't think that will happen, but we've stuck together so far and i think she would haunt us for the rest of our lives if we did."

Violet couldn't help a smile at the thought of Daisy Young standing there judging them and trying to knock down a vase in Rose's house.

"Come on," Lily said getting out and made her way around baby blue to stand next to Violet taking her hand and pulled her along until they reached an empty grave, chairs waiting for them.

"Lily, Violet come and sit down."

Violet looked over to see Mrs. Young sitting down next to her husband. Lily put on a painful smile and led Violet over to them sitting down which Violet was thankful for because she felt dizzy, everything catching up with her.

"How are the two of you holding up?" Mr. Young asked and Violet was taken aback by how kind he sounded, how concerned he was about them as he was burying his own daughter. "I'm okay," Violet said trying to sound convincing but looked away not able to meet his eyes.

"That's good and how is Rose? Daisy would kill us if she isn't doing well," Mrs. Young asked looking tired.

Violet opened her mouth unsure what she was going to say but was thankfully saved by Rose herself walking over alongside Jason. "I'm doing fine for the most part," Rose said sitting down, Jason next to her his black hair messy from the wind.

"That's good to hear," Mrs. Young said her eyes ringed with red.

Violet wanted to say something comforting but didn't get the chance as the Priest walked up to the grave, the casket following behind.

Violet felt vomit in the back of her throat as they lowered it down into the cold ground and the priest started the last word as everyone stood and took up a hand full of dirt.

"For as much as it has pleased almighty god to take out of this world the soul of Daisy Jane Young,"

Mrs. and Mr. Young let their hands tip then, the dirt hitting the wood with a soft sound.

"We, therefore, commit her body to the ground, earth to earth, ashes to ashes, dust to dust."

Violet opened her hand as the rest of his words fell on deaf ears, the dirt turning to dust in the air as it fell to cover her best friend, her savior.

* * *

Rose

Rose let her handful fall to the ground not able to stand throwing dirt onto her best friend's body and stood back letting everyone else take their turn. "How are you fairing," Jason asked joining her. Instead of answering, she asked her own question, "Where were you at the viewing? I never saw you."

"I was in the back there wasn't any room up front with the whole town showing up."

"Why does he act so surprised?" Daisy asked making Rose jump and look at her in surprise as she walked over to them and stopped. Rose cursed at herself for it. She had learned a long time ago to stop looking at the people and things that shouldn't be there making her mother happy in the belief that her daughter was the pretty little girl she raised and not crazy.

"Do you think it's cold down there?" Daisy asked but again Rose didn't reply instead she turned and went over to where Mr. and Mrs. Young stood looking gray and tired. "My mother made a casserole and a cake for the two of you, it's in the back of the car."

Mrs. Young nodded trying to smile for her, "Thank you, we'll take them when we go home for the after service."

Rose simply nodded as everyone started for their cars, she had never known how short the burial service was, she had believed she would be out in the warm sun longer in hopes of warming up because for the past two months she had only felt cold.

"Why aren't you talking to me?" Daisy asked making Rose stop as she moved in front of her blocking her way, "Are you mad at me for earlier?"

Rose rolled her eyes, no why the hell would she be mad, she only had to watch her friend bleed to death at her own funeral! "You know what you'll have to do in order to stop seeing me right?" Daisy smiled and Rose bit her lip letting the pain wash over her, she knew what she needed to do but seeing Daisy made it too hard to go back.

But her attention was caught seconds later as everyone started talking in low whispers as they turned to look at something. Rose looked up and felt her heart drop as she saw both Mark and Chief Thompson getting out of their police car and started for Mrs. and Mr. Young, both looking pained.

CHAPTER 7

Lily

Lily stopped in her tracks as the red and blue lights came into view flashing across the green of the grass, her heartbeat picking up, what could it be now?

She watched as Mark and Chief Thompson started for the Youngs and before she knew what she was doing she moved slowly towards them wanting to hear first hand what bad news was coming.

And luckily for her she was faster than them stopping next to a large gravestone just tall enough to hide her as she listened to footsteps come closer then stop.

"Mr. Young, Mrs. Young I'm sorry to have to talk with you today of all days," Lily heard Chief Thompson say real pain in his voice. "But it's about the boy Tommy Johnson, I'm afraid we can't get anything out of him."

"Let me in the room with him for a few minutes and make sure no one is watching and maybe I can get something out of him," Mr. Young said sounding as dark as Lily had ever heard him before.

"No, that's not what I mean, the thing is another boy has come forward to claim that he was the one to kill your daughter in the same way Tommy did."

Lily felt her eyes widen as the words hit her and both the Youngs must have been just as taken aback as well because it took them a moment to reply. Lily could hear the breath catch in Mrs. Young's voice as she spoke. "How can that be?"

"I believe it's just a game to these boys, but I can promise you both, we will get to the bottom of this," Chief Thompson said. And Lily wondered what Mark was doing as they talked.

"They think this is a game!" Mr. Young said sounding angry and Lily understood the feeling, how dare people play with the death of her friend. But she knew how to get to the bottom of this and if it really was a game there would be hell to pay for whoever came up with it.

"I understand how painful this is I really do, and we will be charging them with obstruction of justice, but they will be lawyering up soon," Chief Thompson said and Lily was surprised to hear Mark join in.

"To be honest Mr. and Mrs. Young the truth is we would like to know why and are they covering something up for-"

"What young officer Hollow is trying to say is we are working around the clock and talking with everyone who we believe could help in the investigation," Chief Thompson said quickly sounding annoyed.

"Yes, of course," Mark said clearly cowed. "May we talk some more?" Chief Thompson asked.

"Of course we were just heading home for the after service with everyone, we can talk there," Mr. Young said his voice hard.

"Thank you, I know today is hard but we will give you closure," Mark said sounding sure. "Thank you," Mrs. Young said her voice small.

Lily stayed where she was until the footsteps faded away. "Lily there you are we need to go to the after service," Violet said grabbing her forearm, but Lily didn't move. "No we need to meet Alex," Lily said her words hard as she adjusted her bag and started for baby blue.

Violet stood there for a moment taken aback by Lily, she had never acted like that before but snapped out of it and followed Lily who was almost jogging now. "Who the hell is Alex?" Violet asked catching up with the taller girl.

"You'll get to meet him soon I guess," Lily said opening the car door and jumped in, Violet following behind. "Where are we going?" Violet asked looking over at Lily turning the key, the engine starting up.

"We need to go to the park by your house," Lily said looking through her bag for something and Violet wasn't surprised when she pulled out a pack of cigarettes but what did was when she rolled the window down and threw them into the grass.

"What the f-" Violet started wide-eyed but Lily cut her off, "Drive!"

"But what about Rose?"

"She'll be okay, she's with Jason after all," Lily said looking up at Violet with a look she had never seen before, a look of determination and without a word Violet put the truck in drive and pulled away as fast as she could.

* * *

Rose

Rose looked after Mark and Chief Thompson just like everyone else, Mr. and Mrs. Young behind them as they got into their own cars. "What do you think they needed to talk about?" Rose said and looked up at her brother who was pale most likely from the cold breeze that had kicked up now.

"I don't know but we need to follow them for the after service so maybe we'll find out," Jason said watching as they drove away and Rose looked around to see people heading for their own cars as fast as they could.

"Come on," Jason said taking her arm dragging her towards the car and almost threw her at it. Rose looked across the car at Jason his hair a mess from the wind as he tried to open the door with his key but he had grabbed the house key instead.

Rose wondered what was wrong? He had never acted like this before that she had seen but now it was like the world was on fire somehow. "Jason, what's going on?" Rose asked wanting to see his reaction to the question. And she was happy to see one as he looked up sharply his eyes dark, "I just want to know what's happening with Mr. and Mrs. Young, make sure everything's okay," Jason said finally opening the door and threw himself in.

She had no choice but to get in having seen the baby blue truck take off minutes ago. Jason turned the key and the radio turned on at full volume "Why do me like this, why kiss me then kill me like-"

Jason cut it off with an annoyed sigh. "Do you think it's about Tommy?" Rose asked as they drove at a speed she had never seen from him. "That's what I hope to find out."

Rose raised an eyebrow at him wondering why he cared so much, he had liked Daisy yes, more in a little sister kind of way, but maybe this had hurt him more then she had thought and said as much to him.

For a long moment, he said nothing and Rose thought he wasn't going to answer until his deep voice broke the silence.

"Of course her death hurt me Rosey, and I need to know the person who killed her is in jail or even better in the grave both for me and you."

Rose opened her mouth to ask why the grave and how that could help anyone when they parked in front of the Young's house and Jason jumped out.

Rose grabbed her black coat seeing the darkening clouds that had grown overhead as the day when on. She stepped out shrugging to get it on when she felt the first drop of cold hit her cheek feeling like the tears that fell this morning.

She followed after Jason through the large dark wooden door and was met with a room filled with people.

Jason broke away from her then starting for the kitchen where Rose heard Mrs. Young's voice, but she didn't follow him this time and instead she headed for Daisy's room.

As she walked she couldn't help be disconcerted that Daisy's and her houses were so similar yet so very different. The interior was decked in warm colors of orange wallpaper and brown carpet with splashes of yellow in the furniture unlike her home so full of white and light blue feeling like ice.

She could hear the radio going as she walked the carpeted floor fewer people around her, a voice reaching her even now and the memory of Daisy singing and dancing along to it only months ago alive and smiling. Rose had been sitting on her bed shaking her head at the silly dance she performed, but a moment later she was being pulled off and handed a hairbrush to use as a microphone to sing along with her, unable to help a smile as their voices mixed, "You're tearing me apart baby boy, I wanted you and now I'm left cold."

Rose closed her eyes as she reached out grabbing the cold handle, then opened them looking at the white door littered with posters of bands and art Daisy had made that she actually felt good about. A water colored blue sky wrinkled from being touched caught her eye, Rose reached out and ran her thumb over the light blue dotted with blackbirds, she stayed that way a moment then pushed the door open stepping into the dark room that smelled of dust and untouched clothes.

The room hadn't been cleaned up once most likely since that morning the police went through it looking for anything to help in their search and Rose felt maybe Mrs. or Mr. Young had stood outside thinking about cleaning it up for when Daisy got home or even throwing away something after her body was found, but couldn't get up the nerve. The thought of those nights and days spent in this room too much to handle for them, of the smiles and all too happy memories keeping them away.

Rose flicked the switch lighting the pink and yellow room, the walls a mess of posters just like the ones on her door but her art covered the walls, paintings of flowers and birds now lay unlooked at and under a layer of dust.

But Rose knew what she was doing, she pulled out a wooden chair from under the desk and over to the air vent and climbed atop it, opening the old grates and waited a moment.

Not a second later she heard Mr. and Mrs. Young's voices because, in the end, Jason had been wrong, they wouldn't talk in the kitchen. No, they would move up to their bedroom and if you were close enough you could hear every word said as if you were in the room yourself.

She and Daisy had found this out when she wanted to hear what she was getting for Christmas and thought crawling through the vent would be the best way but instead found she could hear everything, it was also how she learned there was no Santa but never told them to keep the magic alive.

Rose leaned in closer and listened closing her eyes blocking everything else out.

"Ms. Young I know this is hard but I must know, did she have anyone she was seeing?" Rose heard Chief Thompson ask, his voice tired.

"No, I can't think of anyone she liked or even had an eye out for?" Mrs. Young replied.

"Do you think she told anyone if she was dating?"

"Of course she would tell her friends, but even they said she wasn't seeing anyone right?" Mr. Young answered.

"Yes we have interviewed her friends, but like you said they didn't see or hear anything about an older boyfriend."

"But people said they saw her calling someone, a man the night of the party?" Mrs. Young asked

"A few people yes, but…" Chief Thompson trailed off, …..."But no one can confirm it for sure and it may just be speaking ill of the dead."

Rose had to stand there and blink a moment to comprehend what she just heard, they thought Daisy may have been seeing someone, an older man at that. But they were wrong she would have told her because Daisy told her everything.

"Hey! What the hell are you doing up there?"

Rose jumped and turned for the door to see who it was with her in the room, but forgot she had been standing on a chair. The next thing she knew the floor was coming at her fast, that was until someone caught her in their arms.

The impact made her ribs scream but at least she didn't bust her head open. She looked up to tell whoever interrupted her off but her words died as she looked up to meet the hazel eyes of Mark Hollow.

"Looks like I saved you this time Rosey," Mark said with a soft smile. She made a disgusted sound and pushed him away. "Why the hell are you here?" Rose hissed at him. He raised his eyebrows at her in question, "Really you're asking me that?"

Rose tried to look taken aback. "Excuse me but I'm trying to mourn my best friend!"

Mark crossed his arms and gave her a dry look, "Yes, I too mourn my best friends from atop a chair next to the vent."

Rose bit her lip out of anger and turned away from him. "You were listening to the Young's and Chief Thompson weren't you?"

"What are you going to do arrest me?"

"If you're hiding something it's in my right too," Mark said not sounding very serious, "Was she seeing someone Rosey?"

Rose let out a breath and turned back to face him, "No she wasn't seeing anyone and you trying to focus on it won't help anyone!"

"And how can you be sure?" Mark asked taking a step closer towards her. "She would have told me," Rose said her voice rising in anger. "What makes you think she would tell you?"

Rose looked up at him so they were eye to eye. "After that day a year ago she would tell me if anything happened in her life."

The words hit its mark and he looked away first, she knew that would have been the one thing to break him. "What happened with Tommy?" Rose asked taking a step closer herself, "Will he be moved to a real jail soon?

Mark shook his head anger in his eyes. "He's been let go as someone else came forward and confessed to killing her in the same way as Tommy did."

Rose's eyes went wide as the words hit her in the face like ice water, "Why?"

"That's the part I'm trying to figure out," Mark said scratching at the back of his head, his brown hair a mess. Rose looked away quickly but her eyes caught on the tipped over chair and her breath stopped. "Shit," she hissed and pushed pass Mark to kneel next to it.

One of the old oak floorboards stuck up and Rose prayed it had just been knocked loose and not broken. But as she moved it to see how bad the damage was she found that the reason it was loose wasn't the chair falling but a black book lay under it making the board easy to move.

"Why is there a book under the floor?" Mark asked standing behind her. Instead of answering she gently picked it up and turned it around and found that the cover was of painted daisies, the white and yellow stood out and above it was written 'Je Suis forever' in gold. Rose knew it was French but that had been Daisy's thing, not hers.

"I am forever," Mark said going to his knees next to her. Rose looked at him surprised, "You know how to read French?"

"I have many talents," he said with a little smirk and she rolled her eyes opening the little book flipping to the first page and started to read.

August 14th, 1974.

"Today was amazing, the sun was shining and I couldn't wait to go swimming, but I couldn't stop looking at him, the way he would smile and act as if we hadn't spent the night together, the way his eyes met mine and the twitch of his lips. But on the other hand, I can't stop worrying about Rose. She looks so pale after being in that messed up hospital that her damned mom put her in. I only wish that I could make her smile again, but the pills they have her under make her almost seem like a zombie, as if she's under a heavy wet blanket, but he said that the doctors will give her something a little less strong and hopefully that will help her as school starts again. But I can't help wondering what her mom will make her say to make up for the past six months and when I asked he only said something about an aunt that lives in Arizona. We're meeting tomorrow at 33.714080,-83.291840 to talk more."

Rose raised her eyebrows at the random string of numbers and looked over to see what Mark's reaction was, but he too looked confused just the same as her.

"What do you think it means?" She asked watching as he read over it again and shook his head. "I have no idea what the numbers mean, but what is she talking about a hospital and pills for..." He trailed off as he looked her in the eye, his own now filled with horror, "What happened in those six months you were gone Rosey?"

She stood so quickly she almost fell over as she backed away from him, the book clutched in her hand so tightly her knuckles turned white. He stood up slowly as if she was a wild animal he was trying to calm down. "Rose i need that book, it could be a big help in this investigation, whoever that man is she's talking about could be her real killer."

Rose could barely hear him over her heart beat, pounding in her head as she kept backing away until she hit the wall. She could never let him read this, could never let anyone.

"Please Rosey," Mark said softly putting his hand out for it not understanding her reaction. "N- no," Rose said her voice shaking, "You can't have it!"

Mark blinked at her and opened his mouth to say something but Rose would never know what it was because just then Mrs. Young opened the door coming into the room and her expression hardened as she saw Mark. "Mr. Hollow can I help you?"

"Mrs. Young i- I'm sorry I was just talking with Rose here."

Mrs. Young's eyes caught Rose's and she raised her eyebrows, "Well I hope you're done with your talk because Chief Thompson is looking for you, I believe he's ready to go," Mrs. Young said looking at him steal in her green eyes.

"Of course, I'll be going then," Mark said shooting Rose a look that said this conversation wasn't over. Mrs. Young moved out of the way as he passed her in the doorway, her long black dress swaying around her thin body.

Rose looked at her as they were left alone, "Are you alright dear?" Mrs. Young asked her eyes full of the same kind of kindness as her daughters. "Yes," Rose lied looking down at the black book still in her shaking hand.

Mrs. Young looked unconvinced but nodded, "Well if you're done in here come down and eat something, you're looking too skinny now of days."

Rose had no other choice but to follow her into the kitchen full of people eating and talking in whispers. Rose slipped the book into the inner pocket of her jacket and sat with her brother who looked pissed off.

"What happened to you?" Jason asked his voice filled with annoyance. "I was just in Daisy's room is all," Rose said taking a bite of her sandwich. Jason looked over at her eyebrows raised, "What for?"

And now it was Rose's turn to look at him in confusion, he had never cared about what she did in her time before now, but maybe he was just worried since this day was hard on everyone but she couldn't tell him the truth. "I wanted to be somewhere she loved and we had so many good memories here."

Her words had the effect she wanted as he looked away from her and nodded, but she could still feel the words in the air, Are you okay?

Are you still seeing things no one else can?

Instead of answering his unasked questions Rose got up and left her brother their worried eyes still on her as she made her way into the living room which was empty and dark. Rose found and turned on the light switch to find the reason no one was in here.

Boxes of flyers sat on the coffee table and chairs, there had to be fifty or more of them. She walked over to them and picked up one of the pages and looked down at the blurry photo of Daisy. It was the same picture as the one that sat in front of her casket today, it was taken a year ago in the park by Violet's house the background a blurry green as she sat on one of the swings a smile as bright as the yellow and pink top she wore, her teeth white and hair blowing back in the wind.

Rose smiled to herself putting it back down, but as she did something caught her eye and she moved to another box her brow furrowed. She tipped her head to one side as she tried to figure out what she was looking at, and finally it hit her as she picked it up and held it out to the light showing that it was an X-Ray of someone's teeth.

But why would Mrs. Young keep this with Daisy's missing posters and info on the search...Rose shook her head not understanding. She put the X-Ray back and went looking through the box again and grabbed a file and found that she was looking at dental records.

And as she looked at them closer she saw that the name on them was Daisy's. But Rose knew for a fact that this couldn't be hers, because Daisy had a tooth that was crooked from when a baby tooth didn't fall out right away but the adult tooth grew in making it leaned to the side. It wasn't in the front so it wasn't noticeable if you didn't know it was there so Daisy never bothered to have it fixed. But Rose did know and the dental records she was holding wasn't hers, all of the teeth were perfect.

But... whoms were they if not Daisy's? Rose felt something like hope starting to rise within her from the ashes.

Just then a door slam somewhere in the house and Rose knew her time was up. She quickly folded the X-Ray and stuck it into her pocket next to the book, just in time as right then Mr. Young walked in looking out of it for the most part, his eyes somewhere else but he came back to reality as they focused on her.

"Rose what are you doing in here?"

She swallowed hard giving herself a moment to think of a believable lie, "I-I was kinda just wondering around, I don't know what to do now," Rose said looking down her head spinning with questions that couldn't be asked.

Mr. Young nodded in sympathy, "I know, I keep thinking she'll just walk in one day laughing about something or another but.." he trailed off a moment and Rose could hear the pain in his voice as he spoke, "But that won't happen will it."

Without another word Rose went over to him and wrapped her arms around him, Mr. Young had been like a second father to her ever since she was a little girl. When she got a cut on her knee he was there to clean it up and put a bandaid on it with reassuring words that it would be alright and now it was her turn to do it for him.

"I'll come by whenever I can," Rose choked out, her voice thin. Mr. Young stepped back from her with a painful little smile that looked fake, "Don't you worry about as now, you just worry about your school work and health got it."

Rose nodded not meeting his eyes, "Will do sir," She said walking into the hallway passing by him and touched the inside of her pocket letting out a breath she hadn't known she was holding. She needed to talk with Lily and Violet right now, because Daisy wasn't dead.

CHAPTER 8

Violet

Violet drove following Lily's directions as the day grew darker, the sun setting. The ride, for the most part, quiet as both were too deep in their own thoughts. Violet wondering if this day would ever end, first Tommy's confession then the funeral and now this. And Lily in a world of questions that needed answers.

"Why are we going to the park again?" Violet asked for the fourth time in the last fifteen minutes. Lily rolled her eyes as she kept an eye out for a sign of Alex and his friends. "Like i said before I need to talk with some friends about the guys who confessed to killing Daisy today."

"And how do you know they will have any idea what's going on?" Violet asked looking over at her a moment.

"Like I said I'll tell you when-" Lily started but her words were cut off with a gasp, "Stop!"

Violet's eyes went wide as she slammed on the breaks making the truck stop on the spot next to the sidewalk which Lily had made her drive next to, sending them forward and if Lily hadn't been holding onto the armrest she would have been sent through the window.

"What the hell!" Violet snapped at Lily but she was already halfway out of the truck disappearing into the night. "God damn it!" Violet hissed but pulled out the key and followed after her trying not to fall on her face from the roots of the tall trees all around them.

She caught up with Lily in a minute jogging next to her. "Okay Lily you need to start talking now, we are in the middle of an empty park and it's getting dark and my dad will need a reason as to why I was out so late."

"My friend's have..." Lily paused a moment then when on, "They have connections and have answers we need."

Violet opened her mouth to ask what that meant , but stopped as they stepped into a clearing and found ten or twenty older teenagers smoking or talking around a metal can, a fire going in it. All wearing black in some way or another.

"Jesus Christ we're going to be murdered," Violet said under her breath, stopping before them. "Don't be so dramatic," Lily said walking up to them, "They're my friends."

Violet looked at her and whispered in a rush so they wouldn't hear, "They look like drug dealers!"

"Some of them are," Lily said simply and stopped next to a guy who had his hair down to the middle of his back. "Hey," Lily said looking up at the guy with a dark smile, one Violet had never seen before, this Lily was a new one to her and most likely to everyone else who knew her in the day time.

"Lily, what the hell are you doing here girl? Isn't it Daisy's funeral today."

"It was and I'm sure she was sad not having you there," Lily said taking the cigarette someone passed over and the girl next to her lit it.

"Oh don't lie Lily it doesn't suit you, I know damn well she wouldn't want people like us there for her parents to see, they wouldn't want to know about that side of her," The guy said tipping his head back breathing out smoke and Violet watched it blow away in the wind.

"And anyway we had our own little celebration of life," A girl with a tall afro said a rolled up white piece of paper in hand.

"What did you do? hit a few buds," Lily said blowing a mouth of smoke at her. The girl laughed high and shrill, "You know she liked a good left-handed cigarette."

"That's because she was actually left-handed," Lily said dryly.

"But you're not here just to talk to us are you Lily dilly?" Axel asked.

"I just wanted to buy a few cigarettes."
"I told you lying doesn't suit you," Axel said.

"Fine," Lily said taking a deep inhale and let it out as she spoke, "Today at school Tommy Johnson confessed to killing Daisy in front of Mark and everyone, but then at the burial service Chief Thompson came up to Mr. and Mrs. Young telling them another guy from school confessed to it as well with the same story and everything."

"And you want us to tell you and your friend.." Axel trailed off as he looked over at Violet, his eyes looking black in the night. "Violet," She said crossing her arms pulling them closer to her chest as the night got colder with the sun gone. "You know Violet," Axel said with a smirk, "We have a fire going for a reason right, it's not just to make us look spooky."

Violet opened her mouth ready to give him a reason as to why she shouldn't get closer to the fire because she really wasn't a fan of smart ass's and they seemed to fall so easily, but Lily cut her off. "Anyway, your right Axel, I'm hoping you know something I don't like normally."

Axel shook his head with a little laugh, "God Lily you got any toast for that much butter?"

Lily just gave him a dry look. "Fine, fine," he said, "Yes we know that for a fact about five guys have been paid off to come forward to her murder."

Violet felt her eyes go wide and she was unable to help herself from almost yelling, "Five! Five men have come forward?"

"Not yet, only two so far but, Gage and Kevin have put down a payment on new cars all of a sudden and Jim was able to pay his mother's medical bills, so I have a feeling we'll have more murderer's than we know what to do with," Axel said throwing his cigarette into the fire.

Lily was shaking her head looking confused, "Why would they do that and who the hell would pay for them to confess to a murder they didn't commit?"

"Your guess is as good as mine in that Lily dilly," Axel said looking into the fire as if it could tell them. "How do you know all of this?" Violet asked finally walking over to them looking him in the eye. But to her surprise, he looked over at Lily, "You never told her about us? I'm hurt."

"What are you talking about?" Violet asked turning to Lily now, "How do you know these people Lily?"

Lily looked away a moment the fire lighting her brown eyes up so they looked lighter than normal. "I'll tell you later okay," Lily said leaving no room for disagreement. "Oh come on Lily, tell her about the night we broke into the school a year ago and-"

"Shut it!" Lily snapped and grabbed Violet's hand and started to walk away from them, but stopped as Axel called back to them. "Daisy wouldn't have run Lily dilly."

Violet turned to see what Lily's reaction was and to her surprise, she was smiling. "Oh yes she would have," Lily called back then took off in a run pulling Violet with her through the dark until they reached baby blue.

They got in a little out of breath and were quiet a moment. "Let's go," Lily said in a whisper but Violet was done listening to other people for the first time in her life. "No, we are going to stay here for however long it takes you to tell me what the hell just happened," Violet said with real anger in her voice.

Too much had happened today, too much and she was tired of it, in honesty, she just wanted to go home and sleep for the next week, then wake up and find it was all a dream. But knew it wasn't going to happen.

Lily let out a long breath and swallowed hard, her eyes closing a moment then she spoke. "One day when you had to go with your dad to something or another and Rose was... well, you know where Rose was. It left me and Daisy alone so she took me to a party someone at school had invited her too, and that night I saw a side to her I don't think many people have seen, not even Rose."

"What do you mean?" Violet asked confused. "Daisy liked to hang around with an older group," Lily said looking at her.

"Yeah well Daisy liked to hang out with everyone, that's the best part about her, she didn't care who you were," Violet said not understanding what Lily was trying to say.

"Violet what I'm trying to get at is that she liked to do drugs, all kinds pot, LSD, harder ones, I tried to stop her but after Rose went to that...place she was messed up in the head thinking it was her fault for what happened."

Violet shook her head not believing what Lily was saying, not wanting to. "Why did she blame herself? It was no one's fault."

"You think I don't know that?" Lily said sounding tired, "I tried to get through to her but nothing worked, she would be out at all times of night doing god only knows what. Even after Rose came back she didn't stop, that was until October, when she suddenly stopped and acted as if it never happened in the first place."

"Then why did you know them?" Violet asked. Lily shrugged "I get my cigarettes from them and once in a while I need something a little stronger."

Violet gave her a look but it explained the smell on her at least. "So someone is paying guys off to confess to a murder. Daisy had a drug problem at one point and she liked hanging with an older group," Violet said summing things up. "That's about right," Lily said.

Violet nodded turning the key and the engine came to life, "We need to talk with Rose about all of this," She said pulling away from the curve. "It can't wait until tomorrow?" Lily asked.

"Not this, it could be the reason she was killed," Violet said. "How do you mean?" Lily asked looking over at her. "If she was buying from someone and then stopped all of a sudden that would cut the dealers cash by a lot, than if they found her that night wanting her to start buying again and she refused that could make them angry right?" Violet asked.

"But to the point of murder?" Lily said shaking her head. Violet looked down a moment remembering times she had seen girls at school with new clothes every week, new shoes, new everything. And what did she have? Old dirty shoes and clothes from goodwill from four years ago. She knew what it was like to go hungry, to be without, she had done it for a long time now.

"Maybe, if they needed it that much," Violet said softly. "Alright then let's talk to Rose then we can go to the police," Lily said and Violet without another word turned the truck towards Rose's house.

* * *

Rose

Rose opened the door to her bedroom and shut it quickly throwing her jacket, not even bothering to look where it landed as she jogged to her desk and sat down.

She reached over to the lamp and clicked it on opening Daisy's diary to the first page and read over it again, thoughts racing through her head. Who the hell was the guy she was talking about? And what was the string of numbers?

Rose shook her head in confusion and turned to the next page and read.

October 1st, 1974

> Today was the first day back to school for everyone, no more summer kisses, late nights or ...well that doesn't need to be written down because I will remember those nights for the rest of my life. Instead, we're now back in school and the homework is hell on all of us and I've been feeling so tired because of it. But Rose seems to be okay,

her mother did go with that stupid story about going to see an aunt in Arizona of all places, like anyone would go there by choice, and for six months. Her meds are working well and her scars have faded to white lines. Anyway, I'm going to go now, I need to call him before he has work.

"He, him, us?" Rose said out loud sitting back in her chair, her back cracking from where it had been sitting over the book reading the passage over and over again.

She closed her eyes and breathed out, "Who were you seeing and why the hell didn't you tell me?" Rose whispered. Why the hell would she keep something like this from her of all people? She would have never told anyone about Daisy dating someone, none of them would have.

"So what were your reasons then?" Rose asked as she opened her eyes and looked to the right where Daisy stood over by Rose's tall bookshelf, reading and Rose felt her cheeks heat as she read the cover, it was the bell jar.

"You got this when you first started to hear them didn't you?" Daisy asked turning to face her, she still had blood on her white dress dried now to a rusty brown but at least she wasn't dripping it everywhere anymore.

"You're not answering my question," Rose said. "You didn't find the answers you were hoping for in here right?" Daisy asked still not answering Rose. "No I didn't," Rose said simply watching as Daisy closed the book and placed it back on the shelf alongside hundreds more.

"I'm happy your mother didn't find that book or it would have ended up in the same place as your clothing. What did she say again?"

Rose looked away but her words still found her. "Ah yes, you're slutty clothing was a reason you had to go to that place right?"

"Would you just answer me!" Rose yelled and in a blink of an eye Daisy was there, tipping Rose's chin up to meet her dark green eyes.

"You know I can't answer Rosey, I'm not her and you know it."

"That's the thing, I don't know anymore, it's like before I can't see what's reality and what's just in my head now, " Rose said looking up at her.

"And who's fault is that?"

"Why don't you go and f-"

Rose's words were cut off as the door opened to reveal her mother. "Are you talking to someone Rosalina?" her mother asked narrowing her eyes.

"No mother I don't know what you're talking about, you must finally be losing it," Rose said knowing what it would lead too, but to her surprise, her mother just looked at her with death in her eyes. "You're very lucky your friends are here or I would have smacked you for that."

"My friend's are here?" Rose asked, "This late?"

"Well what can I say you have no taste in friends besides Daisy, but I'll let them up because of the day you and Jason had."

With that her mother left closing her door, but not even a moment later it opened and Lily and Violet came in looking out of it, their normally high hair looking as if they ran through a wind storm. "What the hell happened to you guys?" Rose said standing up her eyes wide, "And why do you smell like my uncle?"

Violet took a deep breath and Rose could tell it was taking a lot for her to be standing at the moment by the way she looked at Rose's freshly made bed. "We need to talk," Lily said pushing Rose back into her chair and wheeled it towards the bed that Violet now sat on.

"Well I have news as well and I was going to call you, but you're mom said you weren't there Lily," Rose said raising her eyebrow at them. "Someone is paying guys to confess to killing Daisy so the cops have no chance to figure out who actually did it," Lily said in a hurry.

"And we know who may have done it," Violet said looking like a wild animal, her dark eyes wide.

Rose opened her mouth to tell them the good news, that in fact Daisy wasn't dead, but was out there somewhere. But her words were cut off as Violet went on. "Daisy was into drugs."

Rose felt the words die on her tongue, choking on them, Violet's words ringing too loud in her ears as Lily explained what they had learned tonight. That when she had been drugged out of her mind in that hospital so had Daisy apparently, along with hanging out with an older group when she had been around nurses who wiped the drool from her chin. Both in worlds of darkness at the same time but Rose had never known about Daisy's. Because of course, Daisy would never want to bother her with her own problems.

After Lily finished Rose sat there a moment trying to remember what she had to say when all she could hear was the word older, older, older, could Chief Thompson be right in some ways?

"I have some news for you now," Rose said taking a deep breath and looked up at them so she could see their reaction, "Daisy is alive."

For a moment no one said a word both Lily and Violet looking at her with eyes that said they knew the number for the nearest Psychiatric hospital.

"Rose don't take this the wrong way, but have you stopped taking your meds?" Violet asked sounding as if she was talking to a child who had a hard time hearing.

Rose stopped herself from looking at the corner of her room where Daisy stood nodding her head. "You know you're not the first person to ask me that today," Rose said getting up from her desk chair and when over to her jacket and pulled out the X-Ray, "But I have proof."

Lily still looked at her in confusion as she took it from Rose and after a moment of looking at it and then the name at the top her face only got more confused and handed it over to Violet who had the same reaction.

"What is this proof of?" Violet asked handing it back to Rose. "Don't you see?" Rose said sitting back down, "Daisy had a tooth that leaned to one side and she never got it fixed, these look perfect. So the teeth that they found on the body isn't her's. Therefore Daisy can't be dead!" Rose said her voice rising in excitement and she could feel the smile on her face.

But Lily and Violet only looked at one another with a look of pity than back at her. Lily bit her lip as she looked back at her, "Rose this doesn't really mean anything."

"How can you say that?" Rose asked, but could understand them because hearing it out loud now it sounded as if she really was crazy. Lily and Violet said nothing in reply maybe scared she would do something if she got upset.

"That's not the only thing I have," Rose said and grabbed the black book from the desk and held it up for them. "I found this in Daisy's room today under a floorboard," Rose said and was happy to find they looked interested now.

Lily reached out grabbing it from her. It fell open to the first page and she started to read Violet looking over her shoulder mouthing along to the words.

"Lily you said you went with her to these party's, do you remember seeing her with anyone?" Rose asked. Lily looked up and shook her head her eyes downcast, "No, in fact, she stayed away from guys who tried to get with her, I thought at the time she just didn't want to be with anyone but…" Lily trailed off.

"You think she was seeing someone like Chief Thompson said?" Rose asked.

"I don't know what to think!" Lily said her voice high as she rubbed at her face and Rose saw the dark circles under her eyes. Rose nodded slowly as a plan of what tomorrow could hold when this hellish day ended started to form. "We need to get some sleep, then we can talk more in the morning," Rose said looking at them both, her blue eyes tired, mirroring their own.

"Right then," Violet said getting up, keys in hand but Rose stopped her gently taking them from her hand and placed them on the dresser.

"You two can't drive with how sleep deprived you both are, I'll tell my mother you will be sleeping over and in the morning we will be going to school together," Rose said opening her bedroom door to go tell her mother and get their old sleeping bags they still had in the attic from when they were teens and had sleepovers at least twice a week.

"What about my dad?" Violet said alarmed, her eyes wide with fear that Rose hated seeing every time her father came up. "I'll have my brother call him and tell him we made you stay the night," Rose said simply and walked into the hallway closing the door behind herself.

Rose closed her eyes leaning against the door a moment looking up at the ceiling. God, what would they do to her when they found out what she had planned for them in the morning. But first, she had to make her plans happen in the first place.

Rose walked into the kitchen to find her mother and father talking about the biggest news of the day, Tommy Johnson. "Rosalina, there you are, I have some questions for you young lady," her mother said hands on her hips sounding angry, but then again when didn't she now of days. "And what are those mother?" Rose said putting sugar into her voice making her sound so fake it made her want to vomit.

"One, why are your friends still here, and two did you give Mrs. Young the food and if so what did she say?"

Really Rose thought, this is what you live your life for? To know who liked your casserole or more likely she was fishing for gossip and right then and there Rose wondered what had made her father fall in love with this woman? Was it her looks that she so desperately wished to have back. Or was it because at one time she had been a kind loving girl who wanted nothing more than to marry her high school sweetheart?

"It's too late for them to be driving mother and their too tired after the day we just had, so they will be staying over for the night."

Her mother narrowed her eyes at her, "Since when did you have to stop asking for permission in this house Rosalina?" her mother asked in a hiss sounding like a snake somehow.

And Rose was taken aback by the question because she didn't know the answer. When had she started to act like this? Was it because of today? A day that she would remember as the worst and the best day of her life because her best friend was alive out there somewhere and that thought kept her standing even when all she wanted to do was fall.

But she knew that wasn't what her mother wanted to hear. "I'm sorry mother, I'm just tired and in pain is all. May my friends stay over tonight?"

"Pain?" her father said sounding concerned, his eyes filled with worry. "It's just a simple toothache father nothing to worry about," Rose said turning to give him a smile but made it look pained and she watched as his eyes grew soft and she knew she would get what she wanted.

"Deborah love, will you make Rosalina a dentist appointment for tomorrow."

Her mother turned to him with a smile so fake it hurt, "I don't know if they will see someone on such short notice honey," She said through her pearl white teeth. "Tell them I will pay extra for the short notice," her father said as he got up and kissed her mother on the cheek, then left for his small office that sat in the back of the house.

"Of course love," her mother said sugar in her voice like the sweet little housewife she was, but she looked at Rose with ice in her eyes as she turned her back on her, moving towards the red landline phone that hung on the clean white wall of their kitchen.

Rose couldn't help a little smile and looked over to Jason who sat at their old dining room table just off the kitchen. She tipped her head to the side not breaking eye contact motioning him to follow after her. He nodded and followed her out into the backyard.

The night dark and spotted with stars, the cold spring air blowing lightly around them making their dark hair blow around their faces. "Can you call Mr. Luiz and tell him Violet is staying over at our request?" Rose asked.

"Yeah, of course, but that's not what I thought you brought me out here to tell me," Jason said crossing his arms, the muscles standing out against his skin. "What do you mean by that?" Rose asked raising an eyebrow at him. "You and Mark talked in Daisy's room today right?"

Rose was taken aback by the question but answered it honestly. "Not really I just wanted to be in there like I said before, but Mark came in and wanted to ask me a few questions is all."

"What the hell did he ask you Rosey?" Jason asked his voice going hard and Rose understood why, after all, Mark was a reason for a cold night that she almost didn't wake up from, but still he had used that tone with her before and she felt that if she brought up the diary it would only cause more anger and she didn't want him to hate his best friend even more than he already did.

"It was nothing just more questions about that party," Rose said feeling a chill go down her body and she couldn't tell if it was from the wind or the way his dark blue eyes looked black in the lighting. "If he tries something like that again come and get me and I'll take care of him okay?" Jason said meeting her eyes and she nodded looking down.

"Thank you Jason," Rose said and Jason patted her head affectionately. "It's what big brothers are for Rosey, you can come to me, you know that right?"

She nodded and headed for the door passing him but stopped not able to help herself, she had to ask and turned back to look at him, her words filling the quiet world around them. "What did you do to him that night?" Rose asked, "Daisy told me he couldn't move his arm for over two months after I was in the hospital."

Jason didn't look at her as he spoke his back to her so she couldn't see his reaction as he spoke. "Let's just say he knows what will happen if he hurts you again."

Rose stood there a moment the sound of crickets all around and she couldn't help the feeling of terror that went through her, because her brother really had taken after their mother in the way he could be terrifying with no outward appearance. It was always just a feeling of what he could do to you.

Rose opened the door and left him standing there looking at the old tree and went to the attic grabbing the box of sleeping bags, blankets and pillows and when to her room finding Lily and Violet half asleep laying back against the wall on her bed looking out of it.

"You guys can wear some of my nightgowns," She said opening her closet, "Then this day can end finally."

They both nodded and got up slowly and without a word took a long nightgown from her and when to the bathroom to change until Rose was left alone to lay out the sleeping bags.

"So this day will finally end," Daisy said sitting on the desk chair, knees pulled up to her chest. "You found out who killed me, went to my funeral and that I am alive in about sixteen hours. I have to say that's busy even for you Rosey."

Rose didn't reply not wanting to respond with Lily and Violet around. "Oh come on now Rosey, you remember those days when you had so much going on you couldn't even have lunch with me, how did those sewing lessons work out for you by the way? Are you going to be a good housewife just like your mother?"

Rose closed her eyes and counted to ten something she had learned to do a long time ago when the screams got to her in the middle of the night and she couldn't get to sleep because of them, though it hadn't worked in the end.

As Rose reached five for the sixth time Lily and Violet came out looking weird in the vintage nightgowns, but it was the only thing her mother had bought her when she got back.

"I'll take the blue one," Lily said. Violet said nothing as she got into the red one. Rose looked over to see Daisy standing over them but in a blink she was gone.

Rose closed her eyes a moment then undressed getting into the pink nightgown and climbed into bed and within seconds she was asleep.

* * *

Lily

Lily opened her eyes to see a world of colors, music thumping through the room making her head pound with the beat. She looked down at her drink, the amber liquid looking dark in the dim lighting of the room.

She put it down on one of the short side tables that sat next to her and started for the hall lined with mint green wallpaper the red carpet soft under her feet, though she couldn't remember taking her shoes off. The sound of laughter drawing her closer to a door.

She walked slowly down the hall which was filled with smoke from drugs of all kinds from the people who sat in the living room on the flower printed chairs and sofa, eyes looking far off to a place she couldn't see.

Lily felt herself tip to one side then the other off balance, her head now spinning as the laughter grew and grew.

Finally, Lily reached the white door and twisted the handle throwing it open to find Daisy making out with someone, a cloak of darkness keeping the other in shadows. "Daisy?" Lily asked her voice hoarse. Daisy broke away and looked over at her, a smile ghosted across her lips never reaching her blown out eyes.

"Lily dear, what did you smoke?"

Lily blinked trying to clear the fog in her head but it seemed to only get worse as she raised a hand to her forehead trying to stop the pounding. "I - I don't know... I can't remember, w- where are we?" Lily asked leaning against the door frame as the world stopped moving for a moment.

Daisy got up from the messy bed pushing the other person away and back into the dark, before making her way to Lily a smile still across her lips in only her bra and jeans.

"Lily, how many times have I told you to stop smoking things you don't know?" Daisy asked her voice high and sweet. "I-I didn't smoke anything," Lily said and she was pretty sure she was right but everything was blurry.

"Alright then I guess it's time to go," Daisy said and looked back into the room. Lily followed her gaze to the figure still in the bed and Lily was surprised to find that she recognized them somehow, but with the dark so thick she couldn't tell how or in what way.

Lily opened her mouth to ask him where she knew him but Daisy grabbed the door handle shutting it. "Time to go Lily," Daisy said taking her hand and pulled her along until they reached Violet's truck that waited for them in the night, lit only by a street lamp above them. And it was there when Lily figured it out, it was his eyes. She knew them but couldn't place them on just one face and with the fog making her eyes heavy it was hard to concentrate but she knew she had to place them...But why?

"Lily."

Lily looked over to her side and found Daisy there looking sad for some reason. "I'm so sorry."

"Why?" Lily asked confused looking around herself to see they were now in a park, trees all around them as they sat on the wet grass a small fire in front of them. "For everything that's going to happen when I'm gone," Daisy said a stick in hand that she poked at the embers with, her green eyes catching on the light making them glow like a cats.

"You're not gone," Lily said but had to stop and rub at her face as the world spun. "Make sure Rose is taken care of okay."

Lily opened her eyes and looked over to tell Daisy that what Rose really needed was her. But then Daisy was kissing her hard and fast, her lips tasting like smoke and green apple. Lily gasped as her warmth disappeared and looked over too see Daisy standing by a tree, her back to her so she couldn't see Daisy's face as she spoke, the words seeming to flow out of nowhere.

"Lily I know you won't remember this but thank you for being here with me, but I think it's time to go back."

"Go back where?" Lily asked trying to get up and follow her but only managed to make it to her knees and watched helplessly as Daisy moved deeper into the trees her long red hair the only thing she could see now.

"Back to bed for you, but for me, I have to go somewhere you can't follow."

"Wait!" Lily called to no answer as she was left alone in the world of darkness, the only sound her own breathing. "I need you too," She whispered feeling the tears she hadn't been able to shed start to fall finally. "Please, I'm no one without you Daisy."

And it was true, Lily knew that. Before Daisy, she was just the school slut and was treated like it. But Daisy came along with all her kindness, her brightness and picked her up like a broken necklace and fixed her up. Taking her to parties, introduce her to all kinds of people Lily knew she would have never talked too if it wasn't for Daisy showing off her new shiny friend.

But what was she now? Some girl who smoked too much? A girl who was so lost after the first week Daisy was gone she slept with her forty-six-year-old Principal feeling nothing.

"How messed up am I?" Lily said but the words didn't seem to come from her lips. Instead, they flowed around her like fireflies, around and around her until she wanted to scream. She felt tears dripping down her cheeks and before she knew what was happening she was up on her bare feet running through the trees.

Branches hit her from every side but she didn't feel it as Daisy's form came into view and she caught up to her. Lily reached out and grabbed her shoulder turning Daisy around to face her, but choked back a scream as what little light from the moon hit Daisy's face and Lily saw the blood running down her chin from a wound Lily couldn't see.

"Are you happy now?" Daisy's said, "No one remembers that messed up girl from before."

Lily took a step back, her mouth open gasping like a fish without water, no sound coming out. But as she stepped back she felt her foot catch on something and the last thing Lily saw was Daisy's face as she fell and jumped awake.

Lily sat there a moment as her eyes adjusted to the dark, her breath coming too quickly. But as the room came into focus her heart seemed to understand she wasn't about to be murdered and went back to beating normally.

She sat up and looked around herself to see the white walls of Rose's room and looked down to see Violet still asleep and from the soft snoring on the bed so was Rose.

Lily closed her eyes a moment letting the nightmare slip away like flower petals on a spring breeze. After a second she let out a shaking breath and stood slowly as to not wake the others, moving towards the desk where Daisy's diary still lay open.

Lily sat down looking at the art on the cover. She knew Daisy was a good artist having seen it all over her room but then again Daisy was good at everything it seemed. Lily opened the little book and read through the pages again over and over.

October 24th, 1974,

"It's been a hard few weeks, I felt sick all day yesterday and today. I don't know why, I can't tell if it's because of stress with what happened to Rose and homework or if it's something more? I mean I did have an uncle that dropped dead for no reason two years ago out of nowhere so hopefully I won't be going the same way. Anyway onto what happened with Rose today, she was talking to herself in class and the teacher yelled at her for it and I could see how much Rose was hurt by it. She had been doing so well lately but now she has to go home with a message for her mother and I can see the pain in her eyes for what will come tonight. I know there is nothing I can do about it, but maybe if I tell him about it he could help with her mother? I don't know how to help but hopefully, I'll feel better tomorrow and can come up with something to make her feel better, I've stopped smoking in hopes that will help."

Lily bit at her lip rubbing at her neck, she didn't believe Daisy was alive. Because she couldn't be right? Not with the bones they found, hell they went to her funeral and Rose could have simply had a delusion. But… Lily looked over at the X-Ray, at the black and white perfect teeth and was unable to help seeing why Rose could think it.

It was a better ending, after all, thinking she had simply replaced her records and ran away and was alive somewhere in the world, but it was a lie and she knew that.

"Lily?" Someone said behind her sleep still in their voice and as she turned around to face them she found Rose up looking at her blinking the sleep from her eyes, her brown hair a mess. The room had lighten now with the sun rising. "What time is it?" Violet asked sitting up slowly looking around.

"It's seven twenty," Lily said looking at the clock on the wall. "What!" Rose said her voice going high, clear with panic as she jumped out of bed almost falling over herself, her eyes wild like a cat who had been shocked.

"What's wrong?" Violet asked looking as if she was falling asleep again but jerked awake as a pair of jeans hit her face.

"We need to get dressed now!" Rose said and threw Lily her t-shirt. "Why? What do we have to do this early?" Lily asked catching her long skirt as it flew through the air.

"I'll tell you after we're out of here," Rose said undressing and stepped into a green dress, but she had been in such a hurry she hadn't seen it was facing the wrong way round.

Lily shook her head and went over to her, taking her by the shoulder stopping her in place and looked her in the eye. "Rose you need to take a breath and tell us what the hell is going on," Lily said trying to sound calm.

Rose looked away and bit down hard on her lip to the point it turned white, "I can't tell you yet, or-or you won't come with me."

"Rose when will you get it through your head, we are here for you no matter what," Lily said and Violet nodded in agreement pulling on her own t-shirt. "I'll drive you anywhere."

Rose swallowed hard still looking unsure, "Would you follow me into hell?" Rose asked looking at both of them, "Because that's where I'm going."

Lily shot Violet a look asking a simple question in the silence, Would we? Is that what friends are? People who aren't blood-related doing anything for one another? Following them with little to no question? And without having to think Lily knew her answer.

"Yes."

"Of course," Violet said.

Rose looked at them for a moment then nodded, "Alright then, get dressed and we'll meet in baby blue then I'll tell you what's going on, but I can't let my mother overhear us, or we really will go to hell."

"Fine by me," Lily said turning and started getting ready.

* * *

Rose

Rose stepped outside into the morning lit by a light pink and yellow sky, making the world around her look like bubblegum, Lily and Violet next to her.

"You know you could have wore a pair of my tennis shoes right," Lily said looking down at Rose's three-inch heels.

"You really think I could have left the house without my mother seeing?" Rose asked her as they walked over to Violet's truck. "I still don't get why she makes you wear those," Violet said opening the door and hopped in.

"It was part of my recovery," Rose said getting into the passenger side seat, Daisy right next to her. "Pretty sure it was because she wanted to dress you up like a doll," Lily said climbing into the truck bed, the back window open.

Rose said nothing in reply already knowing she was right, at least partially. When she had been in the hospital out of her mind on any and all kinds of drugs her mother had come to her and told Rose she was going to clear out her room.

She hadn't known then what that meant so it was a heartbreaking find when she came home to a room stripped of everything that was of her.

Her books replaced mostly with old romances, her clothing now dresses and nightgowns years out of style along with her shoes now all heels, her record's, posters, everything that had made her who she was gone.

Rose never could say if it was because her mother actually believed in some small part of her heart that it helped her or if it was simply her mother wanting even more control over her and maybe she didn't want to know the truth.

"Turn in here," Rose said snapping out of her thoughts and looked up to find they were here. Violet pulled into the mostly empty parking lot and stopped in front of the short building painted in olive green and white trimming.

"Where are we?" Lily asked from the back, a confused look across her face as she looked around and saw only a few cars around. "The dentist," Rose answered grabbing her bag sounding as if this was normal.

"Why?" Violet asked raising her eyebrows at her. "I had my mother make me an appointment for this morning at seven since it's only Doctor Hunt and a nurse this early in the morning, so it will be easier to break in."

CHAPTER 9

Violet

Violet sat there a moment unsure if she had heard Rose right, but as she looked over at Lily to see her reaction it was the same, surprise, confusion with hints of terror. Because Rosalina Waters just said she wanted to break into a place. The girl who in second grade told the teacher she didn't feel comfortable playing outside without adult supervision, the girl who couldn't even try a cigarette without choking up half a lung.

"You want us to what!" Lily said her eyes going wide and voice even higher. "Why?" Violet asked wanting to know where this was coming from, "It's not because of that damned X-Ray right?"

Rose looked her in the eye her own blue ones a burning sapphire. "You said you would follow me into hell, and this is where the road starts. So I need you to prove to me you won't turn back when it's time to cross the fires."

Violet swallowed but there was no going back she made her decision this morning after all. "Alright, what do you want us to do?"

"When I go into the back with the doctor one of you need to distract the nurse somehow, than the other needs to go into the back and look through the records."

"What are we looking for?" Lily asked both eyebrows raised. "Daisy's records along with any large payments made recently and anything else that looks out of place," Rose said opening the door and hopped out.

Violet sat there a moment her mouth open unsure what to say, but she didn't have time as Lily got out and followed after Rose. A few curse's ran through Violet's head as she hopped down and ran to catch up with them just in time to slip through the door and into the brightly lit waiting room, the smell of the fake orange cleaner hitting her nose hard almost choking her.

"How can I help you?" Someone said and Violet turned to see a woman in her late thirties, her makeup caked on so dark it looked as if she dipped her lips in blood, which wasn't a good look when you worked in the medical world.

"I'm here to see Doctor Hunt," Rose said sounding like her mother, voice hard and sure. "And your last name is?" The nurse asked looking slowly through the papers on her desk as if this was the last thing she wanted to do before her morning cup of coffee.

"Rosalina Waters."

At the sound of Rose's name, the nurse looked up her cheeks going pink most likely from the knowledge that her father was one of the most powerful men in the small town being the owner of the only bank.

"Miss Waters I'm so sorry I didn't realize it was you, please take a seat and I'll tell the doctor you're here."

Violet watched as she got up so quickly her nursing hat almost fell off. "Damn," Lily said looking over the desk to watch the woman jog down the hall, "You have them whipped."

"I don't, my father does, I can't imagine how much he paid to get me in on such short notice," Rose said going through her bag for something. "What are you looking for?" Violet asked.

"This," Rose said taking out the x-Ray and handed it to her, "If you have time look for its match because it's not Daisy's."

Violet bit the inside of her cheek, but all she could do was nod because she knew Rose wouldn't believe her until she could prove that Daisy wasn't alive, that this was just another delusion.

"I'll go and look through the back for the records," Violet said looking down at the X-Ray, "And Lily will distract the nurse."

"How the hell am I going to do that?" Lily asked her eyes going wide with worry. "Your smart Lily, you'll figure something out," Rose said trying to give her a little smile.

Lily opened her mouth to say something else but just then the door opened as the nurse returned clipboard in hand and a smile plastered to her face. "Miss Waters, the doctor is ready to see you now."

"Thanks," Rose said going over to the nurse ready to follow her, "Is it okay if my friends stay here? I just feel better knowing they're here waiting for me."

The nurse looked at the both of them narrowing her eyes a little at Violet and her old worn out clothes and most likely her skin, but still smiled as she looked back at Rose. "Of course Miss Waters, they can just take a seat and wait here for you."

Rose put on her own fake smile, her pink lips standing out against her pale skin so unlike Violet's own. "Thank you ever so kindly," Rose said following after the nurse as they went through the double doors, she shot them one last look that said good luck then disappeared.

A moment later they were left in silence the only sound being the radio. "Well this will be interesting at the very least," Lily said rubbing at her face. "Maybe for you, if I'm caught I'm going straight to jail without passing go," Violet said feeling her heartbeat pick up at the thought of what her father would do to her if he had to take off work to come and bail her out.

"You'll be fine," Lily said trying to sound reassuring but it didn't really sound that way. "Thanks a lot," Violet said and looked up to see the nurse come back and sit down opening up a magazine and started to read, not giving them another look.

"So how do we do this?" Violet asked in a whisper. "Why do I have to come up with something?" Lily said her tone matching Violet's own. "I don't know, just-just go up to her and ask about appointments or something."

"And what are you going to do?" Lily asked crossing her arms. "I have no idea but I'll think of something."

Lily let out a huff but slowly made her way over to the woman and after a moment of Lily standing there she looked up, a tired look across her face. "May I help you?" She asked giving Lily a dry look. Violet watched as Lily visibly swallowed and spoke, "I was just wondering about...how much a cleaning is?"

Lily didn't sound very convincing at all, but instead of the nurse telling them to get the hell out of her office she rolled her eyes and got up to look through the dark green filing cabinets that sat against the wall, her short heels clicking.

Violet shot a look at Lily as she started for the door that would hopefully lead her to the records she needed. But god she had never been able to hear her footsteps or breathing more than when she was turning that damned doorknob and of course it had to squeak.

Violet caught her breath and looked over at Lily who's eyes had gone wide most likely matching her own, but somehow the woman hadn't heard and Violet quickly opened the door enough to slip in and closed it so gently she stopped breathing.

She stood there a moment against the door her hand on the handle as she took a deep breath, there really was no going back now.

She took a step forward looking down the yellow lit hallway, the orange and white tiled flooring making even her flat shoes sound loud.   As she passed the long line of closed doors Violet couldn't help the feeling of cold creep into her body making her shiver, everything looked the same, the only color was the walls being a muted green and a few posters of health quotes so cheesy it actually hurt Violet to look at them, "Healthy teeth today is a healthy tomorrow."

"Yellow teeth is not the person you really are, brush today!"

She looked away from the awful posters and started reading the signs on the doors. Violet passed the X-Ray room, a few exam rooms, an office, break room, and at the end of the hall sat a room marked storage.

Violet looked back to see an empty hallway and let out a shaking breath. For a moment she thought of turning back telling them she couldn't find anything but she needed this as proof, otherwise Rose would never let this go.

Violet looked down at her hand, which sat on the doorknob a small cut running along the front of her knuckle and she didn't remember if it was one that her father gave her or if she had done it by accident she couldn't tell anymore.

She bit her lip hard snapping out of her thoughts then turned the handle. The door opened into a dark room making Violet blink in surprise as she quickly went in and closed the door swearing she heard a door open somewhere, but with her nerves, it was probably nothing.

After a moment of silence, Violet let out a breath she hadn't even known she was holding and locked the door not taking any chances and started further into the room.

A window sat on the right side of the room letting in a little light enough to find the light switch at least. She flipped it on the room filling with yellow light and for the first time, Violet saw that the small room was barely big enough for her to stretch her arms out to the side.

Filing cabinets, the same green color as the one behind the reception desk filled the room stacked on top of one another. "Jesus Christ," Violet breathed looking around herself, this was going to take time she didn't have, hell if she was lucky she maybe had ten minutes and that was if Lily could keep talking.

Breathe Violet thought to herself, just look for the D's, Daisy's name had to be in there, but a little voice said what about looking for the matching x-ray?

Violet closed her eyes a moment, she didn't have time for all of this. I'm going to be caught and dad will kill me. But suddenly there was her mother's voice, sweet and calming the kind of calming that made her father's rage not seem so bad. The voice the calmed her down when all she wanted to do was give up after she took on to much at school, the warm hand on her arm as she heard her mother's words. "Violet love, take a long deep breath. Good now one thing at a time, the most important first, then the rest can come next."

"Why can't you be here when I need you?" Violet whispered, but she had been asking herself that question for the past four years. Every time her father opened another beer, someone at school would make a comment about how she should learn better English or go home where she came from.

Her mother had known how to deal with it all and so did Daisy, shielding her from all of it but she was gone too. And Violet hated that small part of her that wanted Rose to be right, for Daisy to be alive and come back and stop all of this pain, the dirty looks, the words said behind her back.

But she was here to disprove all that for Rose's sanity. So Violet took a deep breath and started to look for the D's. And a few minutes later found it against the wall with the window. Violet opened it and found Daisy Young quickly and took out her file, It fell open and the first thing Violet found was Daisy's X-Ray.

She looked at it a moment, then placing the open file on top of another one that sat on top of the paint chipped cabinet and took the X-Ray she had folded and placed in her jeans pocket out. She unfolded it and matched it up to the one in the file and yes it was the same one. Name, number everything and if it was a matching one to someone else's in here how the hell would she find it?

No that's not what she needed. What she needed was to look for any large payment receipts. Violet turned back to and moved to pick up Daisy's file thinking of taking the matching X-Ray to show Rose.

But instead of grabbing just the top she picked up the one that lay under it causing the contents to fall out across the floor.

"Oh you have to be kidding with me," Violet hissed under her breath going to her knees and started picking them up as quickly as she could but stopped dead in her tracks.

There in front of her sat another X-Ray, matching Daisy's perfectly. In every way to the size of the Incisors to the weird way one of the Molars had grown in. "N-no way," Violet said her voice catching as she scrambled to take out Daisy's X-Ray once more.

She laid them out next to one another and felt her eyes go wide as with a fingertip she traced the outline of a tooth to the next to in hopes she was wrong but there was no denying it they were the same mouth, the only differences being a name at the top of the one that had fallen out of the other file.

"Linda Ross." Violet said under her breath moving the X-Ray to the side and picked up her information sheet and looked it over. Linda Ross, age seventeen, came in for a filling on 6/12/74 after her old one fell out after being hit.

Violet scanned it but couldn't find if she lived in Watkinsville, but stopped dead her heart freezing as the door handle turned stopping suddenly as the lock caught. Violet looked at it with horror a moment as whoever it was on the other side tried again and cursed being unable to open it once more.

She didn't dare breathe unsure if someone still stood outside. She quickly grabbed up everything she could carry and stood up looking around panicked. How the hell was she going to get out of here without being arrested? Maybe she could hide behind one of the cabinets but in this small room, it would look too obvious.

No she couldn't hide but she couldn't - Violet stopped moving as the window came into view. It was small yes, making it a small fit even for her short frame but it would have to do. She just hoped she'd make it.

***

Lily

Lily could feel the sweat forming on her neck as she asked another question about the cost and benefits of a whitening. The nurse who Lily had learned the name of was Jesse Williams, mother of three cats all named after a boy group she had never heard of.

But she was running out of small talk and questions about dental work and she could see that Mrs. Williams was getting tired of them too, but Lily didn't know what else to do. Violet was still gone and she had no idea how she would be able to sneak back in without being seen.

Just then the door opened with a loud squeak and Lily's heart jumped into her throat as she turned wide-eyed to see a clean-cut man in his late forties standing there, a doctor's coat hugging his frame. Rose behind him looking away from them and down the hall, her skin pale, a worried look across her face.

"Doctor Hunt, how can I help you?" The nurse asked standing up to greet him. "I couldn't find anything wrong with Miss Waters teeth today even though her mother told me she had a bad ache last night and I just wanted to check her older records for anything, but the doors locked."

"Locked?" The nurse asked clearly confused, "It shouldn't be since it locks from the inside only."

The doctor shrugged, "All I can say is that it's not opening."

The nurse shot a quick look around the room and must have seen for the first time that Violet was missing, Lily watched as her lips curled in as she moved around her desk and grabbed something.

A moment later Lily saw that it was a pair of keys and her heart dropped to the bottom of her stomach as she watched in horror along with Rose as the nurse followed the doctor down the hall, a look of determination sat rock hard on her face.

Lily quickly made her way to follow them trying to stop them if only for a moment, "Hey you didn't answer my question about whitening benefits," Lily called jogging after them, Rose in tow. But it was too late as the nurse shoved the key in the handle so hard the door move back in its frame.

A moment later she pushed it open and Lily felt her heart stop as she walked in turning the light on. But found nothing, no one was in there and there was no way of hiding.

Lily felt her chest relax and she couldn't help a little smile, wondering how the hell Violet got out of that little window. She heard the nurse let out a deep breath and turned on them. Lily could see she was trying to hold back her anger and that was only because of Rose most likely.

"Where is your Mexican friend?"

Lily failed to hold back the smile as she lied through her teeth, "First of all she's Portuguese not Mexican. And second she had to go to the car and get something, didn't you see her leave when I was asking about the right kind of toothpaste?" Lily asked her eyes wide with innocence.

Nurse Williams bit her lip so hard it turned white and clearly wanted to say something but crossed her arms and walked past them. The doctor just raised an eyebrow and went into the room mumbling about women and their emotions.

Lily moved over to Rose and lowered her voice as to not be overheard, "How did it go?"

Rose shrugged, "It's easy to lie when all they see is green, I mean they didn't find anything of course, but you can bet they're going to send my father a bill. But did Violet find anything?"

"I have no idea, I had to keep nurse huffy busy, but I'm sure she's just waiting by the car."

Rose nodded but looked out the window as the doctor came back papers in hand and closed the door, worry in her eyes making the blue a storm on the sea.

"Miss Waters i just need you to sign a few things then you may leave," the doctor said and handed the clipboard to her and pointed to the places she needed to put her name.

Lily stood by the wall next to the door, her foot tapping against the white tile as she watched impatiently as Rose sat in one of the waiting room chairs signing her name for the millionth time. She couldn't help looking out of the tall window that faced the street.

Violet hadn't come back in and Lily felt that something bad must have happened for that, Violet could be laying on the ground with a broken leg from jumping out of a window for all they knew.

Finally, after what felt like a year and a half though it could have only been no more than five minutes, Rose stood up and handed her papers to the nurse who still looked pissed off, but she took them and a moment later Rose grabbed her bag and walked out of the door.

The first thing that hit Lily was the air. It smelled of flowers, the wild daisies just starting to bloom around the town everywhere you look. The second thing Lily saw was the red and blue flashing lights of Mark's police car that sat in front of Violet's blue truck blocking it, Violet in the back looking scared out of her mind. And there was Mark, arms crossed leaning against the front, his hair a mess from the wind. And as they walked up to him his lips turned into a wicked smile.

***

Rose

Rose felt her cheeks heat as she saw Mark's stupid smile that made her want to slap him across his face. How dare he look at her like that after what he said, what he did to her. "Well, it's a surprise seeing you here Rosey and Lily," Mark said tipping his head to the side.

"Cut the crap Mark, why the hell is Violet in the back of your police car?" Rose asked standing right in his face so he had to look her in the eye.

"Well wouldn't you know it, I was just driving by when all of a sudden I saw Violet here jumping out of that window, a file in hand. I couldn't believe she was stealing, so of course, I thought the place must be on fire and pulled in to help. But no, after I caught up to her I found she had Daisy's dental records. Now could you tell me why she would want that?" Mark asked sarcasm clear in every word he spoke.

"Go fuck yourself," Lily hissed from behind her. But Rose didn't look away from him as she spoke, "Let Violet go now or I'll burn the diary which I know is the only reason your here right now."

Mark's smirk grew as he slowly shook his head, "That's not how this is going to work Rosey, I'm going to let Violet go, but I needed you to listen to me first."

"Then speak," Rose said crossing her arms.

"Not here," Mark said pointedly looking up and Rose turned her head to see the nurse by the door as she talked to someone inside but if she turned and saw them with a police officer it would snowball into rumors they wouldn't be able to get out of.

Rose looked back up to Mark. At that moment she would have loved to have her brother here because he seemed to be the only one who could knock him down a peg, but he wasn't and she didn't have the time.

"Come on then, let Violet go and let's talk somewhere."

"Glad to see you've grown up Rosey from your childish games," Mark said as he went and let Violet out with a key.

"And whose fault is that?" Rose said not breaking eye contact with him as Violet jumped out and quickly joined them looking gray. Mark seemed to lose his smile at her words but spoke again as he opened his door and got in. "Meet you at the old diner got it."

"See you there," Rose said watching him pull away. "Are you alright?" Lily asked looking at Violet who had gotten behind both of them. "Yeah, I-I guess so," Violet said not sounding very fine.

"Did you really run from him?" Rose asked an eyebrow raised. "I got scared when I saw him with the lights on," Violet said sounding small, "If my dad ever found out he would-"

Violet stopped herself from finishing the sentence and Rose gave her a comforting look, "It's okay Violet, you did great just getting the file in the first place."

Violet nodded and they started for the truck together. "I do need to let you both know something before we talk to Mark," Violet said handing Lily the file as she unlocked the car door.

"And that is?" Rose asked getting into the passenger side seat. Violet hopped in and looked at both of them her skin the color of ash as she spoke. "You were right Rose, someone is trying to hide something, I don't know if Daisy is really alive, but someone sure is trying hard to make sure no one knows and they have more power then we know."

CHAPTER 10

Lily

Lily felt numb as they drove. She couldn't think right, the only thing that seemed to be going through her head was Daisy could be alive and out there somewhere.

But the idea still felt unreal even now as she sat in the back of baby blue the wind the only thing she could hear besides her thoughts which seemed to scream at her.

If Daisy was alive then she must have been kidnapped because Lily knew she would rather die then leave Rose and her family. And who was the body they found?

Lily had to stop thinking then thankfully as they pulled into the mostly empty parking lot, which she guessed was normal given it was a school day and nine am in the morning when most people would be at work by now.

She couldn't help but think of her mother, wondering if she had even seen that Lily never came back home last night, though it's not like she cared before, why would now be any different.

Lily jumped down and joined Rose and Violet as they opened and walked through the glass door, the neon green sign blinking at them.

Lily was hit with the smell of old oil and burned toast as she looked around herself quickly not surprised to see that the long room was painted in red and orange. Fake green plants hung on the walls along with random paintings of food. Large windows lighting the room so the yellow and white checkered floors shown clean.

The tables and booths were orange as well making her eyes hurt or maybe she was just in a bad mood she couldn't tell anymore. "Over here," Mark said from a large booth that sat in the back, the lights dimmer than the front with no light from the windows reaching that far, casting him in shadows.

They made their way over to him and shared a look between each other wondering who it should be to sit with Mark. Lily seemed to lose with looks that said she hadn't been mentally scarred or chased down by him, so she took her place next to him, the smell of strong coffee all around them coming from the steaming cups that Mark must have ordered.

"So," Rose said slowly, "Where should we start?"

Mark took a long drink from his cup then spoke, "How about where you got the idea that Daisy is alive in the first place?"

"How do you know we believe Daisy is alive? " Lily asked, her heart beating in her ears.

"Why would you want the one thing that proved she was dead if you believed it," Mark answered.

Rose looked him dead in the eye, then looked down and told him everything they knew so far, about the boys being bought off to confess. About the dental X-Ray being someone else's. How someone with money seemed to be trying to hide all of this even in their small town.

Lily watched Mark look at the x-rays shaking his head, chewing on his lip so hard she was surprised it hadn't started bleeding. "What do you think?" Rose asked.

Mark let out a breath and sat back rubbing his eyes. "I have to say this whole case looks weird and has felt off from the very first day. But to think it's big enough to have that kind of money is just messed up.

Rose nodded and seemed to quickly look at something behind them as if for reinsurance but when Lily looked she found nothing.

"Do you really think the X-rays are from the same person?" Lily asked feeling unsure. "There's no doubt about it it's the same one from this Linda Ross whoever she is, I've never heard of her before."

"Do you think she could have something to do with it?" Violet asked. "Doubtful, it's most likely just a girl from out of town that someone is using," Mark said crossing his arms.

"Can't we take all of this to the police to help show them that Daisy is alive?" Lily asked hopefully.

"Ha," Mark said a real laugh in his voice along with anger, "You really think Chief Thompson will believe any of this? The old man can barely make coffee by himself these days. No, all he wants is a cut and dry case like the one whoever is doing all of this wants it to be. And even if we did it's all circumstantial evidence anyway."

"So we're all alone on this," Rose said looking into her coffee now cool. "No, you have me," Mark said.

They all looked up at him, surprised by his words. Lily would have never guessed he would say those words after what happened a year ago, but she never guessed they would be in this situation in the first place.

"But you have to trust me first," Mark said.

"And how do we do that?" Rose asked eyebrows raised.

"Let me read her diary."

Lily felt her breath catch as she turned wide eyed at Rose. She hadn't read much of it herself but the things Daisy wrote was about the mystery man, yes, but also it went deep into what happened to Rose that day a year ago, things no one knew about but them.

For a moment the room seemed to go silent as they held their breath. "Fine" Rose said swallowing hard her skin pink. She reached for her yellow book bag and opened it slowly, taking the diary out.

She paused a moment biting her lip as she looked at the art then handed it to Mark. He took it without looking away from her, "Thank you Rosey."

"Whatever," Rose said looking away and stood up, "I have to go."

Lily started to pick up her bag but stopped as Rose spoke, "I'm going to see my father at the bank, there's no need for the both of you there."

"Are you sure?" Violet asked. Rose tried putting on a smile but it looked so painfully fake it hurt. "Yeah, I'll see all of you later on, make sure to eat something okay."

"Shouldn't someone tell you that?" Lily said but Rose was already making her way towards the door and either didn't hear her or didn't want too.

"She sure hurried away didn't she," Mark said watching after her. "Wouldn't you want to leave if someone was going to read about one of the darkest times in your life from someone else's point of view?" Lily asked looking up at him.

Mark looked down at the black book a moment, his eyes were full of pain, something Lily was still trying to understand as Mark opened to the first page.

***

Rose

Rose felt the cold spring air blow against her too warm cheeks as she walked down the sidewalk, her heels clicking the only sound around her. She loved these kinds of mornings, the ones where the air felt as if it had never been touched before and she could walk with no one around her. The ones where she could pretend she didn't hear Daisy's screaming that night, one where she could run from all of this if she wanted too instead of the truth that she would never leave this messed up little town.

She turned the corner then and was faced with the old red brick building that towered over the other commercial businesses that sat around it, making them look small in its shadow.

Rose let out a breath before she crossed the street and opened the glass door to the smell of overpriced pens and old money as she made her way through the familiar dark wooden floors and ivory walls hung with clocks that seemed to tick too loudly and paintings of long forgotten places. Clerks working with the few people that were there and made her way over to where her father's secretary sat.

"Miss Waters here to see your father?" Mrs. Lion asked. Rose put on a smile for the older woman who still somehow at the age of eighty-five got up and came in every day to work. "Yes," Rose said, "If he isn't busy that is."

"I'll go and ask, but I'm sure he'll make time for you Rosalina," Mrs. Lion said slowly getting up and started for his office that sat in the back. "Mrs. Lion do you know where my brother is, I saw his car out front as well."

Mrs. Lion turned to look at her and Rose saw the gossip in her eyes she saw so often in her mothers. "I believe he is in the back helping one of the younger female interns if you want to see him before your father."

The way Mrs. Lion said 'helping' made Rose think he wasn't helping anyone but himself. "Thanks," Rose said and they went their separate ways.

It wasn't hard to find her brother, no, all she had to do was follow the looks the other employees shot a door as if in hopes of burning it down. She understood why. If Jason wasn't the son of the owner he would be in the street with his pants around his ankles, but her parents always turned a blind eye to his actions. Without thinking, Rose opened the door and thankfully found her brother clothed, but he didn't stop kissing the twenty-something woman that was so deep into the kiss she didn't even notice Rose.

It took Rose actually grabbing her brother's arm and pulling him off her to make him stop. He opened his blue eyes and looked at her his white teeth bright.

"Morning Rosey, what are you doing here so early?"

Rose rolled her eyes so hard it was a wonder she didn't die instantly. "I needed to see the dentist remember, and I wanted to tell father everything was okay," Rose said crossing her arms waiting for his sarcastic remark. But instead, his eyes filled with something she couldn't read, almost like fear than in a flash it was gone and his cocky smile returned.

"Well then, I'll let you do that because I need to get back to work," Jason said and looked at the young woman again and winked. But Rose cut that thought off before it started. "Yes you will, and if I don't see you up front when I leave I'll ask father to put you on paperwork for the rest of your time here."

"God Rosey you're a buzzkill, you know I get so easily bored to the point it becomes dangerous."

"That's not my problem," Rose said then turned away before she saw his reaction and walked across the room and passed through the frosted glass door that Mrs. Lion held open for her with a smile as if she knew what had just happened.

Rose walked into her father's office and inhaled the smell of old cigar smoke, the green carpet and brown wallpaper a sudden change from the lobby.

She stopped in front of her father's desk where he was just finishing up with a call putting the black receiver down with a click and looked up to her.

"Morning Rose, sorry I wasn't at breakfast but I had something to take care of."

"It's okay father, I understand you're always very busy," Rose said with a small breath because it was more than busy for years now. He would stay at the office for hours after it closed, as if he was hiding from something, but she just didn't know if it was because of her mother or because of herself.

"How did the dentist appointment go?" he asked taking off his rounded glasses and started cleaning them. "Fine, they found nothing wrong, I guess it was just in my head."

Her father turned to her with a sharp look at her words and she did her best to hide her smile.

"Well, I'm happy for that at least. But since your here i did need to tell you about-" His words were cut off then as the door opened once more and Mrs. Lion came in, and Rose could hear someone shouting from somewhere in the building.

"I'm sorry, Mr. Waters but one of our customers are refusing to talk with anyone but you."

Her father let out a deep breath and put his glasses back on and stood up making his way for the door as he spoke, "Rose wait here, I'll be right back."

She turned and watched the door close behind them and was left in silence.

"So," Daisy said from where she sat in her father's chair slowly spinning around to face Rose, her white dress still painted in red. "You're working with silly little Mark now I see."

"Be quite Daisy, I don't want to hear it," Rose said turning away from her. "What don't you want to hear Rosey? That your working with a man who almost killed you and it was me who saved your life?"

"It wasn't him who tried killing me Daisy, it was a lot more than that and you know it."

"I guess you're right since I'm one of those things because the real Daisy is alive isn't she.. or is that just what you want to believe?"

Rose turned on her than, anger hot within her veins as she stormed over to the desk and swiped down her nails cutting through the empty air, slamming her hand hard into the wood. Pain shot up her arm as she bit back a cry.

Rose bit down on her lip as she held her hand in the other looking down at the bright red it was turning. She knew it would bruise by tomorrow, something she couldn't afford with her mother watching her every move. With a huff, Rose fell into her father's chair closing her eyes a moment wondering if she would be able to look Mark in the face after he read Daisy's diary.

There were things in there that she wished would never be seen by anyone, even herself. She didn't want to know the pain Daisy felt when she had first seen Rose in the hospital drugged out of her mind, the painfully slow recovery of those six months, the heartbreak of watching herself through someone else's eyes and never knowing how much pain she had caused until now.

Rose opened her eyes once again and turned to get up, her father wouldn't be happy to see her in his chair. But stopped as something gold caught the light and flashed across her vision. Rose looked down and tipped her head to the side as she reached out opening the long drawer that was already cracked open, most likely from when she had hit it.

Rose felt her eyes go wide, breath escaping her lips as a revolver shined up at her with it's sleek ivory handle.

"God," Rose breathed, how could her father have this without her knowing, she had been in this office so many times before now. But that's not the thing that had caught her eye before. No, the gold was from a bracelet that seemed to scream at her for some reason, but she couldn't understand why too focused on the gun.

She started to reach in slowly going for the bracelet. But just then the door handle started to turn and Rose had just enough time to close the drawer and stand up.

For a moment she thought her father would call her out, see the deep pink color of her cheeks and yell, but instead, he shook his head tired and looked at her with a small smile.

"Sorry about that honey, Mrs. Jones was having a hard time understanding what a transit number was, anyway as I was saying-"

Rose cut him off as she quickly grabbed her bag feeling the blood pounding in her head. "Sorry father, I have to go, I-I need to see Lily for... notes on a project were both working on that I just remembered."

"Oh well, tell her I said hello then."

Rose only nodded as she made her way through the door, then she was outside in a blur, her heart racing. Rose ran across the street almost getting hit by Mrs. Marrow if she hadn't stopped in time but Rose couldn't think straight. Her father had a gun she had never seen before and Daisy's golden bracelet.

That's what had been screaming at the back of her head, she had given that bracelet to Daisy. Picked it out and bought it with her own money, even had it engraved with her name. She would have known it anywhere. Rose came to a stop then, her heart falling as she turned slowly back around as red and blue lights casted shadows in front of her.

***

Violet

Violet took a long drink from her cool coffee finishing the last drops as Mark sat back in the booth, looking sick. Both Violet and Lily looked at him from across the table that Lily had moved to after Rose left, to see him slowly shaking his head, opening and closing his mouth like a fish and Violet decided to cut to the chase.

"Now that you know everything, do you have any ideas about what the numbers mean?"

Mark wetted his lips with his tongue before he spoke, "Rose, that night she tried-"

"That's not what I asked you," Violet said trying to keep him on track, "I think it could be a code of some kind, I just can't figure out what word to number combination she used."

But her words didn't seem to get through to him as he kept looking down at his hands. So Lily tried another way to get through to him. "I know you're probably freaking out about Rose, her mother did a good job of keeping it all under wraps, so no one knew besides us and now you, but she's okay now, I promise. But she needs Daisy as we all do and you may just be the only one to help with that."

He looked up then and nodded without saying a word and opened the book and read out loud.

"October 31th 1974,

Today was a nightmare from the second I woke up, I keep feeling tired for no reason from the moment my eyes open. Then in school, I heard some asshole talk bad about Violet and I had to remind them about the time I helped her at the spring dance about the rooms that were never checked on on the second floor. And on top of that now I have to go to a check-up which I don't have time for! But no matter I'll be meeting him tonight at 33.864535 -83.420389 and at least that will be nice and for once I'll be the one taken care of. It feels as though i'm always the one looking after people, Rose has been doing fine for the most part, but I can't help looking at those white scars everytime I see her, see the blood. But I know that as long as she has me she'll be okay."

Mark finished and looked up at them. "You guys really don't have any idea what this is from?"

"If we did we wouldn't be here talking to you," Violet said. Mark gave her a dry look and opened his mouth to say something but stopped and Violet watched his eyes go wide. She turned towards the window where he was looking and saw Chief Thompson pull up.

Violet felt her whole body go cold as he got out and started for the door. "You said you wouldn't tell anyone about getting that file!" Violet hissed looking at him, panic in her chest.

"I didn't do anything I swear," Mark said low as they watched Chief Thompson look around then start towards them as he opened the door. Violet knew he was right, but no one was with him when he drove here, he could have simply radioed in. But would he do that to Rose?

Violet grabbed the diary from the table and threw it into her bag just before Chief Thompson stopped in front of them. "Excuse me, Officer Hollow, Miss Andrews, Miss Luiz I need all of you to come with me," Chief Thompson said.

"Jesus Chief, can you be any scarier," Mark said trying to sound upbeat and it almost worked. "Sorry if I made you girls uncomfortable, it's just that I'm surprised to see Officer Hollow talking with the both of you while the investigation is going on," Chief Thompson said his eyes burning a hole into him. But Mark didn't look intimidated.

"I'm off the clock until noon boss, the only thing I want to talk about is how many cups of coffee you can drink and not die."

"Well you're back on the clock now, so well all of you come back with me to the station?"

Lily and Violet shared a look both knowing if they said no it would look bad, but Violet still had to ask, "What is it that you need us for?"

"I can't tell you that here, I can only say you're not in trouble, now please come with me."

"Of course," Lily said a smile on her face as she got up and grabbed her bag along with Violet's hand.

They followed Chief Thompson out into the sunny day and stopped in front of his car as a door opened. Violet felt shock go through her as she watched Rose step out of the back.

"Hey," Rose said as everyone looked at her. "What the fu-" Lily started but Rose cut her off. "After I went to see my father, I just walked around for a bit but then Chief Thompson stopped me and said I need to come in with you guys."

Violet was surprised at how calm she sounded but could see the fear in her dark eyes.

"Miss Waters, you and Miss Andrews can ride with me. Miss Luiz, you ride with officer Hollow."

"What about my truck?" Violet asked. "Officer Hollow can take you back afterward," Chief Thompson answered as he got into his car. Violet shared a look with everyone, a silent question being asked. What the hell is going to happen now?

CHAPTER 11

Lily

Lily watched the world pass her in a blur as she looked out of the window, Rose doing the same as they sat in silence, the air filled with tension. She looked down at her hands to find them shaking and realized she hadn't had a cigarette in over two days now. It was no wonder she couldn't think.

"Can I light a cigarette in here?" Lily asked already taking the pack out of her back pocket. "You really shouldn't, but I'm not going to tell anyone," Chief Thompson said. Lily rolled down the window and flicked her lighter to life inhaling deeply.

For the rest of the ride to the station, she filled herself with nicotine so when they walked into the police station she felt a sense of calm instead of the panic that would be screaming at her.

Violet walked close to her looking around with her head down as if trying not to be seen. But it was too late for that, because Rosalina Waters walked in front of them next to Chief Thompson as he led them down halls, everyone looking at them as they walked past.

Lily kept her head up not giving them the chance to think she was some little girl to be pushed around, making eye contact with a few who looked at Violet with something dark in their eyes and Lily made sure she looked even harder at them until they finally reached a door.

Chief Thompson twisted the handle and held it open for them as they walked in one at a time. Lily was the last to go in and found a room lit with old yellow lights making it darker than it should have been. A table was the only thing in it besides themselves a window above it.

"What is this place?" Lily asked looking at the bare cream-colored walls and concrete floor, then saw Rose and Violet staring at the window. Rose's eyebrows raised and Violet had her mouth open a little. Lily wandered over and felt her own eyes widened as Mark answered her question.

"This is the opposite side of the lineup room, where we have witnesses identify people."

Lily shook her head as she looked at the men behind the one-way mirror, she knew them all from school. Tommy was there looking sick, Jim looked as if he hadn't slept in days and the others looked much the same. "Who are you trying to identify using them?" Violet asked.

"We wanted to ask you all if you recognize any of these men from the party that night, if maybe Daisy was with one before she was killed?" Chief Thompson asked.

For a moment the room was quiet all knowing what he wanted them to say then Rose spoke. "No, I don't remember seeing them that night."

"I don't think I saw them as well," Lily said and Violet nodded along. She looked up then to see that he didn't believe them, but couldn't say that out loud.

"Are you all sure? These men have all confessed to killing her that night."

So, Lily thought. Mark was right he really did want a simple cut and dry case. Otherwise, maybe he would have found what they had.

"May I talk with you a moment," Mark asked the older man. With a set jaw, Chief Thompson nodded and they walked out of the room. But Lily saw that Mark had left the door open a crack.

Lily shot Rose and Violet a look and without saying a word they moved closer to listen. "What the hell are you trying to do Chief?"

"I'm trying to end this case that everyone wants closure for already."

"It's not closure if you put the wrong people behind bars," Mark hissed. "You think I'm not doing my job boy?" Chief Thompson asked. For a long moment, there was only silence then Mark spoke his voice hollow. "My answer won't change anything whatever I say will it?"

Lily waited to hear an answer but instead jumped back as the door opened again. She looked up to see Chief Thompson's cold face and Mark behind him surprised that he had just been pushed aside. But he was even more surprised at what happened next, then again so was everyone else.

Lily yelped as Chief Thompson grabbed her upper arm and dragged her through the door and out into the hall, everyone else following behind Rose asking what the hell he was doing alongside Mark who was asking for him to stop.

But the older man kept going until they stopped at a door with his name on it at the very end of the hall. Chief Thompson grabbed the handle and opened it dragging her in, the whole time she felt frozen only moving because she had no other choice, the only sound she heard was her heart pounding in her head.

But now she stood in front of a map pinned to the wall showing all of Georgia, her eyes flicked around looking at all of the red push pins that sat everywhere but mostly Watkinsville.

"What is this?" Lily asked her voice dry. "This is everyplace one of those boys said they killed Daisy Young, Tommy killed her at the river after being rejected. Jim killed her at the park because he wanted to know what it was like to watch someone die with his own eyes. Gage killed her outside his own house!"

Lily felt the words hit her as he wanted them too, but her eyes were trained to the side of the map her breath catching as a piece of this messed up puzzle came together.

"Chief!" Mark said anger clear in his voice, "Stop this now before it goes too far and you can't back out."

"No, they need to know this, otherwise we'll never end this damned case!"

Rose stepped up then gently taking Lily's arm and pulled her away to stand next to Violet who looked about ready to pass out from fear. "We're going to leave now, if you try to stop us I will have my lawyer on you faster than you can say sorry, got it."

No one said anything but after a second Chief Thompson nodded, still looking pissed off. "Officer Hollow take them back to their car please."

"Fine," Mark said hard not looking at his Chief Officer as he guided them out of the building and into a blue day.

They piled into his car and as soon as they pulled out Rose turned on him like a wild animal. "What the hell was that?"

"You think I know?" Mark said with a cold laugh, "I think the old man finally lost it to be honest."

Rose shook her head biting into her lip hard looking ready to say more, but Lily decided to cut her off guessing it was more telling off.

"Mark do you have a map in here?"

"Um yeah, I have one in the dash, but why?"

Lily didn't bother answering instead she turned to Violet. "You have the diary right?"

"Yes," Violet said taking it out of her bag and handed it to her a confused look on her face. "Great, now pull over Mark."

"First tell me why," Mark said. "Just do as she asked," Rose said. Mark let out a hard breath but didn't argue with her. Simply pulled off to the side of the long road, empty houses on both sides as everyone was at their jobs or school.

"Hand me the map," Lily said excitement in her voice for the first time in almost three months. Mark opened the dashboard and went through it a moment before pulling out a new most likely never touched map and handed it back to her.

Without a word, Lily grabbed it and hopped out of the car and started for the front unfolding it until it showed all of Watkinsville and the surrounding outer cities. She laid it out on the hood and started to flip through Daisy's diary and found the first set of numbers.

Lily was just about to start going through them but was stopped by a hand on her shoulder spinning her around where she found Violet looking at her worried, Rose and

Mark beside her. "Lily tell us what's going on because this day has already been too crazy and hard to keep up with."

Lily knew she was right, that for the last three months everything felt as if it was on fast forward and it was a bitch to keep up with. So she took a deep breath and spoke. "When we were at the station and Chief Thompson showed us that map I figured out what the numbers mean in the diary."

Lily watched with a smile as all of their eyes grew bigger. "What do you mean?" Rose asked breathlessly a smile on her own lips as she walked up to stand next to the map, Mark with her.

"It's so easy, I can't believe we didn't see it before," Lily said pointing down to the numbers at the side of the map and Violet gasped. "It was latitude and longitude?"

"Yeah," Lily said smiling. Rose shook her head slowly, "I should have known, my father taught my brother it, then tried to teach me and Daisy and she must have remembered."

"You're kidding," Mark said sounding amazed kneeling down running his fingers down the numbers. Violet opened the diary and started to read out the numbers for him to follow along, his fingers running smoothly up and down the paper until he came to a stop.

For a moment they all stood there looking down at the words his finger had stopped at. "The Iron Horse," Rose said, "She was meeting someone at the iron horse at night?"

"Best place to go really, if you want to meet someone secretly," Mark said, "It's out of the way, no one lives around there to see or stop you."

"Let's do the next set," Violet said and started to read out loud again and this time Mark stopped by the river they had found the body. They all stopped a moment looking at one another the memory of a skull looking at them going through their heads. "Let's do the next one," Lily said her voice shaking a little.

"November 15th, 1974,

> I woke up today knowing it could end, I've made up my mind and I'm going to tell him, I only hope he'll help me otherwise I don't know what I'll do. It's also the last day of school which will be for the best. Rose has done so well but I haven't told her anything and I never plan too. I never want to see her face if she knew what i've done, she would hate me. I have to go meet him now at 33.875030 - 83.412590 a place we once loved to go to and wake up with no memory of. I wish i could go back to that kind of life but I can't. Wish me luck future me."

Lily finished reading out the numbers and Violet quickly found the place and looked up at them confused, "Main street?"

Lily shook her head having no idea what she was doing at Main street and by the look on Rose's and Violet's face, they didn't either. Then Mark spoke up making them jump from the sudden noise. "Jolly's! She must have been going to Jolly's to meet whoever it was."

"What's Jolly's?" Rose asked crossing her arms. "It's a disco club, it's a pretty good time if you enjoy loud music, drug use, and drinking too much."

Rose made a face, "And as a cop, you haven't shut it down?" Mark shrugged, "It's not my job to ruin a perfectly good business that's not meaning to hurt anyone."

Rose shook her head but Lily spoke up before she could go into the evils that were alcohol. "We need to go there and ask if everyone saw Daisy with someone that night, maybe it could lead us to her kidnapper."

"So we really are going with she was kidnapped?" Violet asked her eyes filled with horror. "It's the only answer isn't it?" Rose said, "Whatever she was going to tell the person she was seeing maybe it didn't turn out well."

"But that was in November and she never seemed scared of anyone, why wait so long?" Violet asked. "That's why we need to go to the club," Lily said, "Someone out there has answers."

"I'm sorry to say lady's, as good as that plan is it's not going to work," Mark said cutting them off, "Jolly is only opened three days a week, Friday, Saturday and Sunday."

"Friday is only two days away," Rose said, "We'll go then."

"Not without me your not," Mark said.

"Why afraid for us or something?" Lily asked an eyebrow raised. "No I just don't want to miss happy hour is all," Mark said but he didn't take his eyes off of Rose as he spoke. "Right," Lily said rolling her eyes, "Well, in that case, we'll all meet up Friday then."

"Fine by me," Mark said and started for the driver's seat. Lily grabbed the map, diary still in hand as they all got back in and started down the road. Lily couldn't help but think it was going to be along two days of waiting.

****

Violet

Violet awoke the late afternoon of Friday in pain, her whole body aching and screaming at her to stop moving from the bruises and cuts across her whole body. But with one last deep breath, she stood and had to bite down on her cheek to keep from crying out as she made her way to the bathroom, the cut on her ankle killing her every time she took a step.

But finally she made it and looked into the mirror seeing her face for the first time and a whole new wave of pain washed over Violet. Her right cheek had a purple and blue bruise looking dark and painful, there were matching ones on her arms and chest, small cuts lined her fingers and ankles from the glass.

The fight came back to her as she started the water in the tub. After they had figured out the meaning of the numbers Mark had driven them back to the diner and they walked over to her truck.

"So do we go to school or skip it for today?" Rose asked hopping into the back. "I say just skip, I'm sure the whole school is talking about how you were dragged into the police station, so it should be best to just lay low for today, " Mark said.

Lily nodded, "What should we tell our parents?"

Mark shrugged, "Tell them what happened at the station and say you didn't feel well after, and that I said go home."

"My mother will be overjoyed that I'm laying low," Rose said sitting down in the bed of the truck, but Violet knew that her mother wouldn't be happy about more news that had to do with her daughter just like her own dad.

"I'll see you all Friday," Mark said.

They nodded and he left with one last look at Rose, and with that she drove Rose and Lily home, wondering how her dad would take the news tonight, he didn't like her missing school, but maybe she could make him a warm dinner and it would help soften the news.

But when she pulled in his car was already there. Violet paused a moment thinking of what would happen if she ran. Ran to Rose like she had been telling her she could, but she wouldn't leave her dad, her mom wouldn't want that. She had loved her father since they were children living in Portugal, they had moved here together to give her a better life. If Violet abandoned him her mom would hate her. Yes, he got mad sometimes but he was always sorry afterward.

She stepped out of her car and slowly made her way towards the house. She reached out opening the old squeaking door, the smell of cheap beer hitting her as she walked into the living room and found her dad in his bright red chair, the tv on a soap opera her mom had enjoyed.

"Hey dad, how was wor-" Her words were cut off as a beer soaked her front making her take a step back in surprise and hit the bookshelf. Violet stood there the cold beer chilling her as her father got up from his chair, his eyes were red from all the alcohol or crying she couldn't tell.

But she guessed the alcohol from his breath which she could smell as he grabbed her upper arms and pushed her against the wall hard enough to make the painting shake above her. Fear ran through her even more than from anything that had happened today.

"What the fuck were you doing with the police today!" her dad yelled his voice sounding like the edge of a blade, sharp and hard.

"N-nothing, I was asked to look at a line-up and see if I remembered them from that night at the party," Violet answered, her words shaking as she turned her face away in the hopes he wouldn't see the sacred tears that pricked the corners of her eyes.

She had seen her dad like this before yes, but never had she been cornered to the point she couldn't get away if she needed too.

"And that was it? They didn't ask about any bruises or cuts?" her dad asked his voice now low, filled with anger.

"N-no Sir."

"Good, because if I get fired from my job we're both fucked, got it!."

"Yes sir," Violet said the tears falling finally to drip off her chin. She could feel her hands shaking with how scared she was, she tried to stop them but it was no use.

"Go to your room," her dad said stepping back. She took off for the stairs then, not daring to look back and she made it just in time as a beer bottle hit the bottom of the first step and shattered. The glass cutting into her heel as she kept running the sound of her heart pounding in her chest.

As soon as she made it to her room she closed the door and fell against it listening as her dad threw around more bottles and what sounded like books.

She had closed her eyes tears falling for what felt like hours, the sound of her sobbing breath muting the breaking of glass. But it still hadn't been over because of course it wasn't.

The next morning she had made her way downstairs slowly not only because of her foot but also looking out for glass. But was surprised it looked to have been cleaned up the night before by her dad, who she found in the kitchen placing fried eggs on a plate which already held toast and bacon.

"Morning honey," her dad said as if nothing had happened last night, as if she wasn't limping or had new bruises on her arms. "Morning," Violet said trying to sound normal but she wasn't sure it had worked. Though he didn't seem to care as he when on. "Come and sit down Violet."

She did as she was told and sat down quickly at their old scratched table, her dad sitting across from her. "I need to say sorry about last night, I really have no idea what got into me, work has been crazy lately, can you forgive me?"

No Violet wanted to scream, no, how many times can I keep forgiving you until I drown in them, until I am nothing more than a sorry to you?

But she put a smile that was so forced it hurt. "It's okay, I understand."

Her dad smiled and moved to pat her hand, but she flinched away without thinking, the memory of last night flashing through her eyes and a moment later she knew that it had been the wrong thing from the look in his eyes, which shown with a burning anger that had only been growing for the past four years of stress and overwork.

"I-I I'm sorry I didn't mea-" Violet started but her words were cut off by a slap to her cheek so hard it felt numb a moment until a burning pain replaced it seconds later. "If you want something to flinch at I'll give you it!" her dad hissed as he got up so fast it knocked the mug full of coffee over spilling across her food and down on to her lap.

Violet opened her mouth in a vain hope of lessening his anger somehow but he was already starting for the front door. He stopped his hand on the handle and looked back at her once as he spoke. "Your mother would hate to see you flinch away from me."

With that, he opened the door and left her alone, his words filled with hate swimming around her in the quiet. The next thing she felt was the warmth of tears on her cheeks for the second time in twenty-four hours, wondering what she had done wrong.

And even now as she turned the water off they hurt almost as much as her wounds. Would her mom really hate how weak she was? Her life could be far worse she guessed, but here she was crying because her dad yelled and hit her sometimes. At least she had food, a roof over her head, clothing, and friends who were most likely worried about her given she hadn't gone to school yesterday and today, pain making it hard to walk.

But as she slipped her brown skirt and yellow t-shirt off and stepped into the water she knew she had to go pick her friends up and lucky sitting down in the warmth her muscle settled and the pain lessened.

After a good thirty minutes, the water had gone ice cold and Violet took a long breath knowing she had to get up.

And on the count of three, she pushed herself up and grabbed a towel. She passed through the hallway of old photos were she had smiled without thought and into her cold room, the floor creaking as she made her way over to her small dresser.

She took out a dress the color of blue cotton candy, the sleeves falling down to the middle of her arms in puffy waves and the skirt going to her knees. Next, she stepped into her platform shoes the color of burned orange, then threw on an old ripped jean jacket.

After the pain of pulling that on she turned to the portrait mirror that sat on the dresser along with her meager amount of make-up and picked the pink lip gloss and green eyeshadow. As she put them on she was surprised to find how much she looked like her mom, with her kind brown eyes, wavy black hair and thin lips.

She reached out a fingertip and ran it down the cool mirror over her own cheek. The memory of her mom holding her close in a warm hug washing over her. But a moment later she closed her eyes and turned away because her mother was dead, gone and she couldn't keep wishing her back to protect her anymore.

She stepped into the sunset for the first time in over two days. She looked up to the darkening sky and couldn't help a smile as she spotted the first stars coming out to greet her.

The drive to Lily's was quiet and almost peaceful for her but the worry of what her friends would say about her face broke it. And as she pulled up outside of Lily's house Violet knew any story she tried to come up with wouldn't work given they all knew her dad could be violent, but they didn't know it was that bad and she didn't want them too.

So all she could do was hope the shadows covered it, though Lily always seemed to know what was going on with her. "Hey Violet I got the outfit for you and Rose since you weren't at school today, but-"

Lily's words broke off as she finally closed the door and looked up at her and Violet watched as her skin paled.

"What the hell did he do to you?" Lily said, her voice filled with the anger Violet knew she should feel but didn't.

"It's nothing," Violet tried, "It doesn't hurt much or anything."

"Doesn't hurt! Damn Violet, it shouldn't have happened in the first place, you need to tell Mark and get him are-"

"No," Violet said cutting off her words, "I know it looks bad but he didn't mean too and I'm not going to turn the only family I have left into the police."

Lily opened her mouth again to argue but Violet cut it off before it even began. "I won't do it, okay."

Lily shut her mouth a moment but then said quietly, "If he does it again you need to call us so we can get you out of there, promise me alright."

After a few seconds, Violet nodded unsure if it counted if she didn't actually say it out loud. The rest of the ride was quiet as they drove to Rose's house but Violet couldn't help asking. "Lily, do you think Rose is okay?"

Lily looked up then from where she had been staring out to the blurry world that passed them, her eyes full of something Violet couldn't read. "I have no idea, you know that she keeps everything so close because of her mother."

Violet bit her lip a moment rolling her words around then spoke. "I think she was talking to someone that wasn't there the other day."

"I know I saw it too, do you think she went off her medicine?" Lily asked. "It's worth believing at the very least," Violet answered as they turned into the Waters driveway.

"If that's the case can we really trust her after what she did?" Lily asked. "Do we have any choice in the matter?" Violet said, "We promised her that we would go to hell and back and I know Daisy would want the same, for us to keep her safe if she can't."

Lily let out a long breath and nodded, "Hell just seems to keep getting closer is what I'm worried about."

* * *

Rose

Rose stepped out of her house and closed the door as quietly as she could, her mother was in the kitchen making pies for the church this Sunday. How she had gotten so lucky enough for her father and Jason to still be out she didn't know, but she wasn't out of the woods yet. If her mother found her gone she would kill her, and Rose knew it wasn't a joke because she didn't know how too.

So as soon as Rose saw that baby blue truck she walked as fast as she could in the stupid heels her mother made her wear and hopped into the back giving a wave to Lily and Violet. A moment later they were off, the wind blowing her hair back.

For the next fifteen minutes they road through the town they had grown up in for their whole lives, saw people they had known forever.

But all Rose could think about was her father, the gun and bracelet going around and around in her head to the point she wanted to scream. She hadn't said anything to anyone not even Lily or Violet and she didn't know why. Something didn't feel right, yes, but the question was which part?

The gun was new and it scared her, because her father didn't seem violent, and it could just be for protection. Then there was the bracelet. That was harder to explain because there's no reason he should have it because it had been with Daisy at the party... that was in less it had been a delusion and that's what she was scared of.

"Was it real?" Rose whispered looking over at Daisy who sat next to her. But Daisy once again didn't answer. She hadn't for over two days now, simply would sit next to Rose and look at her with her dress covered in red and Rose was tired of it.

She looked down at the back of her hand that had turned a deep purple and yellow. She wasn't in the right state of mind but at least she could ask people at the disco club if they had seen him with Daisy because a man even as good looking as her father couldn't hide is age.

Rose held onto the side as they turned into the parking lot of the diner, Mark's old ford already sitting there. With a breath she jumped down and met Violet and Lily as they walked into the quiet room, once again almost empty and Rose wondered how they stayed open with so little business, but on another note as she looked up at the waitress and found her counting a stack of money in the corner she probably didn't want to know.

"I've got your outfit," Lily said, "let's go change."

"Sure," Rose said as she met Mark's eyes with her own from across the restaurant and she was surprised to see him in normal clothing of dark jeans and a white t-shirt, a brown jacket over it after seeing him in nothing but his blue and black police uniform since the party that fateful night.

Even his hair looked different in someway maybe it was just a little wilder than most days. But her eyes turned away as Lily grabbed her arm and pulled her towards the bathroom Violet already gone in. Rose quickly followed and once they were all in she closed the door after herself and slid the deadbolt in place locking everyone out but themselves.

Rose looked over to her friends and stopped dead as she saw Violet's face for the first time in the light, the dark mark standing out like a burning house. "What happened?" Rose asked going over to her and looked at the bruise, it had to hurt like hell. "Is this why you didn't go to school?"

For a moment the room was quiet then Violet spoke shooting a look at Lily, "No, I just fell on a door handle and my dad kept me home to make sure I was okay, it was stupid really but what can you do," Violet said her voice light. But Rose knew too well what a hand could do, but there had to be a reason they were trying to hide it, so she would let it go for now and put on a smile. "Well, in that case, I hope it doesn't hurt too much and that you gave that door handle what it deserved."

Violet nodded looking away, her cheeks filling with color. Rose looked at Lily then who had started to take out makeup and outfits from her bag and Rose felt her eyes grow wide at the one Lily handed to her.

"This is a dress?" Rose asked holding the thing out in front of her. It was a golden sheer gown that looked to only go down to her mid-thigh, the collar line went miles pass what she had ever worn before.

"You like it?" Lily asked taking out a similar dress, this one black and the other red and three pairs of white knee-high boots.

"What look are we going for?" Rose asked looking over at her with an eyebrow raised. "The twenty-one and over kind of look," Lily answered handing Violet the red one. Rose bit her lip thinking of what her mother would do to her if she even saw her holding it, but she wasn't here. And if she was honest Rose was tired of the pointless worry because she had bigger things to care about at the moment.

With that thought she went into one of the stalls and dressed as quickly as she could without touching a thing. A second later after trying to pull the damned thing down as much as she could she came out and found Violet in her own dress as well looking like a model with her bright red lips and wavy dark hair.

"You look great Violet."
Violet gave her a little smile but turned her bruised cheek away.

"Let me see if I can fix that," Lily said turning the shorter girls cheek towards her and Rose saw the thankfulness in her brown eyes. "Rose, can you manage yourself?" Lily asked as she started looking through her things.

"Can't I always?" Rose said and quickly applied a dark red lipstick and even dark blue eyeshadow. She looked up at herself in the long mirror that ran across the sinks and she had to say she looked at least twenty-one with her blue eyes shadowed in dark colors and lips blood red. Plus the amount of chest that she was showing had to help.

She passed Lily and Violet heading into the diner, her boots clicking until she stopped next to Mark who didn't notice her too deep in thought as he looked out of the window. She cleared her throat making him jump and look over at her with wide eyes, but somehow they grew even bigger as he looked her over.

"You-I-look-"

"Like a hoe?" Rose laughed cutting him off as she sat across from him. For a moment he sat there looking like a deer in headlights trying to look everywhere but her chest until he spoke. "N-no, I was going to say you look amazing."

"Thank Lily for that, but what were you looking at so deeply out there?"

Mark opened his mouth but stopped as he looked down at her arms that sat on the table crossed in front of her. She followed his gaze and saw the white lines that ran across her wrists.

She quickly sat up letting her arms fall to her sides, heat flooding her cheeks along with shame. "Nothing," Mark said softly, "Just work is all."

"You know," Rose said hoping to break the tension, "Why did you want to be an officer? Since we were kids you never cared about the law or stopping bad guys. You only cared about parties and girl's."

Mark took a deep breath looking down at his hands, "I changed."

"When?" Rose almost whispered, "When did you stop being the boy who ran after us on sunny days to the man who barely spoke to me for over a year?"

Mark looked up at her his eyes hard. "Rosey you have-"

"Ready to go?" Lily asked her black dress shining and blonde hair wavey as she came up to them, Mark's words once again cut off.

Rose looked up at them and smiled as if they had only been talking about the weather. "Let's go, I'm ready to get this over with already," Rose said as she stood and took a little white bag from Violet.

Mark stood up a moment later smiling as well.

"One of us need to ride with you Mark because we can't ride in the back of the truck with these dresses on," Lily said as they stepped outside into the night air, the wind blowing Rose's hair around her face.

"Fine by me," Mark said walking in front of them as he unlocked his car, "Who is it going to be?"

Rose looked over at Lily who in turn was looking at her, "You go," Rose mouthed. Lily shook her head and mouthed back a no, her eyes wide maybe thinking she was helping Rose in some way.

"I'm not going with him by myself!" Rose mouthed her eyes filling with panic. Lily bit her lip and looked up at the stars but shot Rose a look that said she owed her.

"I'll go with you," Lily said her voice light, but Rose could tell she wasn't happy as she closed the passenger side door with a bang. "Come on," Violet said taking her hand and gently pulled her over to baby blue.

They both jumped in and started after Mark, quiet falling around them. "Why didn't you want to go with

Mark?" Violet asked finally breaking the silence after a few minutes.

Rose looked up from where she had been looking out the window the dark world passing her by, "The real question is why did Lily try to make me go with him?" Rose asked tipping her head until it rested on the glass.

Violet took a deep breath, "Haven't you noticed how hard he has been working to help us?"

Rose blinked a little confused, "Sure, but what does that have to do with me?"

"God Rosey, you're blind aren't you, " Violet almost laughed, "He likes you."

For a moment Rose just sat there her mind had gone white as if she was lost in a snowstorm. "W-what do you mean he likes me?"

Violet let out a sigh and took her eyes off the road a moment to look at her, eyes filled with pity, "Likes-likes you Rosey."

"He can't like-like me, Violet, not after what he did to me last year."

"I don't know what to tell you Rosey, but he's trying so hard, sticking out his neck like this for us and it's for a reason. He doesn't seem like the same person from before."

"It's not just for me," Rose said trying to find any other reason besides that even if it seemed like the most obvious one, "He's doing it for Daisy too."

Violet just shook her head as they pulled into the parking lot of Jolly's beside Mark. Rose watched them get out, Mark's hair catching in the pink neon light that streamed from the large sign displaying the name of the club high above the cream building. And she was taken aback that when she looked at him it was like the first time, making her heart jump. And maybe it was, at least it was the first time she had looked at him and understood that the boy she knew was gone replaced with someone she didn't know yet.

CHAPTER 12

Lily

Lily looked up from where she had been looking at the line of people that seemed to go on for at least half a block and found Rose and Violet quickly joining them. The wind blowing Violet's wavy hair around her face looking like a long forgotten goddess. "Ready to go in?" Mark asked all of them, but she couldn't help notice he was looking at Rose as he spoke.

"Yeah," Lily said, "But it looks like it's going to be a long time until we get in it looks like."

"Oh we don't have to worry about the line," Mark said and started for an alley that sat to the side of the building. Lily shot a look to her friend's eyebrows raised, but Violet just shrugged and went after him Rose behind her. Lily looked after them a moment then over at the line, she guessed whatever Mark had in mind was better than standing around all night.

Lily caught up with them as they approached a door the color of the sidewalk and looked just as dirty. She could hear the music pounding through the walls the beat fast and heavy. Mark stopped and gave a few quick knocks and for a moment they stood there, the beat going faster and faster, until finally the door opened and a guy that looked to be in his late twenties looked down at them, then up to Mark.

"Well if it isn't Officer Hollow, here to shut us down tonight?" The guy drawled leaning against the door frame, the baby blue suit he wore catching in the rainbow of lights that flowed out.

"Well Chris, I was really thinking about it but I want to have a little fun beforehand, so let us in and I'll see how I feel in a few hours, what do you think?" Mark said his tone cool.

Chris seemed to think a moment and Lily saw his eyes cut to them and she watched as his lips tipped up.

"Are they legal?" he asked looking at Rose. Mark seemed to be taken aback by the question unsure how to answer as he looked at Rose. "I-I-"

Lily stepped up then until she was in front of the guy and was happy to find she was taller than him. "What do you think?" She whispered tipping his chin up to look at her red lips. She watched him swallow and couldn't help her own little smile showing him her teeth.

God she hated being able to do this, play a man with a simple look. Hated how easy it was to get them to do as she said. But it had been like this since she was thirteen and her father ran off to marry another woman half his age.

The first week she had just wanted to understand why and so she had kissed Tommy Johnson, letting him touch her were no one else but herself had in the warm heat of the summer in her room and found it so so so painfully easy to fall into a world of nothingness only feeling pleasure. But by the next year after watching her mother break down countless times trying and failing at dating she wanted more of the nothingness. The emptiness of the aftermath, going to boy after boy as she slowly started to be known as a slut, but it never felt like enough.

Then Daisy had shown up one day, somehow already knowing her name and asked her to simply sit with them at lunch. The memory of looking at her and Rose who tried giving her a bright smile still made her chest hurt.

And after that day all she wanted was to feel alive like Daisy did. Following her to parties, trying her first cigarette and other drugs and things she only thought about at night, for the first time at the age of fourteen when she figured out no man could ever give her what she really wanted.

She had been happy that at least one person knew what she was and didn't care, But it was taken away from her in a blur of a night and now that she had a chance to get her back she wasn't going to let it go.

Chris stood there only a moment more looking at her like a deer ready for the ax, then moved aside for them, "Go right in."

"Thanks," She said her voice filled with sweetness as she passed him, the others following after her until they reached a door that lead into the back, the music rattling its frame.

Lily took a breath and opened the door and was hit with a rainbow of colors from everywhere she looked.

From the walls that glowed orange compared to the dark wood of the floor. To the bright lights that hung from the ceiling all around the room flashing colors. Lily felt her mouth open a little as she walked in Violet at her side as they looked around themselves.

A DJ sat at the back wall his table filled with things she couldn't name. Then there was the dance floor lit up with colored tiles in the middle of the room filled with bodies dancing on top of one another, a disco ball hanging over them flashing like a star.

"Jesus," Violet said under her breath moving closer to her as someone pushed passed them trying to get to the bathroom looking as if they were going to vomit. "I don't think Jesus is here at the moment," Lily answered.

"Where should we start?" Rose asked looking around herself as if she was going to be murdered any minute. "Let's talk with the staff first and show them a photo of Daisy," Mark said digging through his pocket and pulled out photos of her.

"Where did you get these? Lily asked as she was handed one and looked down at it and found it was a school photo from last year. "Mrs. Young gave the police a lot of photos when she first went missing in hopes it would help," Mark replied looking down at the picture, his voice filled with pain, maybe wishing he could tell the Young's their little girl was alive if nothing else.

"Won't people know her just with her name after the last three months?" Violet asked.

"A lot of people aren't from here and it will help jog their memories, it's hard to say no when you're looking at a photo," Mark said.

"Alright," Lily said letting her arms drop to the side with the photo. "I and Rose can start by the bar and work our way out from there."

Mark nodded and looked at Violet, "You want to start by the lounging area?"

Lily looked over to where he was talking about and found a small area where loveseats and chairs sat around a table full of every kind of drug you could think of and many you couldn't.

"You really want to start with that?" Lily asked worry spreading through her chest but she couldn't think of why, maybe because Violet would be around them? But Mark would be with her the whole time so there was no need to worry.

Still as she watched them step away Lily wanted to run after them grab Violet's arm and walk away from all of this, but instead, she turned away and looked at Rose.

"Let's head for the bar and start asking if they ever saw Daisy with anyone, and maybe there will be some loose shots," She said trying to make her voice light. Rose only nodded still looking down at the photo and Lily saw she had another one in her hand, this one looking different.

"What's that one of?" Lily asked as they started weaving through the crowd. "Nothing," Rose answered too quickly putting the picture away. Lily shot her a look but didn't push it, if she was really off her meds then there was a chance she could be having delusions or even a hallucination and she didn't want her to get violent. She would just watch her like a hawk.

Lily looked up then as they finally made their way to the bar and stopped in front of the waiter, who was pouring a shot for a woman who looked only a year older than themselves. Lily put on one of her most eye-catching smiles as the guy turned to them a dry look across his bearded face.

"May I help you two?" The guy asked sitting down a cocktail glass and started to pour gin into it. "Well I sure hope you can, but it's a little weird you see," Lily said leading into him across the clear glass countertop of the bar, "We need to know if you or anyone may have seen this girl coming in around November of last year. Maybe hanging out with someone most likely an older guy," She said pushing the photo towards him.

He looked down at it a moment before shaking his head, "Sorry but can't say I have."

Lily bit her lip hard as she pulled away trying to think of what to say next but was gently pushed aside as Rose came forward and placed a picture in front of him next to the other.

"Did you ever see this man then?" Rose asked her voice strong even if her hand shook a little. Lily watched the guy look down at it a moment then he picked it up and squinted, "Yeah actually… well kinda, this photo isn't very good but it looks a bit like a guy that comes in here once in a while."

"And do you think he could have brought that girl here with him once?" Rose asked her voice sounding hollow. "Maybe, to be fair i don't look too closely at the women he brings in but she seems his type, who is he to you anyway?" The guy asked really looking up at them for the first time.

Rose paused a moment her mouth open a little, her blue eyes downcast making them look almost black as she answered. "His name is William Waters. My father."

* * *

Violet

Violet turned back only once to look back at Lily and Rose to see them trying to get to the bar as she and Mark walked over to the people who sat watching the club dance and party as they smoked and drank until there was nothing left in their eyes.

"How are we going to talk with them?" Violet asked seeing that many looked spaced out and wouldn't respond to a truck driving right at them.

"I've had to deal with people in this state, hell I've had a few friends but it's kinda like talking with a child," Mark said.

"A child?" Violet repeated unsure.
"Yeah just use small words."

"Great," She said, sarcasm clear in her voice as they stopped next to a guy smoking a roll up his eyes bloodshot. "Hey man, you come here often?" Mark asked sitting down next to him.

Violet cautiously sat next to him as the guy looked up, his long blonde hair catching in the lights. "Sure, I love this place been coming here for years," The guy said blowing out a puff of smoke and offered it to her.

"Really, mind if we ask you a few things?" Mark asked taking the roll-up that the guy still held out to her and put it out in a tray full of ashes. The guy looked down at his hand a moment confused before his smile returned. "Of course my man ask away."

"Have you seen a girl that looks like her," Violet asked passing him the picture. The guy looked down at it only a second before nodding, "Yeah that's Alison Marry." Violet felt her eyes go wide and looked at Mark who looked just as bewildered. "No this is a girl named Daisy Young," Mark said, "She was missing for two months this year, before being found dead."

"No way that's Alison Marry I remember that red hair anywhere, Kelly come here and tell these people that this is a picture of Alison," The guy said turning to a woman who stood by the wall, her dress the color of key limes and matching platform heels making her tower over them.

The woman walked over to stand behind them and leaned over the sofa, her black hair stiff with hairspray as it brushed past Violet who tried to lean away as far as she could. "Yup that's Alison alright, I know those lips anywhere."

Violet whipped her head around to stare at her. "Lips?" Violet said her voice going high. The woman laughed a little at her reaction, "Oh I saw her kissing a guy many times, on this very sofa for that fact and more, but she didn't mind trying it out on other...people if you know what I mean," The woman said with a little wink.

Violet felt her cheeks go hot but Mark shook it off as if it was nothing. "What did the guy look like?" Mark asked his eyes alert. The woman shrugged, "Dark hair, blue eyes, tall."

"That's it," Violet asked disappointed. "If you want to know what he looks like he's here," The guy said making both Mark and herself look at him as he lit another roll-up.

"What did you just say," Mark said slowly getting up. Violet right next to him, fear going through her. "I saw him a few minutes ago before you sat down, it looked like he was trying to find someone."

Mark turned to her panic in his eyes. "We need to get to Rose and Lily."

Violet nodded but turned back to the guy, "Where did he go?"

"I don't know dude, it's kinda hard to see in here, he had a lighter so probably for a smoke."

"He likes girls that look like you, young," The woman said still leaning against the sofa and gave Violet a wink. Violet felt her face go hot. "Thanks," Mark said and grabbed her arm dragging her through the crowd the light blinding them.

Violet hung on to him as she was pushed every which way by bodies of people moving to the music, her heart pounding in her head the fear of being knocked down and crushed under heeled feet felt all too real, but the thought of Daisy's kidnapper even more so.

They were almost at the bar when suddenly an arm came flying out of nowhere and hit her in the cheek right were her bruise was. She felt herself cry out and let go of Mark as pain made everything go white.

Violet stopped in the middle of a wave of bodies holding her cheek, her eyes closed as pained tears wet her cheeks. "Damn it," she hissed as she slowly opened her eyes to see a blurry world in front of her. Lights dancing as someone stopped in front of her. "Mark?" Violet asked trying to no avail to blink the blurriness away. But the person said nothing in reply and before she knew what was happening they grabbed at her arm, catching her off balance and started to pull her towards the front door.

At that moment she felt her heart stop, air seeming to leave her lungs and all she could think was, I haven't lived yet, I haven't got to see the world like my mom wanted, I haven't proved I'm not a coward to her yet, I haven't even gotten to kiss anyone.

With that last thought of brown eyes and blonde hair, she gritted her teeth and pulled her arm away with all her force and to her surprise, it came free. Without looking back she ran through the crowd and right into a body. She looked up fear making her blood buzz and found Mark looking worried.

"Are you okay, what happened?" Mark asked his voice quiet in the midst of the music even when he was yelling. Violet shook her head, "No someone just tried to pull me outside."

"Shit," Mark said looking around himself, "We need to get to the others and get out of here."

Violet nodded her breath still coming too quickly as Mark took her hand once more and they once again made their way through the crowd and finally, they made it to the bar where they found Rose looking down at a photo and Lily downing a cocktail.

"We need to get out of here," Mark said going up to them as Lily slammed down the glass making the bartender give her a dark look.

"Yeah well, you need to hear what Rose has to say first," Lily said her eyes dark. "No, you don't understand Violet was-"

Mark started but Violet cut him off. "What does Rose have to say?"

Rose looked down at the picture only a moment more, then she looked up and spoke, her words like Ice water. "The man that Daisy was seeing was my... My father."

Violet felt cold go through her whole body as the words hit her. "H-how?" She asked.

"I don't know, I don't know anything anymore," Rose replied and Violet saw tears in her eyes as her hands shook so hard the photo fell to the floor. Mark looked just as surprised as them but moved closer to Rose who looked ready to have a breakdown.

"I know this is all a big mess, but we need to get out of here."

He moved a piece of her brown hair behind her ear, "We're in danger right now but we'll figure this out."

Rose looked up at him, her eyes shining but she nodded. "Alright then," Mark said taking her pale hand and looked over at them, "We need to stay together and go through the back and head for the cars, once-"

Suddenly his words were cut off as the world when black. For a moment Violet froze, thinking the lights would be back on any second and everything would be fine. But the dark went on as people started to talk low all at once.

"Lily," Violet whispered, the darkness making her go cold. "I'm here," Lily said from somewhere beside her, then a moment later she felt the touch of warm skin taking her arm.

"Are you all alright?" Mark said his voice low. "Yes," they all answered in unison. "Good, Rose find Violet's hand and hang on, we need to get the hell out of here because someone is doing this to get to us."

Violet heard someone moving around them then she felt Rose small hand take her own and she moved her own hand to take Lily's. "Ready?" Mark said.

"Let's get out of here," Violet answered and with that, they started forward.

They shouldered pass what felt like a never-ending sea of people and as her eyes adjusted to the dark found they still had a ways to go until they reached the door, but she didn't dare try to move quicker in fear of losing hold of anyone. But it seemed as if the world hated them because in that moment someone started to scream.

Violet stopped dead as it seemed everyone in that club did, as the word "Fire!" Rang out across the room. For a second they stopped breathing, then like a breaking dam everyone moved like a wave of water, sweeping them away from one another running for the door.

Violet couldn't help but yell out as she hung onto Rose and Lily as they were bodily pulled towards the back door by Mark. But with the smell of smoke filling the room another surge of people pulled at her and finally Violet felt her grip loosen. With a gasp, she felt the loss of Rose's hand and she watched Rose look back at them her eyes wide as she called out. But it was too late, She and Lily were already lost in the sea of people.

***

Rose

Rose felt her heart fall to her stomach as Violet and Lily disappeared into the crowd. She tried to pull away from Mark and follow after them but he held onto her as if she was a lifeline until they made it to the back wall where the crowd had lessened.

"We need to go back for them!" Rose shouted turning to Mark as he undid the locks on the door, smoke filling the room now making his hands shake as he tried to slide out the deadbolt.

"We can't," Mark answered as he finally got the damned thing open. "We can't just leave them here with Daisy's kidnapper," She said anger in her voice but it cooled as Mark looked at her and she saw he didn't want to do this as well.

"I know but I think they'll be safe if you're with me."

"What do you mean?" She asked as they made their way through the back trying not to breathe too much. "I mean if it's really your father doing all of this he will follow after you."

"Why would he do that?" Rose asked. "Because getting you out of the way would be too easy, " Mark said looking back at her in the dark, his hazel eyes looking black as the night. Rose looked down at her hands a moment thinking back to everything.

Her father had the money to pay off the men to confess and confuse the police. The power to switch out Daisy's dental records and the reason behind it made sense. If he had an affair with a girl four times younger than himself it would have ruined him. His career, his marriage, his relationship with his children everything. So kidnapping Daisy or at least had someone take her and was keeping her somewhere would be for the best in his reasoning.

"It's really him," She said feeling as if she was cracking more and more every second knowing it was real.

"I'm sorry," Mark said as he opened the back door and walked out into the cold night, Rose behind him looking around as they breathed in the clean air.

"We need to get to my car so we can-"

His words were cut off suddenly as they were blinded by headlights that sat at the end of the alley facing them. They stood there like deer's caught in literal headlights, her breath catching in her chest feeling as if she was about to pass out from the lack of oxygen. It was too dark to tell if it was her father's car but if it was, would he kill her to keep his secrets?

She was snapped out of the thought as she jumped when whoever it was that drove the car revved the engine. Mark took a step back his arm out shielding her.

"What do we do?" Rose hissed as the car once again revved it's engine and inched forward. Mark shook his head and bit the inside of his lip, "Run."

"Run?" Rose repeated as they both took a step back as the car inched at them. "Run!" Mark shouted as he grabbed her hand and they took off in the opposite direction. Rose gasped as her feet slipped on the ground but she caught herself as the sound of tires sliding on dirt road rang out around them.

She looked back as they reached another side road that the alley let out of to see the car headed straight for them and she felt her heart stop, her blood turning cold then the next thing Rose knew she was pushing Mark into the line of trees just as the car would have hit them.

They fell to the cold ground, the impact sending pain through her as she landed on a fallen tree, the branches cutting into her. They laid there a moment, Rose's breath coming too quickly, blood in her ears as she slowly looked over her shoulder and saw the car start to turn around heading for them once more.

"Shit," She hissed and quickly forced herself up grabbing Mark's hand and helped him up and without a word, they started to run this time she was in the lead as she knew where to go.

For the next ten minutes she and Mark ran through the dark of the tree's only stopping to catch their breath, but every time she saw headlights they would run a little faster, their hearts beating just as fast until they reached a house Rose knew better than her own.

"The Young's?" Mark asked out of breath as he leaned against a tree, his hair a mess even more than before from all of the running. "Yeah, I can't go home and their like my family, so they'll let me stay over."

"What if they call your parents?" Mark asked. Rose shook her head, "If I ask them not too they won't."

"You're that sure?" Mark asked raising an eyebrow. "I'm like a second daughter to them," Rose answered as she started for their door.

"And what should I do?" Mark asked not moving from his place. "Head into the backyard and wait by the second window, that's Daisy's room, I'll let you in when I can," Rose answered looking back at him. Mark nodded and started for the gate as she took a deep breath heading for the door.

She stopped on the porch and looked down at herself a moment. Her once white boots now dirty, the dress she wore was ripped in a few places and she knew her hair was a mess. "You know you can't just stand there all night right?" Daisy asked in a mocking tone. She had been getting meaner and meaner for the past month just like they had before, but still seeing her was better than nothing at the moment, even if the comment still hurt.

Rose gave a few fast knocks and waited, less then a second later the door opened and Mrs. Young stood there, a dark silhouette in the yellow light. "Rose?" She asked surprise in her voice.

"Evening," Rose said trying to be normal but it didn't really work with the way she looked. "What happened to you darling?" Mrs. Young asked stepping out and looked her over.

"I went for a walk and fell is all," Rose said hoping it sounded convincing. Mrs. Young just shook her head, "Oh Rosey you better come in and clean up, your bleeding you know."

No, Rose thought, I didn't but it wouldn't surprise me at this point.

They walked into the Young's kitchen, the light hurting her eyes from running in the dark for so long, but when she saw Mr. Young a new kind of hurt hit her. He looked years older, his hair graying where it had been red only four months ago. His eyes were red as if he had been crying as he looked at something in front of him.

"Mr. Young are you alright?" Rose asked forgetting the pain she was in. The older man looked up then and she watched his eyes widen at her. "I should be asking you that Rose, you look as if a bear tried getting you."

The comment made her smile for the first time in weeks but it didn't make her feel much better. "Sit down Rose, I'll get a cloth to wash your cut with," Mrs. Young said going over to the sink. Rose did as she was told and sat down across from Mr. Young, her feet hurting from the heels, she turned to ask if it was okay to take them off but stopped as she spotted what Mr. Young had been looking at.

The black and white grainy photo looked like the surface of an alien planet. She tipped her head to the side trying to see it a little better but she still couldn't tell what it was. "I see you've seen the ultrasound," Mrs. Young said sitting down next to her and pressed the warm damp cloth to her cheek where she guessed she had the cut, though she didn't feel it the word ultrasound muting everything else.

"You're pregnant?" Rose asked her voice a whisper. Mrs. Young nodded and Rose saw the shine in her eyes, "It's a miracle isn't it, I went to a doctor to have them checked on today since I'm older now, but everything thing looks good."

Rose nodded not sure what to say, of course she was happy for them, they believed their daughter had died and now out of nowhere had a baby on the way. But Daisy was alive somewhere and she wanted nothing more than to tell them. But she couldn't, not with her father out there especially now. "I- I'm so happy for the both of you," she finally said wrapping her arms around the older woman pain echoing through every part of her body as Mrs. Young hugged her back.

They stayed like that and for the first time she noticed boxes everywhere and saw that a lot of furniture was gone and the pieces came together, hitting her like ice water.

"Your moving?" Rose asked hollowly pulling away to look at them. "Yes," Mr. Young said, "To Chicago next week, we were planning to tell everyone this Sunday about the baby and the move."

"Too many memories here," Mrs. Young said trying to give her a smile but it still looked painful. Rose took a deep breath and put on her own smile, "I'm so glad for the both of you."

"Thank you honey," Mrs. Young said and stood up, "I'm going to call your parents to come and get you alright."

"No!" Rose said too loud her heart jumping. Mrs. Young turned back to her giving her a concerned look and Rose quickly went on. "I-it's too late, their probably already asleep and I don't want my mother to be mad at me for waking them up, you know she likes her beauty sleep," She said trying to give a little laugh at the end but Mrs. Young simply looked at her worried.

After a moment Rose stood going over to her and took her hand, "Have you packed up Daisy's things yet?"

Mrs. Young shook her head, "No it's been too much to even think about still."

"I'll stay here tonight and go through it for you, see what you may want to keep and all of that," Rose said giving the older woman a smile. After a second she nodded looking tired.

"Thank you Rosey," Mr. Young said looking up at her a deep sadness in his eyes. She couldn't answer afraid her voice would break on the words but nodded and headed for the hall.

When she reached Daisy's room she shut the door and slid to the floor, a hand covering her mouth, heat burning behind her eyes from tears. Her father had done all of this. Was the reason the family that had always loved her for no other reason than that she was herself was leaving. The reason they were in pain and the reason Daisy may be hurting at this very moment.

Why, why, why did her family have to be so messed up. Her mother and needing control over everything she could get her hands on. Her brother and his need to be loved no matter what and so bored with life. Her father never being there when she needed and now all of this.

Finally, the sob she had been holding in was let out in a painful breath, chest aching as her body shook. But a knock came from the window a moment later. Mark was standing outside waiting for her, for a second Rose thought about what she would look like to him. A child crying over a life she believes to be unfair, but at the same time, she didn't really care anymore about looking like that perfect little girl for everyone.

She got up and went over to the bed and slid the window up finding Mark standing in front of her the night air cold on her cheeks, she moved out of the way as he climbed through. "That took you long enough, what kept you?" Mark asked the boards creaking under him.

Rose turned away from him tears still running, "Nothing," she said her voice feeling dry. "Why are you crying?" Mark asked and she couldn't tell if it was curiosity or sympathy in his voice. "I'm not."

"Rosey you know I've known you since we were children, I know when you're crying," he said moving to stand in front of her. She gasped as he tipped her chin up to look at him, she couldn't remember when someone had touched her like this, and with a look she couldn't read.

"What's wrong?" Mark asked again the words sounding real.

"Why is my family so messed up?" She finally whispered turning her eyes away from him. "It's not," he said then thinking a moment he went on, "Well at least you're not messed up."

"Your blind then," Rose said anger in her voice as she turned away from him, "I'm the most messed up out of all of them."

"You mean being schizophrenic," Mark said softly, "Rosey that doesn't mean your messed up or crazy, it just means you're dealing with something, sometimes you see things others can't but it's not the plague. You have people around you who understand and will help you through it."

Rose felt heat rise in her cheeks because he didn't understand and she turned on him. "I'm more than just not perfect! I tried killing myself last year! Did you know that? For those six months I was gone I wasn't in Arizona with an aunt but in a psych ward drugged out of my mind! I can get violent sometimes and I'm scar-"

"I know that Rosey, but the thing is I don't care, it doesn't make me see you any differently," he reached out and took her wrists, "These don't make me see you as crazy but someone who survived, survived sometime no one should have to go through but you do it everyday, His voice cracked than and she saw his eyes were wet.

"Did you know I tried seeing you every single day as I trained to be an officer."

Rose felt her eyes go wide from his words and had thousands of questions but the only asked one thing

"How?"

"After what I said to you that night I knew it was my fault you were there, I didn't know you were schizophrenic at the time. But I know you hurt yourself and all I wanted was to tell you sorry, but Jason never let me, hell he beat the crap out of me the first time."

"After what you said to me?" Rose asked shaking her head, "Mark it wasn't just your words that night that made me do it. There was so much more going on."

The memory of that night came back to her every now and then, the coldness of the basement air as she sat in an armchair watching Jason and Mark play on their Atari.

She watched a grainy white ball bounce around the screen the sound echoing through the room. "Do you think your mother is going to put the pork blood into your drink?" A voice asked her. "No," Rose said trying to be quiet. "You're an idiot you know that?" Another voice said from behind her.

She had closed her eyes wishing for them to stop but they didn't, they rarely did in those days. At first, it had started as whispers in the night, simple things like her hair needed a cut or that her makeup looked bad.

But when she turned fifteen it got worse, so much worse. They would tell her how stupid she was, that her mother hated her, she was a failure, nothing but a worm in this world ready to be stepped on. They would stand over her and scream in the night until she couldn't sleep, couldn't eat, couldn't think.

She stood up hoping to get away from them but still they followed her to the door and she couldn't take it anymore. "Shut up!" She screamed at them turning around but only found blue and hazel eyes looking at her.

"Jesus Rosey, you take some crazy pills today?" Mark said with a laugh. "Dude stop," Jason said but he had a smile across his face. "Why she's clearly lost her mind if she's screaming at the air like that," Mark said looking up at her, "Next thing you know you'll be in the crazy house."

"You think I'm crazy?" Rose asked her voice small. "Yeah, you talk to yourself and look at things that aren't there I would say your pretty fucking nuts," Mark said.

She could tell he was joking but still, the words hit her like a slap to the face and the voices laughing didn't help.

He was right isn't he, I'm crazy and there's nothing I can do to stop them. She had opened the door and walked upstairs to find her mother cutting up fruit for a Jello and as she watched her put the knife down on the counter Mark's words repeated over and over again, he was the only one of her brothers friends she had ever liked and maybe it had been a little more and now that was gone.

"No one wants a crazy person," A voice said as she watched her mother turn around, the knife just laying there calling out.

She had quickly grabbed it and headed for the front door, the voices egged her on telling her it would be a way to make them finally stop, maybe in her last few minutes she would be able to sleep in peace.

She had walked into the bright day and over to the line of trees that went around their home ready for them to finally stop. But what she hadn't known was Daisy had been walking across the street on her way to see them and had watched Rose walk mindlessly through the tall weeds something sharp catching the light.

Rose didn't remember much from the time after she had watched her own blood start to run bright across her pale skin, the pain blinding. But the sound of her name being shouted with so much fear by Daisy as she caught Rose in her arms, her body giving out as the world turned blurry. The knife falling beside her stained with red the color of her namesake was the last thing she remembered before waking up.

"I had been so tired and worn down from trying to hide it all for so long, they finally got to me."

"But my words didn't help," Mark said angry, but it sounded like he was madder at himself than her. "Don't do that to yourself," Rose whispered taking his hand, "Stop thinking it's your fault, which I know is what you're doing."

"Do you know why I became a police officer Rosey?" Mark asked looking down so she couldn't see his eyes in the shadows. "No," Rose answered her heart racing. "The first time I tried visiting you Jason dislocated my arm and told me to never talk to you or your family again, to never come near you or he would kill me."

"He what? " Rose asked jolted by his words, Jason had never talked to her like that, but she knew he could have that side to him, an angry side that would come from nowhere when he would get in trouble and knew he couldn't get out of it. But to say that to Mark, his best friend since childhood.

"He shouldn't have done that to you," Rose said his hand squeezing her own.

"He was right to say what he did, it made me take a long look at my life... I wasn't a good person Rosey, I and Jason would do awful things, skip class to go and mess around with the wrong kind of people" Mark said making a face at himself.

"So I decided to become the very thing I ran from, to do good, look after others, help the people I had hurt and somehow it led me back to you Rosalina Waters. Somehow the world forgave me and sent me you when I needed it the most and I can finally tell you how sorry I am. I know a can't defeat your demons for you, but I want to be by your side as your flight them and I only hope you will give me that chance."

Rose looked up sharply at the way he said her name as if it was a prayer that could save him. Before she knew what she was doing she grabbed his shirt collar and pulled his lips down to meet her own, a feeling of warmth washing through her as he wrapped his arms around her. And she knew they both must have been wanting this for a long time as they both pulled at one another with so much need it was as if they were drowning and the other was oxygen.

Somehow she managed to take off his jacket the sound of it hitting the floor made her take a breath pulling her lips away, "Bed," She moaned.

Without stepping away from each other they climbed into the bed, the smell of old laundry and night air around them as they kissed until it seemed they would run out of breath.

Rose stopped only a moment to help him take off his shirt letting it fall to the floor next to his jacket and he did the same to her. Leaving his muscled chest bare and her own body in nothing but underwear.

For a moment they laid there looking at one another taking each other in as if it was the thing that kept them going. But at the same time tiredness spread through her from her words that she had never spoken to anyone else, from the months spent worrying, from finally telling someone about that day because no one ever wanted to talk about it with her.

Rose's eyes felt heavy and if she was honest, she didn't feel ready for this, to have this with him. Not just yet. "Mark?" She whispered her voice laced with heat. "Yes?" he said his voice just as heavy. "Can we stop here?" Rose asked quietly. For a moment he just looked down at her, his pupils blown then reached down and kissed her once more but this one was gentle like the touch of flower petals, soft and smooth.

He pulled away and laid down beside her, his body warming her own. "Of course, it looks like you need to sleep," Mark whispered running a fingertip down her cheek, "You look so tired."

"I can't, Lily and Violet are out there somewhere. What if my father went back for them?"

"No, he went after us so they're fine."

"How can you be so sure?" Rose asked. "Because they have each other," Mark said.

"What do you mean?" Rose asked her words quieter as the world turned dark. "Oh Rosey, you'll know someday."

She wanted to ask what he meant, but sleep had her in its arms and they pulled her into the darkness.

CHAPTER 13

Lily

Lily's only thought as she and Violet were pushed away from Mark and Rose in the tide of people was simply fuck, they are fucked. The next thing she knew was the feeling of the night air on her skin and Violet's hand in her own.

She didn't know how they made it outside without being crushed but they had and as she backed away with Violet she looked back at the building and found it filling with smoke. "Someone really started a fire," Violet said looking sick.

Yes someone had, but the real question was were they still here? Lily looked around herself fear running through her and found people rushing passed them, crying or just looking at the building numb.

"We need to get out of here," Lily said pulling Violet towards her truck snapping her out of the daze she was in, making Violet finally look at her and Lily saw that her hair was a mess blowing around her dark face in strings, her red lipstick wiped across her face looking like blood.

They ran over to blue baby making sure to look behind themselves, the feeling of being followed was too real and Lily was surprised when they made it out of the parking lot with no one stopping them.

She turned around in her seat watching blue and red lights come closer and closer to where they had just almost died. And the thought of the person who had almost done it made her blood boil. Rose's own father had done this to them and she knew it had been him for some time. "I'm going to kill Rose for not telling us before now," Lily said her voice low with anger.

"She didn't do this," Violet said somehow calm as they turned on to a quiet street. "How can you not be mad?" Lily asked looking at her and saw the bruise standing out against her cheek.

"Because I have been around violence all of my life Lily, Portugal was a war zone when I was born, then we came here running from it only to find it here as well. My mom was shot and killed simply because she was different and it ruined my dad, making him just as angry as everyone else. I have seen that anger and it helps no one and does no good."

Lily shook her head "You're so much braver than me Violet, I can't do that."

After a long moment, Violet spoke again and Lily was surprised to hear tears in her voice, "I'm not brave Lily I'm a coward, I used Daisy as my shield from people in school for years."

Lily opened her mouth to respond, to tell Violet she was wrong, that she was the strongest person Lily knew but they pulled up outside Violet's house and saw her father sitting on the steps waiting for her, cans of beer around him.

"Shit," Violet hissed looking panicked as he got up and started walking for them. "It's okay," Lily said giving her a comforting smile, "He won't do anything to you if I'm here."

"I don't know what he'll do when he's like this, he's been getting worse," Violet said looking ashen. "I won't let him do anything to you," Lily said trying to sound reassuring but didn't know if it worked as she saw only fear in Violet's eyes as her dad stopped on Lily's side of the truck.

Lily looked up at him and as always wondered how this man had made the kindest person that Lily knew, with his angry bloodshot eyes and scowl. Why did Violet always feel the need to protect this man who had only been hurting her for all of the time she had known Violet and it was only getting worse.

He knocked on the window and Lily slowly rolled it down only enough for a hand to get through. "Get out of the car Violet," Mr. Luiz said his voice hard. Violet started to open her door but Lily reached over closing it, then looked back at the older man. "No, she will be staying with me tonight," Lily said filling her voice with venom.

He narrowed his dark eyes at her, then at Violet, "Who is this girl to you?" Mr. Luiz said, "Is she the reason I never see you with any boys?"

"Dad don't do this," Violet said her voice cracking. "Don't do this!" he shouted slamming his fist into Lily's window so hard she was surprised it didn't break. "You live in my house, you eat my food, everything you have is mine! Now get out of the car before I make you.“

They sat there a moment simply looking at him, Violet‘s shaking hand in her own. “Fine,” Mr. Luiz said through his teeth and before Lily knew what was happening he opened her door.

Everything happened slowly for a moment as Lily was pulled from the seat and thrown to the ground so hard she knew she would have matching bruises as Violet. Her world went white as she hit the cold sidewalk her arms giving out, her head connecting with the concrete.

Lily heard Violet cry out but she didn't see at what until she looked up and found Mr. Luiz standing over her, his hands in fists, rage burning in his eyes as his breath came to fast.

“You think you can tell my daughter what to do and defy me!“ he shouted down at her, but Lily didn't feel scared because the man in front of her was weak, all he really wanted was to keep things the same, keep things the way he wanted them after he lost so much, but it didn't give him the right. “She isn't yours,“ Lily coughed tasting blood from her lip, “She's her own person, you can't keep her in the same place forever, and you know it.“

She didn't see the punch coming but the impact to her stomach knocked the breath from her lungs. “Fucking dyke!“ he hissed at her before another hit to her shoulder made her curled into herself in hopes of protecting her body as she waited for the next blow only to find it never came.

The sound of someone crying out made Lily look up through tears to find Violet standing over her father, tire iron in hand and tears in her own eye's. “Don't you fucking touch her!“ Violet said her voice filled with so much hate Lily wouldn't have believed it was Violet if she didn't see it with her own eye's.

"Don't talk to me like that," Mr. Luiz said running for her. But he had been drinking for sometime before they had pulled up so all Violet had to do was move out of the way and the older man missed her. His arm out as he swung but it only caused him to be off balance and fall to the ground.

"I will talk to you however I want," Violet said pointing the tire iron at him, "Because you're not my father anymore, you haven't been since mom died. Only a ghost of the person I knew and I've just been hoping in vain that he would come back. But I see now that's not going to happen," she said looking over at Lily who was slowly getting up now.

"That man is dead and replaced with someone mom would hate."

Mr. Luiz looked up and into his daughter's eyes, "And what about you Violet? You're a scared little girl your mother would hate, using people for protection instead of facing them head-on."

Violet shook her head and Lily saw the tears in her eyes as she stood next to her looking down at the bastard. "What do you think she's doing right now?" Lily said holding an arm across her stomach, pain going through her with every movement.

"Then why doesn't she just beat me?" The older man asked trying to get up but fell back down a moment later. "Because," Violet said sounding hollow, "I'm not a weak worm who has to beat someone they care about after getting drunk to get my feels out."

"Bitch," Mr. Luiz hissed.

"Maybe," Violet said dropping the tire iron into the back of the truck then took Lily's arm helping her into the passenger seat, "But at least I'm my own person, meaning I can be a bitch or whatever else I want."

With that Lily watched Violet get into the driver's seat and they took off a moment later. "Where are we going?" Lily asked sleepily, ether from the night or the punches, maybe both. "Your house," Violet said her words choked and Lily saw the shine in her eyes from unshed tears.

Lily reached over and rested a hand on her lap, "You did the right thing you know that right?"

Violet nodded but Lily knew that leaving her father like that was like losing her mother all over again, and Lily couldn't understand the pain Violet was in right now because at the very least she had her mom.

They pulled into her driveway the lights out meaning her mom was still at her job or on another date, it was a coin flip to which one it was most nights.

Lily started to get out but the pain made her stop as she gritted her teeth, then suddenly Violet was there helping her down from her seat with an arm slung over her shoulder until they reached the front door. "Where's the key?" Violet asked looking across to her and Lily didn't know if it was from the pain but Violet's hazel eyes looked like warm coffee in the lighting making her heart jump.

"It's under the flower pot," Lily said gesturing over to the pot of marigolds as she rested against the wall, her head spinning. Violet went over and lifted it up and grabbed the key opening the door a moment later with a creak, then turned back to Lily and helped her inside until they made it to her small bedroom, their heels clicking on the wood.

Violet helped her sit on the bed then went back and turned the lights on showing the light purple room with its messy closet and books laying everywhere. "Sorry about the mess," Lily said.

"I'm not worried about that," Violet said going over to her dresser and grabbed a t-shirt and shorts, "I'm worried about that hit to your head."

"My head is fine," Lily lied everything hurt at the moment, "It's my stomach that hurts like hell."

Violet bit her lip concerned as she knelt in front of her. "Can I see?"

"Are you asking me to undress?" Lily asked unable to help herself. Violet rolled her eyes but Lily saw the little smile on her lips that she was going for.

She quickly took off her dress leaving her in the lacey underwear men loved for some reason, the smile dying as she saw the large dark purple bruise to her abdomen. "Shit," Violet breathed pain crossing her face, "Lily I'm so sorry, this shouldn't have happened, it's all-"

"It's not your fault," Lily said cutting her off, "Don't think for one moment this is your fault or that you had anything to do with it."

Violet had tears in her eyes once again as she shook her head, "But-" "No Violet, that man is the monster here, he did this himself and I know he did worst to you."

Violet looked down a moment but stood slowly and undid her straps letting her own dress fall to the floor. Lily felt Vomit in the back of her throat seeing Violets body covered in old and new bruises even small cuts.

"I'm going to kill him," Lily breathed. "There's no point in that, he's already dead to me," Violet said sitting down on the bed as Lily got up slowly and started to pull on the t-shirt and shorts.

"What do we do now?" Violet asked finally, "I mean about Rose's father that is?"

"Well if he really has Daisy somewhere we'll find her, that's all there is to it," Lily said handing Violet a long green shirt that would pass for a nightgown, "But that can wait until the morning right now I just want to sleep."

Violet nodded and stood up putting the shirt on as Lily laid down and pulled the cover over herself. "Where should I stay?" Violet asked looking around herself hugging her arms to her chest. In answer Lily lifted the covers, "With me."

Violet's eyes went wide a moment and Lily watched heat turn her cheeks pink, but she got in any way after turning the lights off. "Is this really okay?" Violet asked in a whisper right by Lily's ear. "Violet you're not the first person I shared a bed with before."

"Oh," Violet said looking down. Lily couldn't help looking at her hearing hurt in her voice. "It may not be the first time I shared a bed with someone Violet, but it's the first time I feel comfortable with it."

"What do you mean?" Violet asked turning to look her in the eye. "Violet Luiz you are the only person I don't have to be sexy for you to look at me like you do, and I love you for that. I love that I don't feel like I'm bored out of my mind with you or grossed out, I feel alive."

For a silent moment Lily believed she had messed up, normal people didn't say that about someone of the same sex, didn't feel what she did for them. "I-" Lily started but Violet cut her off with a kiss so soft it brought tears to her eyes. She had never felt a kiss that made her want to stay in one moment for the rest for her life.

"Lily Andrews, you made me stand up for myself for the first time in all of my life and from this day on I will never let another person mark me again," Violet whispered and kissed her again. This time it could have been for minutes or it could have been hours Lily didn't care, but she could feel sleep taking over Violet's body heavy and eyes red. So she pulled away.

"Sleep," Lily whispered and wrapped Violet into her arms getting as close to her as she could and for the first time Lily understood this is what she had needed, needed Violet Luiz.

* * *

Violet

Violet awoke to the smell of old hairspray and smoke, opening her eyes to an unfamiliar room fear went through her until she looked down and found Lily next to her. The memories of what happened last night coming back to her in all its horrors.

Lily laying in the ground her father over her, his anger on someone else this time making it easier for her to grab that tire iron and hit him in the back. She couldn't help a shutter at the thought that she was now alone in this world.

But as she looked down at Lily who was in a peaceful deep sleep the knowledge she was safe was enough for her at the moment, she would just figure it out as she went.

A phone started ringing from somewhere in the house and Violet waited a moment for Mrs. Andrews to answer it but it seemed she was either still out or she slept as deeply as her daughter.

With a deep sigh Violet got up as quietly as she could and made her way through the house until she found the bright pink phone, which sat on a side table by the front door which would be the last place she would have looked. Violet grabbed the receiver just in time and answered.

"Hello?" Violet said wondering who would be calling this early. "Good morning mother, sorry to wake you so early, but I was hoping you could pick me up at the diner you dropped me off at last night?"

Violet blinked in confusion for a moment, the voice was Rose's and she was happy enough to hear it but the forced lightness in it made her worry. "Rose is someone there with you?"

Rose's laughed sounded hard and cold to Violet as she spoke, "No mother I wasn't drinking, I'm with Mrs. Young, I fell last night and their house was closer so I stayed the night."

"Okay, I'll meet you there Rose, is Mark with you?" "Yes, I'll make sure to thank Mrs. and Mr. Young, talk more than, bye mother."

With that Rose hung up and Violet was left there looking down at the phone, the ringtone still going. She was so lost in thought that when Lily came up behind her and wrapped her arms around her waist she jumped.

"Woh there it's just me," Lily said into her ear and Violet wasn't going to lie it felt amazing to be touched by someone and knew the next moment they wouldn't be throwing things at you. "Who was that in the phone?"

"It was Rose, we need to get dressed and meet her at the diner with Mark to talk."

Lily pulled away then and Violet turned to see she was angry but she didn't know why, "What's wrong?"

"I'm tired of this now, we almost died last night in a fire Violet, and it's her father's fault."

"Lily don't do this," Violet said going over to her and grabbed her hand lacing her fingers with her own, "We promised."

"Not until death do us part Violet, I will not die for her family."

"No one is asking us to do that, " Violet said and raised Lily's hand to her lips and placed a kiss to her knuckles, "Please come with me and we'll just see what she has to say."

Lily bit her lip a moment but nodded, "fine I'll go, but I'm not promising anything."

Violet could see how mad she was and understood it, they couldn't trust Rose with the knowledge she may not be on her medicine and it was her own father doing all of this to them.

"Let's just get dressed okay," Violet said pulling Lily over towards her room, "I can borrow some clothes right?"

"That depends," Lily said and Violet could hear the smile in her voice now, "Can I watch you change?"

Violet couldn't help but scoff but a smile found her way to her lips anyway.

They dressed quickly enough and the next thing Violet knew she was looking out of the front window at the diner as she put the truck into park. She didn't see Mark's car but he may have left it at the club last night given she didn't know what had happened to them after they had been split.

"Ready?" Violet asked looking over at Lily who was putting her short blonde hair into a ponytail, the yellow crop-top falling down one of her shoulders and for a moment Violet thought of pulling it up, but didn't want anyone to see. She was fine with doing things like that where no one could see them, but she knew what would happen if anyone found out about them and it wasn't good.

"Let's go," Lily said giving her a smile and jumped out leaving her to follow after her. They entered the now familiar building and found Mark sitting at the same booth in the back they had first met him in, but Rose wasn't with him.

"Where's Rosey?" Lily asked standing in front of him narrowing her eyes.

"Jesus I didn't do anything to her, she's in the bathroom is all," Mark said, "Now sit down we have breakfast coming."

"We?" Violet repeated in question sitting down across from him, Lily next to her. "You're really questioning us?" Mark said looking down at Lily's shirt and when Violet followed his gaze found pink lipstick on her neck.

Violet felt her cheeks burn knowing she had the same color on, but Lily just smiled at him as she dipped a napkin in a glass of water and started to wipe the kiss away, "Are you jealous Hollow?"

He gave them a smirk, "No, and before you ask I don't care if you're making out in your free time."

Violet opened her mouth to tell him they hadn't been making out but Rose arrived then and quickly sat down beside Mark. Violet felt her eyes go wide seeing her in a t-shirt and jeans that once had been Daisy's.

"Thank god you're both okay, I was so worried about you last night, but a car followed after us, so I knew they weren't going after you both," Rose said.

"You mean your father went after you," Lily said her words hard. Rose looked at them pain crossing her face, "Yes, I guess so."

"And you mind telling us how you figured that out?" Lily asked acid in her voice. Rose swallowed and looked down, "When I went to see my father that one day at the bank, he left me alone in his office and I ended up finding Daisy's golden bracelet she was wearing that night and..." She trailed off a moment biting the inside of her lip before going on, "A gun."

Everyone stopped dead and looked at her, even Mark. "Why didn't you tell us he has a gun!" Lily said and Violet could hear the fear in her voice.

"Because I know he wouldn't use it," Rose said her voice rising alongside Lily's. "How the hell could you know that!" Lily shouted anger making her cheeks burn pink and Rose looked just as angry.

Rose opened her mouth to shout back but just then the waitress came over placing plates of eggs and bacon down, along with cups of coffee in front of them. Everyone went quiet and eyed one another until she left.

"He wouldn't hurt us, he could never do that," Rose said softly watching the waitress walk away. Violet shook her head, "Rosey you believe he has Daisy somewhere and we don't know if she's hurt or not," Violet said taking her hand across the table.

"And don't forget the girl he killed," Lily said and Violet felt her blood go cold as she looked over at her.

"What do you mean?" Rose said defensively. "I mean the body we found, because if it wasn't Daisy's then it was somebody's wasn't it, and he must have killed them," Lily said coolly.

Violet knew she was right but it felt unreal to her that the man she used to wish was her own father could be a kidnapper and a killer.

"You don't know it was him, Rose said, "He's not a killer!"

"How the hell would you know?" Lily said, "You're not even on your meds I bet! So how can we trust anything you say when you could just be seeing things, for all we know the bracelet you saw was just in your head!"

"Hey don't talk to her like that," Mark said jumping in for the first time. He and Lily looked at one another as if they were about to attack each other but Violet just looked into Rose's eyes wanting nothing more than the truth, "Did you really stop taking your meds?"

For a moment Rose simply looked at her then closed her eyes and nodded. "I stopped taking them when the body was found."

"Why?" Violet asked softly wanting to understand what her friend was going through.

Rose let out a shaky breath, "At first I wanted to think clearer, the pills can make it foggy at times and then I just wanted to see her."

"Daisy?" Violet asked in a whisper. Rose nodded and for a moment everyone was quiet, then Lily spoke up her words still filled with anger. "Still how can we trust anything you've seen?"

"You don't believe me do you?" Rose asked hurt in her voice. After a second Lily shook her head her eyes closed as if she was disappointed, "No."

Rose got up then so suddenly it made the cups clink as the table was pushed back and she started for the door. Violet got up and followed after her stopping Rose just as she was about to open the door, her hand on the handle.

"Rosey where are you going?" Violet asked catching her hand making her stop in her tracks. Rose looked up at her and Violet saw the pain and anger in her blue eyes, like looking at a storm.

"I'm going to get the bracelet to show you I'm not crazy!"

"You know we don't think you're crazy," Violet said lowering her voice as the waitress passed them. "Really?" Rose said not bothering to keep her voice down, "Because I think that's exactly what you think of me, I'm the girl with schizophrenia, who hears voices and sees things that aren't there. The girl who spend six months in a mental hospital. The girl who wanted it to stop so badly she tried killing herself. The girl you can't trust anymore."

Violet opened her mouth but had no idea how to reply and seeing that Rose opened the door and walked out into the growing gray day.

* * *

Rose

Rose didn't remember the walk or more likely the run to the bank. Didn't remember opening the door and walking up to where Mrs. Lion's desk was. And seeing she was gone went into her father's office not sure what she would say or do to him. But found it empty.

And in that moment she stopped, anger leaving her and the knowledge she could have just been alone in a room with a kidnapper and maybe even a killer sent a shiver down her spine.

She looked around herself and found for some reason the room felt off, in what way she didn't know maybe it was because it was so quiet all of a sudden. Shaking it off she moved towards the desk and sat down in her father's chair and reached for the drawer and pulled it open.

The second Rose touched it something felt off but still, her heart found its way to her throat as she looked down and saw that both the bracelet and the gun were gone. Rose let out a breath that seemed to squeeze her insides, pain going through her along with the feeling of tears.

"Shit, shit shit," she hissed getting louder and louder as she hit her fist into the hardwood but that pain did nothing to the panic going through her. "I really am crazy," Rose whispered, her head falling into her hands.

"Guess so," Daisy said standing in front of the desk her dress stained even more, "What are you going to do now?"

Rose just closed her eyes knowing there was nothing she could do, nothing at all. Maybe all of this really was in her head and Lily was right.

She opened her eyes and slowly stood up, her knees weak. Ready to go back to the diner and tell them all just how wrong and crazy she really was. She was halfway across the room when she saw Daisy at the corner of the room looking down at a letter on the floor over by a paper shredder. "You know I hate it when people litter."

Rose couldn't say why it made her stop and take note, why she walked over to Daisy and picked it up. But she would be going to church more after, because as she read she couldn't help but think there was something out there looking out for her.

"Mr. Waters,

> Thank you for checking in, the apartment is great and so is everyone. Food and water are low but I will pick more up soon when I have time. Besides a few neighbors, there has been no one around this place who has looked at us twice, we look forward to the visit."

It had been signed by Mrs. Lion meaning she knew where Daisy was, most likely at this apartment. Rose looked around hoping to find an envelope and after a heart-racing moment she found Daisy next to it, blood dripping on to the white paper as it lay behind the paper shredder, somehow it had been missed. She looked down and saw an address.

"Guess you're not too crazy after all," Daisy said smiling and in the next blink of an eye she was gone.

Rose couldn't help a relieved breath as she tipped her head back, the knowledge she had at least something to show them that could maybe lead them to Daisy made her shoulders relax.

Rose turned to the door folding the letter and envelope and tucking it into her bra, knowing it would be safe there.

She reached for the door handle ready to leave and hopefully get out unseen. But before she could open the door someone pushed it open from the other side so quickly she had to step back to avoid being hit. She looked up ready to tell Mrs. Lion she was just leaving when the words died as she looked and saw her father standing in the door frame.

Rose couldn't help the gasp that left her lips as her eyes widened and the only thing she could think to say was "Father."

He stood there a moment just as surprised to see her as she was to see him, but He smiled seconds later. "Rosalina thank god," he said moving forward his arms out as if he wanted a hug, but Rose took a step back her heart sinking.

He stopped seeing the look of fear on her face, "Rosalina what's wrong? What happen to you last night, your mother was in here saying you were missing."

Rose only shook her head, the color draining from her face as she stepped backward.

Her father gave her a confused looked not understanding why she was so scared, then he looked over at the drawer and his face changed into something she couldn't read.

He walked over to his desk and looked down at it for a long second before looking up at her, ice in his eyes, something she had never seen before.

A new kind of fear went through her then and before she knew what she was doing her feet were moving towards the door in a run, but she was sent flying backward as she slammed into a body and it was all she could do to stay on her feet.

She looked up to see Jason standing there a smile on his face, "Rosey there you are, I heard mother and father were worried about you last night, where were you? They kept shooting me dirty looks like I knew."

Rose felt panic go through her as she regained her balance and grabbed Jason's arm, "We need to run!" Rose shouted starting for the door again but her father grabbed her other arm and pulled her off him.

Rose tried pulling her arm away but it was no use, he may be older but far stronger. "Rosalina, stop fighting!" her father said his words hard, not letting go.

"Father what are you doing, let go of her," Jason said looking concerned moving forward into the room. "Jason, Daisy is alive and father has been hiding her somewhere with Mrs. Lion, we need-"

Rose's words were cut off by her father's hand over her mouth. "Jason go back to work, I need to talk with Rosalina alone," her father said and a cold fear went through her at those words.

Jason just shook his head, looking even more confused than before, "Father what is she saying? What the hell is going on?"

Rose kept trying to get free but to no avail. "Nothing Jason, now leave us."

"No," Jason said simply, "Now let her go."

Her father took a deep breath and looked at Jason. Rose saw that his eyes seemed to go even harder when he looked at his son. "I'm not letting her go, Jason, my gun is missing and Rose may have it, making her a danger to herself and others, so I'm going to take her to a psychiatric hospital for her own safety."

At his words, Rose stopped fighting her heart turning to stone as every vein in her turned cold. "Gun, what gun are you talking about?" Jason asked worry now on his face. "I keep a gun in that drawer and it's gone now," her father said as he started dragging her towards the door, her body had gone limp as the words went around and around in her head. The psychiatric hospital, he was going to lie to them and have her locked away to keep his secrets for the rest of her life.

In the last effort of being saved she turned her head to her brother, "Jason, please you have to listen to me, Daisy is alive and out there."

But Jason didn't look at her like he normally did, with kind eyes and a smile but this time with no emotion at all.

"Father wait a moment," Jason said his voice flat. Her father stopped and looked at him, "What?"

"Rose hasn't been taking her medication for a long time now."

His words hit her like a blow to the head, her vision going white for a moment as her last hope was taken from her.

Rose felt tears in her eyes as her father started once again dragging her out of the room and she looked back once to see Jason watching her with a cool smile. After that, she let her father pull her through the lobby and out into the afternoon air having no more fight left in her.

She looked up as they approached a black Ford, her father held on to her arm as he opened the back passenger side door and pushed her into it and closed the door, locking it with a key before walking around and getting into the driver's seat.

He started the engine and Rose said nothing simply sitting there, the image of her brother's face still imprinted forever in her mind. Why, why, why, had he done that to her? She couldn't understand what had made him hate her all of a sudden because that's what the look had been, hatred, no not hatred but almost nothingness, like this was a game.

But she didn't have time to think of that as her father started to pull away from the sidewalk and start down the quiet street, no one knowing what was happening to her.

Rose's heart fell knowing it wouldn't take them long to get to the psychiatric hospital. She wondered if her mother would help her but the thought almost made her laugh because she wouldn't, hell she would probably be happier throwing away the key.

Rose looked up watching her whole world pass in front of her, but something caught her attention out of the corner of her eye. When she looked Daisy was standing at a corner, her arm out pointing to something behind Rose. She turned in her seat and felt her eyes go wide at the sight of baby blue driving behind them.

CHAPTER 14

Rose

Rose couldn't help a smile at the sight of that ugly old truck. She watched it move into the next lain driving right next to them and saw that Mark and Violet were kneeling in the truck bed holding on to the sides as their hair blew around their faces.

She looked up then as her father finally spoke, "Rose did you take the gun?"

"No, of course I didn't father," Rose answered looking down at the lock on the door then back up at her friends who had gotten closer and saw that Lily was mouthing something to her.

For a moment she had no idea what it was they were trying to say, then her stomach fell as she recognized the word, "Jump."

Rose shook her head unsure if it was at them or herself, she couldn't jump from a moving car for god's sake....But another voice chimed in asking her a question, are you willing to go back into a mental institution or even worse? Because how easy would it be for him to kill her and tell everyone it was an accident, that she was trying to hurt herself or even better him.

"Rose I need you to listen to me now okay," Her father said trying to sound soft. "I am," Rose said her words distracted as she slowly unlocked the door praying it wouldn't make a sound and be noticed. So far her father had been too busy driving to see her friends and she wanted to keep it that way until she was ready.

"Good because I'm-" Rose blocked her father's words out as she closed her eyes, her hand on the handle, trying to stop them from shaking but she had bigger things to worry about.

She nodded to Violet and watched her drive forward until the back was lined up to her door, Mark, and Lily at the ready to catch her.

Rose could feel every heartbeat as she bit down on her lip, on three Rose thought as she sucked in a deep breath and started to count.

One, this will be easy, just like jumping out of her window back home. Two, of course, her window didn't move at 40 miles an hour.

Three, I'm going to die Rose thought before she threw open her door and leaped.

She couldn't help but cry out as the air rushed around her muting the sound of the cars, the world a blurry watercolor until it came to a sudden stop as she slammed into the body of the truck, her vision going white.

For a moment as she was left hanging there the image of her falling and being crushed was all too real until she felt the warmth of hands pulling her up and over. They all fell into the bed holding on to one another and stayed there as Violet stopped the truck and turned so quickly it sent them sliding to the side as they started heading in the opposite direction.

Rose looked up for a second as they turned the corner and saw her father standing in the middle of the road. He must have stopped when she had jumped out, he looked so worried and she couldn't help but wondered if it was because of her or something else.

"Rosey are you okay?" Mark asked turning her chin to face him. "F-Fine," Rose said trying to decide if that was true, but at the moment she had too much adrenaline going through her to tell. "Thank you for coming to get me."

"It wasn't me," Mark said looking over at Lily. Rose looked over at her friend to find Lily looking paler than normal and her hair was a mess but she was still holding on to Rose's hand from went she had pulled her up. "Thank you Lily, I'm sorry for leaving without talking more."

"No," Lily said looking down ashamed, "I shouldn't have said what I did, you can't help what you're father has done, and you can't help the way you are."

"It doesn't matter now," Rose said squeezing Lily's hand, but let out a yelp as Lily pulled her into a hug suddenly. She stayed there like that a moment, head buried into Lily's shoulder as the truck stopped, the feeling of someone's warmth sending feelings of comfort through her that she needed more than ever.

They pulled away and looked around to see the truck had stopped at a back road, trees blocking them from view. Violet came running around to the back a moment later and jumped into the bed pulling them all into another hug talking a mile a minute.

"Rosey are you okay?"

Rose opened her mouth to answer but Violet kept going. "What am I saying of course you're not, you jumped from a moving car for god's sakes you could have died!"

Rose couldn't stop the laugh from escaping as she grabbed Violet and pulled her into another hug but the sound of muffled crunching made her pull back and the memory of the letter made her gasp.

"What was that?" Mark asked raising an eyebrow. Instead of answering him Rose pulled the letter and envelope out from her bra making them all look at her as if she had taken it off instead, eyes wide and Mark's mouth hanging open like he hadn't seen her in a bra the night before.

"The bracelet and gun were missing from the desk when I looked. But when I was about to leave I found this letter on the floor," Rose said passing it to Lily.

She read it quickly her eyes going wide and looked up at Rose. "Is this what I think it is?"

Rose nodded her eyes downcast, "After I found it my father found me and he told Jason I had taken the gun and… " She trailed off a moment and swallowed hard, "Said he was going to take me to a psychiatric hospital for my own safety."

Everyone looked at her with a different emotion, Violet was understanding because her own father was a piece of trash too. Lily with sadness knowing what hell she had been through those six months. And Mark with anger, for the people who should love her no matter what only causing her pain. She took a deep breath letting it go for now. "Anyway, I think that address is where they're keeping Daisy with Mrs. Lion."

Violet took the envelope and read it over, "I know where this is, she looked up at everyone, "Me and my father stopped there when we moved here, It's about two hours away… if we want to go."

They all looked at one another, "Shouldn't we get the police?" Rose asked looking at Mark but to everyone's surprise, he shook his head. "There's no point, not with Chief Thompson, he thinks he has this case closed and we have nothing solid to show him he's wrong still, because that letter could be written by anyone."

"Than what are we waiting for?" Lily asked standing up and jumped to the ground, "Let's get this show on the road."

***

Violet

Violet looked after Lily for a moment her heart pounding fast from the last few minutes of craziness then looked back at Rose, who still laid in Mark's lap. "Do we really want to do this?"

Rose bit her lip a second then nodded. "We have to end this, not only because we don't have a choice anymore, but this hell can't go on, what my father has done will ruin him," Rose said looking down at her hand, small cuts lining her palms from holding on to the side of the truck.

"Is that what you want?" Violet asked, "You'll have nothing if he goes to jail."

Rose said nothing a moment then spoke, her voice almost a whisper "Yes, I don't care if I have to start over, at least I'll be free with the knowledge he can't hurt anyone else."

Violet nodded standing up and hopping down, starting for the driver's seat, only looking back once to see Mark whispering into Rose's ear. For some reason that sent pain through her chest knowing that she would never be able to do that with Lily.

"Ready to go?" Lily asked looking up from the map she had in her lap as Violet closed the door and turned the key, the roar ringing through the truck. "Yup," Violet said as she put the stick in drive and started down the dirt road until they hit pavement starting on their two-hour drive.

"Are you okay?" Lily asked after a few quiet minutes. Violet wanted to say yes, that everything was okay like she normally had in the past. But the thing about the past is that it was behind her now. "No, Lily, I don't think I am."

"Why?" Lily asked now concerned, her eyes filled with worry. "A lot of reasons, like what happens after all of this? Everyone has a home more or less to go back to but… I don't anymore."

"That's all?" Lily said relief in her voice, "Violet you can stay with me and my mom until we graduate, then maybe we can get a place together-"

"No," Violet said cutting her off, "Lily we can't be like other couples, we can't date or get a place together without people looking at us like we're demons or worse, hell we get looks from people now just because of my skin color god only knows what they would do to us if someone saw us kiss."

"Are you scared?" Lily asked.

Violet was quiet a second before answering, "Yes," She almost whispered, "I'm sorry."

"Don't be," Lily said softly moving her hand to Violet's thigh giving it a comforting squeeze, "I understand, but Violet, you have to know that I will never let someone hurt you again. And I don't care what people think of us. Let them judge us, let them look at us with hate, let them wallow in their little worlds because as long as we have one another I don't care if the world burns down around us."

Violet looked up for a second tears burning in her eye's "You mean that?"

Lily smiled at her, then took off a mood ring and gently took Violet's left hand from the wheel and slipped it onto her ring finger, "Violet Aline Luiz, I promise to stay with you for long us we live, and maybe someday this world will be a kinder place where we can say that out loud, but for now it's enough to have you as mine even if no one knows it but us."

Lily raised her hand to her lips and placed a kiss on the ring and let her hand go a moment later.

Violet let the tears spill over then and drip down her cheeks unable to think of anything to respond with, no one had ever promised her the one thing she wanted, love that wasn't limited by blood.

The memory of cold metal against her chest came to her and without thought, she pulled over to the side of the road and grabbed the cord with one hand and pulled it off letting the ring fall onto her lap. With shaking fingers she picked it up and looked over at Lily, her eyes the color of warm coffee.

Violet took Lily's hand and slipped the ring that had once been her mother's onto her pale ring finger, then looked back at her tears streaming down her face.

"Lily I can't tell you what will happen tonight, but I know at this moment all I want is you, I don't know when I decided that. But I'll make sure that no matter what we'll be together, even if I have to face a thousand men like my father, I'll be by your side, i-i love you."

Violet felt her eyes go wide at the words she had just said, those three little words meant to be said when you were sure, when you had been together for a long time, but they had felt right at the moment.

"I love you too," Lily said softly, laying her head on Violet's shoulder, her eyes closed.

Violet felt her heart jump and for once in her life, she felt like everything would be okay, she wouldn't have to worry anymore about glass bottles and yelling. Wouldn't worry about what everyone thought because why would she when she had at least two people in her life that loved her, who wouldn't hurt her. And this time she knew she could be someone to save Daisy instead of the other way around.

* * *

Lily

Lily awoke to the sky on fire, she sat up a gasp escaping her lips only to see it was a sunset of yellow and orange as gray clouds started to cover them, a storm coming fast. "You okay?" Violet asked looking over at her quickly. "I-yes, I'm fine I just didn't know where we were for a moment is all," Lily answered her heart still pounding.

"Well if it helps we'll be at the address soon, maybe ten more minutes," Violet said. Lily nodded sitting back and looked into the rearview mirror to see Rose in Mark's lap, both asleep with his jacket over them. "Have they been like that this whole time?" Lily asked watching as Rose moved in her sleep getting closer to Mark.

"Basically, they seemed to talk for a long time about something, but I don't know what," Violet answered squinting at the buildings as they passed them, looking for the address. "It's probably about what will happen to her father after all of this," Lily said looking away from them and out the window.

"It's pretty easy isn't it, Violet said, "He'll go to jail for the rest of his life."

Lily nodded looking down and bit her lip before speaking again, "What about your father Violet? What he did to you after all of that time, don't you think he should go to jail too?"

Lily looked over at her to see that she was gripping the wheels so hard her knuckles had turned white, "Lily I know what he did to me was wrong... But I can't turn him in, he's still my family even after all of it."

Lily could tell Violet thought that she would fight her on this but it was her choice and all she wanted to do was support her on it, after all, it was her family, and she knew he would never touch her again. "Alright then," Lily said gently touching her hand, "If that's what you want I understand."

Violet turned to her with a smile, "Thank you."

"It's no probl-" Lily's words were cut off then as the truck came to a sudden stop jerking her forwards and if she hadn't caught herself she would have hit her head on the dashboard.

"What the hell!" Lily said looking up thinking they were about to hit a child or something but saw an empty road.

"Sorry," Violet said looking up at a tall building, "But we're here."

Lily felt her eyes go wide as she looked out of her window and up at the tall apartment building that they sat in front of. It wasn't a very pretty building by any measure, with dirty cream-colored walls and dry yellowing grass in the yard with sad looking willow trees in the front. But she guessed that's what they had been going for, a place no one would look twice at.

She and Violet got out and walked around to the back where Mark was helping Rose down. "So this is the place?" Rose asked moving to stand next to them.

"It's the address alright," Violet said. Lily looked at Rose who in turn looked sick and pale, and Lily didn't blame her, she had gone through hell since day one after Daisy went missing, but never gave up hope.

She reached over and took Rose's cold hand, "This is all going to end tonight, hell can't go on forever after all."

Rose smiled at that and nodded, "Let's go."

With that everyone started up the short staircase and stopped at the glass doors looking down at the buzzers. Lily had to squint at the names they were so faded, but after a moment she found the one marked Ms. Lion under the number six and with a breath she pressed it.

For a moment they stood there waiting to hear a voice asking what they wanted but instead they were simply buzzed in with no questions. Lily swallowed and looked over at her friends who looked just as unsure as she felt. So with a shaking hand, she pushed the glass door open and walked in, everyone following after her as they walked down the dimly lit hall.

"This place is giving me goosebumps," Rose said looking around at the old chipping paint on the wall the color of dirty snow, the white tile was stained and made their shoes echoe as they walked.

"I know," Lily said, a shiver running down her spine like fingertips as they reached the elevator and clicked the button for it.

"It's like no one lives here," Mark said looking around. He was right there was no one in the lobby or the hall which was weird given it was early evening when most people came home and the rain that had started to fall didn't help. But they didn't have time to think about that as the doors dinged open.

They all stepped in and Lily clicked the button for the sixth floor, the door closing on them slowly like in some kind of horror movie. Even the music sounded like it was out of hell with the speaker muffling it beyond understanding.

Lily looked over at Rose who stood next to Mark, her hand in his, looking so much smaller, and Lily couldn't help but take Violet's. She was surprised to find it so warm in the cold building, "Your freezing," Violet whispered into her ear.

"How come you're not?" Lily asked, "This place is super creepy."

"I've lived in worse when we were moving here," Violet said simply. Lily was about to ask if ghost's lived at her apartment too but jumped instead as a ding cut through the silence as the doors opened onto a dark hallway.

"Jesus Christ," Rose breathed out, "What next? A man with an ax chasing after us?"

"Don't give the world any ideas," Lily said stepping out looking down the hall. "What room are they keeping her in?" Violet asked Rose. But she only shook her head, "I don't know, the letter didn't say."

"Guess we'll just have to start knocking," Mark said going over to a door and raised his fist. "No, wait," Lily said stopping him as she looked down the hall her eyes on a door, the only one that looked clean.

She made her way slowly down the hall and stopped in front of the red door, her heart finding its way to her throat as she looked at the bright daisy chain hanging on a hook. She reached out gently and held it in her hand, it could only be days old if it still looked like this.

Someone gasped behind her then and she turned to see Rose, who moved to stand next to her and reached out a fingertip running it down the petals.

"Daisy…" She whispered under her breath.

"This is where they're keeping her?" Violet said more like a question. "They don't want it to stand out I'm guessing," Mark said in answer, "Make it look nice on the outside and no one will think something bad is happening in the inside."

"Should we knock?" Rose asked looking at them. " Yes," Mark said pulling out a handgun he had under his jacket in a holster, "And as soon as she opens it I'll arrest her."

Rose nodded and looked at Lily, her blue eyes burning, "Together?"

Lily bit her lip and looked at Violet who seemed ready to punch whoever was dumb enough to open it, "Let's do this," Violet said her voice low.

They raised their fists together and knocked once, the sound so loud in the quiet it seemed to echo through the building. Lily could only hear her breath at the following silence as they waited there for a long moment nothing happening.

"Alright," Mark said moving to stand in front of them, "I'll just have to break the door down then."

They moved out of his way quickly as he got ready to kick it down, moving a little ways back, then he ran forwards ready to kick. But stopped short as the door opened, only catching himself on the doorframe just in time. Rose grabbed his hand and pulled him back to reveal a woman standing there, her hair black but her surprised eyes showing greener than ever.

"Daisy!" Rose said, sounding out of breath as she stepped in front of her. Lily felt her eyes go wide not seeing it for a moment, then it hit her like a truck that this woman really was Daisy, with her pink lips the color of strawberries and heart-shaped face.

But in the months they hadn't seen her she had changed so much, not just the dyed black hair. Her skin was paler than before and she had put on some weight making her look older in ways she hadn't before in the hips and chest.

Daisy looked at them like a deer in headlights, her mouth open like a fish out of water. "W-what are you doing here?" She asked her voice hoarse as she looked into the hall clearly scared of something or more likely someone.

"We're here for you," Lily said moving closer and looked her over but couldn't find any wounds, not even a bruise. "I see…" Daisy said trailing off biting the Inside of her cheek then sighed, "Come in, I think we need to talk."

"No, we need to get out of here," Violet said, "Mrs. Lion or Mr. Waters could be coming back any moment."

Daisy just gave her a tired smile and shook her head, "Let's just talk a moment okay, I think you may be off on some thing's," Daisy said moving to the side so they could come in.

Lily looked at Mark wondering what he thought of all of this and he simply shrugged, "Fine with me, if anyone tries anything, I've got bullets to outnumber them."

"Well can't argue with that," Lily said with a raised eyebrow and walked in.

CHAPTER 15

Rose

Rose followed after her friends into the small apartment, it had the same colored walls as the hall but Rose saw that someone had tried covering them up with hand-drawn art, the floor covered in a bright yellow wool carpet.

"Go ahead and make yourselves comfortable," Daisy said going into the kitchen and started filling mugs with coffee. Rose sat down carefully on one of the floral armchairs, Mark sitting down next to her, as Lily and Violet took a seat on a loveseat with the matching pattern, leaving one chair in the front of the circle for Daisy.

They said nothing, the only sound coming from the t.v. as they watched Daisy move around grabbing a bottle of milk and a bowl of sugar setting them on a tray with the cups, a ghost returned to them after months and watching her do normal things like this felt out of place. Finally, she came and sat down placing the tray on the coffee table that sat in the middle and for a moment they were all too busy pouring sugar or milk into cups, but Rose could only sit back and look at her best friend.

She seemed like the same person she had been all of those months ago, but somehow she had changed and she hated that she couldn't tell how.

"Rosey you like your coffee black right?" Daisy asked handing her a cup. "Yeah, thanks," Rose said taking it into her shaking hands, looking down at the pool of black. "So," Daisy said sitting back with her own cup, "How did you find me? How did you know I was alive in the first place?"

"That's a long story," Rose said, "But to make it short I found your dental x-ray and we started from there."

"Then we found your diary, and it led us to Jolly's and that somehow led us here," Lily said.

"Really? How did you break the code?" Daisy asked taking a drink of her coffee.

"Lily figured it out when she saw a map," Violet answered. Daisy looked over at Lily a proud smile on her lips, "Good job Lily."

"Where is Mrs. Lion?" Rose asked cutting in, noticing the closed door in the short hallway, "I thought she was keeping you here against your will."

Daisy's smile fell then, her eyes turning dark, "She passed away a few weeks ago in her sleep, in her own home."

"Then why are you still here?" Violet asked, "Why not come home and tell everyone what happened?"

Daisy looked down her eyes soft, "I have many reasons."

Rose felt anger go through her then and slammed her mug down making them all look at her. "You have reasons? Rose said her teeth gritted, "What about us? What was the reason to leave us believing you were dead? What do you think we felt going to your fucking funeral? What was your reason for making your parents suffer? Do you know how much pain you've caused with your reasons?" Rose shouted and she could see the pain in Daisy's eyes, but she didn't care, she had believed she would be happy to see her best friend alive again, but she didn't know how angry she had been until now.

"Your mother is pregnant do you know that? Because you better have a good damn reason for making them grow up without an older sister!"

Daisy had gone even paler than before with every word until she looked like a ghost, her color running like the rain on the window. Then a cry rang out, loud and high pitched, a baby's cry.

For a moment no one moved to look at the closed door as the crying went on, not wanting to believe what they knew was behind it. "That's my reason," Daisy said softly getting up and opened the door and disappeared. A moment later she walked out holding a pink bundle.

Rose felt her anger fade away like mist as she looked at the baby Daisy held as she sat back down again. "Meet Emily Lion, my daughter."

"Your daughter?" Violet repeated in question, her eyes wide, "How? You weren't pregnant."

"You said you read my diary meaning, you must have read about the night I told him in November."

"We did," Lily said, "But it didn't mention what happened after or what it was about."

"Let's just say he wasn't happy about it, he told me to get an abortion and I told him I would, because I have never seen him so angry before as if he could kill me. But I couldn't do it so I started a plan to save my baby."

"But you didn't look pregnant that whole time," Lily said. "I got lucky in that I'm small and I didn't show under loose clothing, even Mark himself noted it," Daisy said looking over at him.

"How old is she?" Mark asked, his brow creased as if he was thinking.

"She's a month old now," Daisy answered rocking the baby back and forth slowly, then she looked up at Rose, "Do you want to hold her?"

Rose could only nod and hold out her arms as Daisy carefully placed Emily into them and sat back down. Rose saw then that the baby girl had her mother's green eyes and red hair, nothing of her father could be seen in her besides maybe his nose but her brother had the same one.

"So my mother is pregnant then?" Daisy asked, her voice cracking. Rose looked up and saw that everyone was looking at her, she hadn't told anyone but Mark on the way here, meaning it was just as much as a surprise to Lily and Violet. "Yes, I-I'm sorry I didn't mean to throw it in your face like that, I-"

"It's okay," Daisy said cutting her off, "You're angry and I understand but I was in danger and I had no other choice but to run, not only for myself but Emily."

"But you don't have to hide anymore," Lily said, "We can go home and end this."

Daisy only shook her head, "I don't think you understand, I'm dead, I'm now Elizabeth May Lion, and it has to stay that way, no one can know I'm alive."

"But why?" Rose asked, "My father will go to jail for the rest of his life if you come back with us, he can't hurt you."

Daisy blinked at her a moment, confused, "Your father?"

"You don't have to play dumb," Rose said softly, "We all know you were dating him and it's okay, I'm not mad."

Daisy looked between them still confused, "Rosey, your father saved me."

"What do you mean?" Violet asked.

"Oh god," Mark said his eyes going wide as he looked up at Daisy from where he had been staring at Emily.

"What?" Rose asked fear creeping into her voice.

"Emily isn't Rose's father is she?" Mark asked. Daisy shook her head, "No, she's Jason's."

* * *

Violet

"What do you mean Jason's?" Violet asked her voice hollow.

Daisy took a deep breath and let it out slowly, "It started after Rose went to that... hospital, while she was there me and Jason saw a lot of one another, and then a few months in we started dating. It was perfect timing because he had just broken up with his girlfriend and I needed something to keep me from thinking too much, the drugs weren't helping anymore, but he would take me to clubs under a fake ID and we would dance until i couldn't remember my own name. And it went well for the whole time Rose was there," Daisy said with a little smile but it died a moment later.

"But then Rose got out and Jason had to go to college and we had to go back to school."

Daisy looked at them then and Violet saw the tears in her eyes as she swallowed, "I thought it was just going to be a one-off thing, that we wouldn't see much of one another after that, but then I found out I was two months pregnant with Emily on Halloween."

"How come the doctor didn't tell your mother," Lily asked.

"I made sure the doctor didn't tell my parents with the knowledge that he kept refilling people's pain medication years after a broken arm or hurt back," Daisy answered and Violet felt a cold shiver go through her at that.

The one thing people always forgot about Daisy is that she could put you at ease, making it easy to talk to her about anything and everything.

"Anyway that fall break I saw him again, well I actually had to corner him at the bank because he wouldn't see me and I told him. I didn't know what to expect from him, but he got so angry, I mean I've seen him mad before, but not like this. He told me to get rid of the baby or he would kill me."

"But he couldn't have meant it," Rose tried. But Daisy shook her head, "Rose, he slammed me into the back wall and hissed those words into my ear with a look in his eyes that I had never seen before, it was so blank and cold as if he was empty, and it that moment I knew he would kill me if I didn't do what he said. After I said yes, he let me go and I fell to the floor, he ended up leaving me there without a second look. I can't tell you how long I sat there on the floor when Mr. Waters found me and took me into his office, I was so lost and scared I just ended up telling him everything. When I was done he looked like he had seen a ghost, but he wasn't surprised as if he had seen Jason do this before."

"What do you mean? Jason did something like that before?" Violet asked, but Daisy only shrugged.

"I don't know if he ever did, but it seemed like it. Afterward, Mr. Waters started to come up with a plan to keep me and his grandchild safe. I would go missing the first week of school in hopes I would either be named a runaway or a kidnap victim, I would stay with Mrs. Lion as her daughter with a new name and ID."

"But that's not what happened," Violet cut in, "You went missing at the spring break party."

Daisy nodded, "Jason wasn't supposed to be there, Mr. Waters believed he was going to be in New York until October, so when Mark told as he was there I ran and called Rose's father, he sounded more scared then I did to be honest and for good reason. He told me to wait outside for him to come and pick me up, that I would just have to run that night. So that's what I did, but Jason found me anyway in the front yard," Daisy said and took a deep breath and moved a piece of her hair back to show a long scar.

"I tried running through the trees in hopes of losing him, but he caught up to me..." Daisy trailed off a moment, her voice shaking as she went on.

"He hit me on the head with something hard, I-I don't even know what and I fell, then he was on the top of me.... choking me. I don't remember what happened after that I think I passed out and he believed I was dead because he was carrying me to the river."

"Oh god," Rose said. "What?" Mark asked. "I found flower petals leading to the river the next day, but Jason must have covered them up."

"He's good at that," Daisy said, making you believe you're crazy when you're not."

"How did you get away from him?" Violet asked.

"I didn't," Daisy said simply, "Jason dumped me into the water and I was so out of it I couldn't move, it was Mrs. Waters who saved me. She got me out of the water and helped me to her car, we drove to Mrs. Lion and she stayed with me until a doctor got there and paid them off to keep quiet."

Violet felt the surprise go through the room and she couldn't help look across to Rose, who looked as if someone had poured Ice water on her. "My mother saved you?" Rose asked her voice cracking like an iced over river.

"Yes, she knew about me and the baby and got to me before it was too late."

"Why didn't they just turn him in?" Violet asked, "If he's really that dangerous."

Daisy looked over at Rose who had her eyes downcast as she looked at Emily, "Because my family will do anything to keep their names clean," Rose said.

"I have a question," Lily said and they all looked over to her, "Who was the body we found and why pay people to confess to killing you If that was never part of the plan?"

"That wasn't Mr. Waters," Daisy said, "The only thing Mr. Water did was pay to have my dental record changed and he didn't have a choice with who's it was, and for this apartment."

"Oh fuck," Rose said her eyes widening.

"What's wrong?" Violet asked she could feel her heart start pounding faster as she looked across to Rose who stood up looking panicked, "It was Jason this whole time."

"That's what I was saying," Daisy said confused just as much as the rest of them.

"We need to get out of here right now!" Rose said as she started for the door. "Whoa, Whoa Rosey what's wrong, " Mark said getting up and grabbed her arm to stop her. "It's not safe here anymore and it's my fault," Rose said, then looked behind her at Daisy, "Do you have a baby carrier for Emily?"

"I do, but Rose why are we in danger?" Daisy asked still confused.

"When I was at the bank today Jason came in when I was talking to my father, I believed then that my father was holding you somewhere, so I told Jason you were still alive and that our father was hiding it," Rose said clearly mad at herself. "Father started acting weird and I should have seen why, he was just trying to protect me from the real threat."

"But Rose he can't find us," Lily said.

"Daisy said my father was paying for this apartment meaning he most likely hid the records for them somewhere in the bank," Rose said her voice hollow and Violet felt cold go through her blood at that.

"Do you think he could have found them so quickly?" Mark asked. "He's been working there since he was a teenager, of course he knows where my father hides the things he wants no one to find," Rose answered.

"Well shit," Daisy said slowly, her face growing paler, looking just as scared as Violet felt.

For a moment they sat there trying to understand where in their lives they had gone wrong to end up here, then Mark stood taking command. "Let's start moving, if he started looking right after we left he wouldn't be that far behind us."

They stood at his words and started grabbing their things as fast as they could. "I can go and start the truck up so we can leave right away," Lily said and Violet looked up at her, fear going through her whole body making her chest hurt but she didn't know why as she reached into her jean's pocket and pulled out the key's handing them to her.

"Be careful okay," Violet said low as Lily passed by her. "I always am," Lily said as she opened the door and disappeared.

"I'm sorry," Rose said, "This is all my fault."

"Don't blame yourself," Violet said, as she moved to take Emily and handed her to Daisy who wrapped her in a blanket quickly, "This is no one's fault but the people who wanted to keep this all quiet and hide it because they were willing to let others hurt to keep their names clean."

Rose nodded understanding her words far too well than anyone should. "Ready to go?" Mark asked looking around at them all, his hand on the door handle.

"We're ready," Daisy said and Mark nodded as he started to open the door but before he could it burst open knocking him back.

Violet couldn't help a gasp as they all took a step back as Lily slammed the door close, leading against it as she tried to catch her breath. Violet felt her heart stop at the look of fear on Lily's face as she looked up at them all.

"What's happened?" Violet asked worry clear in her voice as she went over to Lily and took her face into the palms of her shaking hands so she could look into her coffee brown eyes.

"I-it's too late, Jason's already here," Lily said trying to catch her breath. Violet felt her eyes go wide as she looked over at everyone, her heart pounding in her ears so loud she almost didn't hear Mark's next words.

"Did he see you?"

Lily shook her head in reply, "No I was just stepping out of the elevator when I saw him pull up a little way down the street."

"Okay, so we need another way out then," Mark said looking at Daisy who nodded, "There's a fire escape outside of that window," Daisy said pointing to the window by the loveseat she and Lily had sat in before.

"Good, get it open and get out I'll go last," Mark said. "Why can't you just arrest him?" Violet asked as she took Emily from Daisy as she started to open up the window.

"Because he most likely has Mr. Waters gun, like Rose said it was gone and I can't risk confronting him and any of you being hurt, it's better to get as far away from this place as possible for now until I have back up," Mark answered and Violet couldn't argue with that so she nodded and watched as Rose and Daisy worked together finally getting the window open, the cold wet night air making goosebumps run down her arm.

"You go first, then I'll hand you Emily," Rose said as Daisy started out of the window but stopped suddenly one leg still inside as a soft knock rang through the room from the door sending fear running through Violet's veins like ice, freezing her in place.

"Daisy I know you're in there so why don't you open this door and we can talk a little," Jason said and even though his words were muffled by the door Violet noted how wrong he sounded and she wondered if he had always been like this and simply hid it from everyone or if people didn't want to believe that boy with a kind smile could be a sociopath.

"Keep going," Mark whispered as he grabbed Lily and pulled her away from the door where she had stood frozen and guided her into Violet's arms, then pulled out his gun and pointed it at the door as Jason spoke once again.

"You know I have to thank you Rosey, I would never have found out where Daisy was, I mean I figured it wasn't her body found at the river bank but after you confirmed it, it was easy to find father's record's hidden away."

After a moment of silence as Violet helped Lily out of the window, Rose and Daisy already out and holding onto Emily and couldn't help but jump as Jason banged on the door, so hard it sounded like it could break any second.

"Come on now don't make me break this damned thing!" Jason shouted. The pounding getting even harder matching her heart beats as her turn came to slide out of the window and into the rainy night, lightning crossing the sky as Mark backed up slowly as the sound of wood cracking came from the door.

"Mark hurry," Rose said her voice sounding as if it was on the edge of tears. Mark looked back at them then at the door as the frame cracked inwards. "Hell," Mark hissed as he dropped his arms that were holding the gun and ducked through the window.

Violet ran forward with Lily and slammed it shut just as the front door burst, but Violet didn't look back as she grabbed Lily's hand starting down the winding staircase. The sound of metal creaking and rain that soaked them all around them as they ran passed windows of people who had no idea what was happening to them, the fact that they could have a murderer after them never known. And in that second as they reached the muddy ground Violet found it almost funny how easy it was for people to simply be looking the other way as people were hurt all around them.

"Violet catch!" Lily shouted as she threw the keys. Violet caught them and was just about to open the door when her foot connected with something that made her heart drop to the bottom of her stomach. "No," Violet breathed as she knelt in a puddle and felt the flatten tire that Jason must have slashed open, she moved over to next and found the same on the back one as well. "Shit."

"What's wrong?" Rose asked standing next to her. Violet stood slowly than, on shaking legs and turned to her every ounce of warmth leaving her body cold as she looked into Rose's eyes, "We're not going anywhere."

***

Lily

"What do you mean?" Lily asked her voice coming out high as she joined Rose and Daisy next to Violet who was shaking now.

"The tires have been slashed, the trucks not going anywhere," Violet said fear clear in her voice.

"What do we do then?" Lily asked turning to Mark, but he looked just as unsure as they all did his eyes trained on the front door as his hair dripped rain water.

"We need to run," Rose said sounding sure, "If we go through the trees over there I remember seeing a police station a few miles away."

"But how can we be sure," Violet asked. "We can't," Daisy said her eyes wide, "But we're out of time to talk, look!"

They all turned to look where she was looking and saw the elevator doors open and Jason stepped out.

"Damn it," Mark hissed as he looked towards the thick tree line that sat a little ways from the building then at his gun biting his lip, but his jaw set then and nodded making up his mind.

"Start running, I'll stay here and cover you," Mark said. "No!" Rose said, "I'm not leaving you here!"

"I'll be fine," Mark said trying to sound reassuring, "Now go!"

Lily looked at Rose who looked about ready to cry either at the thought of Mark shooting her brother or

Mark being hurt, maybe both. But she started to back away with Daisy and Violet as they took off.

"Follow after them," Mark said not taking his eyes off the doors as Jason stepped outside a wicked smile across his face, as if this was a game he knew he could win.

"Can you really do it, shoot him I mean?" Lily asked quickly. "We'll find out won't we," Mark said as Jason stopped a few feet away from him.

Lily backed away and took off as the two faced one another but still heard their words as it carried in the rainy wind. "You know they can run and hide but it won't make any difference, and do you really think you can kill me, Mark we've been friends for so long now."

"Go fuck yourself!" Mark said.

Their words were cut off then as Lily made it to the tree line and met up with Rose, Violet, and Daisy who was waiting there for her, Emily seeming to somehow be asleep in her mother's arms.

"What's happening?" Rose asked her eyes almost black in the dark as she grabbed Lily's upper arms. "Mark is talking with Jason," Lily answered turning around to see if she could make them out but the dark made it impossible to see anything.

"Should we wait here for Mark?" Violet asked. "No, I think we need to get to the road and find that police station as soon as we can," Lily said and grabbed Rose's hand and pulled her forward.

"But what if Mark needs help, Rose said, "Because I won't put anything against Jason now."

"Mark will be fine," Daisy said as they started walking through the trees, branches breaking under them. "Plus he's the one with the gun," Lily said and as if god had heard her words a gunshot rang out through the air stopping them dead in place as lightning lit the sky with the crack of thunder.

"No," Rose cried out and turned back ready to run back but Lily grabbed her and slammed her back into a tree. "What the hell are you thinking! " Lily hissed, rain making her hair stick to her forehead, "You can't just run out there, we need to wait for Mark's say so to make sure everything's safe."

After a moment Rose nodded and moved to hide behind one of the other large trees as Violet and Daisy did the same. They waited there for what felt like days in the silents, the only sound being the rustle of the wind through the trees, thunder in the distance and her own heart pounding faster and faster the longer they stood there.

Then like a blessing, footsteps approach them, Lily was about to step out but stopped her blood freezing as Jason spoke. "You know I've never used a gun before, but it's surprisingly easy when it comes down to it, just pull the trigger and bang you're dead."

Lily covered her mouth to keep from crying out as she looked across to Rose who had fallen down to her knees the glint of tears on her cheeks mixed with rain.

"So Daisy if I were you I would just come out, so I don't have to shoot anyone else tonight," Jason shouted but Lily was surprised to hear it sounded further away now. She turned to look at Violet who looked panicked but her eyes were clear as she looked up and met Lily's.

Lily tipped her head towards the way they were walking before and hoped she understood as she moved as quickly as she could to Rose and knelt next to her.

"Rosey we need to go now," Lily whispered and helped her stand. "He's dead isn't he?" Rose choked out looking up at her.

Lily wouldn't say no, she couldn't lie and tell her Mark would be fine because Jason had the gun and that really meant only one thing she could think of. "Let's go," Lily said taking Rose's arm and helped her walk.

They moved as quietly as they could through the trees until they finally saw a street a little ways off. "Thank god," Lily whispered as she moved forward and stepped on a branch. It was something out of a horror movie with how loud it was in the quiet, but for a moment Lily believed it had simply been in her head, of course, luck wasn't on their side tonight.

Emily's cry sounded like a death sentence at that moment as they looked at one another, fear going through all of them and without a word they took off running for the street giving up on being quiet.

The trees were a dark blur as they ran pass them, the lower branches whipping at their arms and faces as they tried not to fall on the uneven ground, the road getting closer and closer as Rose and Daisy ran ahead, Violet a few feet ahead of her as she ran in the back.

Then the sound of footsteps behind them made Lily look back which was a mistake because the sight of Jason right on her heels made her lose her footing, then the next thing she knew was the feeling of the ground, the impact knocking the breath out of her.

Lily reached out a hand trying to get to her feet as she watched her friends turn around and call out her name, but it was too late as Jason grabbed her hair and pulled her bodliy up by it, ripping a scream from her already pained lungs.

"You know you'll never be as fast as Rosey but nice try," Jason hissed into her ear as he placed the barrel of the gun under her chin tipping her face up so she was looking into his dark eyes.

"Go screw yourself," Lily said her voice rough as sandpaper. "Cute," Jason said, "I always liked your will power Lily, but unless you want a bullet through your skull start walking forward."

Lily sucked in a breath the gun cold against her skin as she started walking and saw her friends eyes widen as they backed away from him, but refused to leave her and it was that which made her heart break, because as much as she wanted to scream at them to run and leave her, there was a smaller part that was happy she wasn't alone.

They walked until they stood in the middle of the road, not a car for miles and Lily didn't know if she should be grateful that she wouldn't be hit or sad because she would most likely die from a gunshot instead.

"Where's Mark!" Rose shouted, her skin so pale in almost glowed in the lightning. "Dead hopefully, after I grabbed the gun I didn't stay to watch him bleed out," Jason said sounding bored.

Rose shook her head not understanding, "He was your best friend how could you, how could you do any of this?"

"How? Oh, Rosey you don't understand anything because you don't even know the half of it. Mother and father have kept you so innocent to the point of stupidity," Jason said, and Lily could almost hear the eye roll in his voice.

"Then tell me," Rose said unshed tears in her eyes, "How much of all of this are you responsible for?"

Jason let out a breathy laugh at her words, "All of it, I only fucked Daisy because I was bored, but then she had to go and get herself knocked up with my kid which was her first mistake, I already killed once because she wanted more than I was ready for," Jason said and Lily felt her legs go weak.

"Linda Ross," Daisy whispered from where she stood behind Violet Emily moving it her arms. "That's right," Jason said as if he was proud, "I killed her the same way I almost killed Daisy, but she stayed dead and that's your second mistake."

"Mother and father knew didn't they?" Rose asked and Lily felt Jason nod, the gun slipping down to rest against her neck. "They had a feeling after Linda's parents started calling and told them she had come down to visit me, but what were they going to do? Throw their son to the dogs and worse have their names in the paper with a murderer?"

Jason laughed at his own words, "No they paid off her roommate at college to tell them Linda had run away to canada for another boy after breaking up with me, It's amazing what money can buy you," Jason answered.

"They kept you on a short leash after that," Lily said hate in her voice.

Jason shrugged, "They wouldn't give me as much money to live on after and made sure to check up on me, but then they had bigger things to worry about, right Rosey?"

Rose didn't take the bait as she went on, "You paid off the dentist to switch the record's so everyone believed it was Daisy's body found and the men to confess to killing her."

"Of course," Jason said, "I told you this is all me."

"Why pay them to confess though? " Violet asked, "It didn't help you in any way."

"To be honest it was fun just watching everyone lose their minds, and it kept the police off of me as I tried to figure out if Daisy was really alive or not and here we are."

"I don't know why you think you're so smart," Rose said, "You've been caught and will go to jail for the rest of your life."

"Is that what you think?" Jason asked and Lily felt the cold metal of the gun leave her as he pointed it at Rose. But she didn't even blink twice at it, Lily could feel the anger going through him and Lily understood then. Jason got high off their fear so if they didn't show it there was no fun to have.

"I'm going to kill you one by one until only Daisy is left and then I'll put a bullet through her baby's head that she threw her life away for," Jason shouted making Lily jumped. But the sound of a car getting closer sent a wave of fear through her, being killed by a hit and run was one of the too real possibilities at that moment.

"Then shoot me," Rose said steel in her voice, "End me and let's see if mother and father will still stand by you."

Headlights got closer and closer as Jason's breath became heavier with fury. "You think I won't do it!" Jason shouted as he pushed Lily to the ground the impact hard to her already bruised body.

"Lily!" Violet and Daisy cried out as they raced to her side, Violet knelt down and helped her sit up, but Lily couldn't look away from where Jason was pressing the barrel of the gun to Rose's forehead.

Rose stared into her brothers eyes as if she was trying to read something that wasn't there. "What are you waiting for?" Rose asked her voice so low it was hard to hear over the squeaking brakes of the car that stopped behind them, headlights lighting everything up to the point it hurt.

"Aren't you scared?" Jason asked. Rose looked away from him then and for a moment Lily believed it was at them, but Rose's eyes were trained on the car behind them as she spoke. "No, but if you really love me, pull the trigger and this hell."

"Famous last words," Jason said and as if in slow motion Lily watched him pull the trigger.

CHAPTER 16

Lily

The bang echoed through the air like thunder as they all screamed out as they stared in horror at Rose's body hitting the ground. Jason took a step back and started to turn around but his footsteps were uneven and as he turned the light caught on his chest, showing the blood that bloomed across his white dress shirt from the bullet hole going through his heart.

Lily let out a gasp as Jason looked down at his own blood for a long second, pain in his eyes before falling to the ground in a lump and stayed there unmoving.

"Rosalina!" Someone shouted from behind them and ran past, Lily felt her eyes go wide at the sight of Mrs. Waters, gun in hand as she went to her knees next to her daughter.

Without thinking Lily got up, barely feeling the pain in her ribs as she ran to where Mrs. Waters was hugging Rose to her chest, tears dripping from her cheeks matching the ones falling from Rose's own as rain soaked them.

"I had to do it, I had too," Mrs. Waters repeated over and over again, her body shaking.

"I know mom, it's the best way out for him, he can't hurt anyone now," Rose said her words choked and opened her eyes to look at her friends then her eyes went wide as she looked at something behind them.

Lily turned on her heel and found Mark standing there, looking out of it as he pressed a hand against his right side blood dripping through his too pale fingers. "Looks like I missed the party then," Mark said looking around then stopped next to Jason's body.

"Your shot," Daisy said, "You need to lay down and keep pressure on your wound until we can call the police."

"I'm fine, and I already called the police from a payphone," Mark said kneeling next to Jason's head and pressed two fingers to his neck. For a beat no one moved then Mark closed his eyes, "He's gone."

"Are you sure?" Rose asked and Lily couldn't tell if it was relief or pain in her voice

"Yes," Mark said finally looking over at Rose and Mrs. Waters who nodded.

Rose peeled herself from her mother and crawled over to Mark and cupped his cheeks in her hands, "I thought you were dead," Rose sobbed. Mark leaned into her hands and it looked like he was having a hard time staying awake. "The bastard tried his hardest, after Lily ran he went for the gun and we struggled for it, then it went off and got me in the side, but I'm not one to die so easily. So I guess you're still stuck with me."

Rose let out a choked laugh as she pulled him into a hug his body going limp as unconsciousness took him, the sound of sirens getting closer.

Lily looked at Violet and took her hand into her own, "It's over."

***

Rose

Rose opened her eyes to find the sun up and ready for the day unlike herself. She let out a long breath as she sat up in the uncomfortable chair and found Mark smiling at her. "Why are you so happy?" Rose asked blinking the sleep away.

"You're cute when you're asleep you know that?" Mark said from his place in the hospital bed, his eyes tired but to her, they were the most beautiful things she had ever seen in all of her life because for the last four days they had been closed and the doctors weren't sure they would open again after his surgery.

"How the tables have turned, from me wanting nothing more than to sit by your bed to you sitting by mine," Mark said taking her hand. "How long have you been sleeping by my bed?"

"Since the moment they let visitors in, to closing time," Rose answered squeezing his hand.

They sat there a moment in comfortable silence enjoying simply being with one another until Mark spoke. "So... I heard the nurses talking earlier, it's his funeral today isn't it?"

Rose looked down and nodded, her eyes dark, "It's this afternoon, I actually have to go soon to meet Violet and Lily were going together."

"I wish I could be there for you," Mark said squeezing her hand back, "But at the moment I'm on so many pain killers I can barely think."

"I know that feeling far too well," Rose answered and Mark raised an eyebrow at her. "Are you back on your antipsychotics?" Mark asked.

"Started them a few days ago," Rose answered and Mark was surprised to see her smiling.

"They've actually been working pretty well, no more Daisy, no more blood."

"You know I would be with you no matter what right? Pills or no pills you're still my Rose, and I'll help you through anything."

Rose raised his hand to her lips and kissed his knuckles slowly, "And that's why you're my boyfriend, I mean if that's what you want to be of course..." Rose said trailing off her cheeks turning pink as she looked away, but Mark just smiled.

"Of course, it's like a dream come true, to be honest, I've had a thing for you since we were kids. But you don't mind dating an older man?"

Rose rolled her eyes, "Your only four years older than me, that's nothing."

"Until your father finds out that is," Mark said with a smirk. "My parents have no say in what I can do and what I can't...After what they knew about Jason and did nothing leading to all of this," Rose said, "Their lucky I haven't gone to the police myself, but Daisy would be hurt more than them."

"Maybe that's why they were so controlling," Mark said, "It was too late for him, he was too far gone. But they made sure to get you to doctors and on antipsychotics even if it was in their own messed up way after they found out."

Rose bit her lip and nodded, "Maybe, but it's going to take me a long time to forgive them."

"And that's fine, you can take however long you need, after all, you'll have me and your friends."

Rose leaned in placing a kiss to his cheek and whispered, "Thank you, you'll never know how much that means to me."

She pulled away and stood then, grabbing her backpack from where it sat on the back of the chair. "Where are you going?" Mark asked his words filled with sleep from the painkillers bringing him back under.

"Lily and Violet will be waiting for me downstairs, but I'll come back tomorrow morning okay,"

Mark tried nodding but he was already asleep. Rose couldn't stop the little smile that formed on her lips as she looked at him, peacefully asleep, but it died a moment later as she turned for the door and walked through the halls.

Today would be the final step out of hell and into something new but it was one of the hardest steps to take, but she guessed the end chapter of any story was the hardest part.

She stepped out into the sunny day, the spring air feeling warmer and warmer as summer got closer to them.

"Rose over here."

Rose turned at the sound of her name and saw baby blue sitting at the sidewalk, Lily leaning out as her hair blew around her face.

Rose walked over quickly and leaned into the window and found her friends already in the same outfits as Daisy's funeral, the only person wearing something different was herself.

The day after everything had happened and the nurses kicked her out from trying to see Mark she had gone to a store and gotten everything she had once wanted, putting it on her parent's credit. They had said nothing to her when she had brought the bags upstairs and went through all of the outdated dresses and heels bringing them to a goodwill and happily donated them all.

She now wore a long black skirt and matching v neck, her shoes flat and hair up in a simple ponytail. "Ready to go?" Violet asked and Rose noticed that she looked better then she had seen her in years, no dark bruises or cuts across her body.

Even Lily looked better somehow, and then it hit Rose that she hadn't seen her smoke a cigarette for a while now. Not since Violet had moved in with her after getting her things from Violet's father who had agreed to start looking into Alcoholics Anonymous meetings, though no one was hopeful, he had far more problems he had to face.

"Just ready to have this nightmare over," Rose said as she hopped into the back as Violet started the engine.

* * *

Violet

Violet watched as they lowered the sleek black coffin into the cold ground for what was far too many times in her short lifetime. She looked up then and looked around herself, everyone but Lily, Rose and herself had tears dripping down their faces.

After all, Jason had been liked by almost everyone he met, and Violet wondered what they would think of him if they knew what he had done. Even the Waters had tears in their eyes, maybe they believed they failed him when all they wanted to do was protect the angel they had made. But they had failed to understand that too many monsters wore the faces of angels.

She stepped away then Rose and Lily following silently as they made their way through the graveyard, knowing no one would notice them missing far too caught up in the gossip of why they were there in the first place. They came to a stop as they reached a small pond, willow trees all around them blowing in the breeze and under them a woman sat on a bench, a baby sleeping in her arms as she looked out across the still water.

"How are you Daisy?" Rose asked sitting down next to her. "Fine as you can be as the man who fathered your child and wanted to kill you is buried."

"Are you sure you still want to do this?" Lily asked crossing her arms, "You can still come back."

Daisy shook her head, "You know my answer by now Lily, I died. My parents are starting over with a new family and have closure for me even if it's false. I can't ruin that for them, and to be honest I don't know if I can go back to living that life anyway, I'm going to be moving to Virginia and starting a new life."

They nodded, then Rose picked up her bag and took out a jacket. They all looked down at it as she slowly unwrapped it to reveal a gun, blood on the ivory handle.

"You know the story of Jason's death right?" Rose asked looking down at it, "We called Jason after we found that Violet's tires were slashed when we got back from helping clear up Mrs. Lion's belongings. Jason had been with my mother and Mark at the time catching up and decided to come with just in case. When they got there they found us cornered on the road by muggers after we ran from them. Mark went after them with his gun but in a struggle was shot and in an effort to save his best friend Jason fought them off until they took off but was fatally shot in the process," Rose finished looking up and threw the gun into the calm water, the ripples fanning out across the pond.

Violet felt bitterness go through her at the idea of Jason being a hero but it was better than Mrs. Waters going to jail for killing her own son. "Me and Lily tried finding Linda Ross's parents, but it looks like they both died in a plane crash a year ago and she had no other family," Violet said.

Rose closed her eyes pain crossing her face, "Is it really right to keep letting everyone believe it's Daisy?"

"None of this is truly okay," Lily said, "But in the end there's nothing else we can do unless we want more people to hurt because of one person's actions, I think this is the best ending we could have hoped for, after all, no one likes to believe angels want to set the world on fire."

"Even those boys who confessed to killing Daisy will get out of jail next month," Violet said.

Rose looked over at Violet who was looking at Lily in turn. "What do we do now?"

"Live as normally as we can," Lily said with a laugh, "Live like everyday could be our last."

Rose rolled her eyes but couldn't help a smile then reached into her bag and pulled out a golden bracelet and looked at Daisy.

"My mother gave this to me to give back to you, she grabbed it when she found my father's gun when she went to his office to ask about me."

Daisy took it and looked down as she spoke, "Why did she take the gun in the first place?"

Rose took a deep breath looking at the water, "My parents had been scared of Jason for a long time now, my father got it after Jason killed Linda Ross and when I went missing my mother took it just in case."

"How did she know where we were?" Lily asked.

"My mother knew about Daisy, she was the one who lost the letter and when she noticed it gone started driving for the apartment. It was just luck that she got to us when she did," Rose answered.

"That reminds me," Daisy said getting up and grabbed three Daisie crown's and handed them out. "I'm not sure we'll see each other again but I hope you all find happiness wherever life may take you all."

Violet looked down at the small white flowers made into a ring and brushed a finger down the soft petals. When she looked back up she found Daisy walking away from them, Emily sound asleep. "You know we're not the same people we once were three months ago," Violet said looking at her friends, "I think it's time for Daisy chains to be in the past as well."

With one swift motion, Violet threw the flowers as hard as she could. For a moment it stayed there on the top floating in the sunlight then slowly sunk under the clear blue water and out of sight, Rose and Lily following after.

They stood there a moment unsure what was going to happen to them in the future, sure they would finish high school but where would they go afterwards?

Violet guessed that was the only sure thing in life, that you simply couldn't know where it was going to take you or who you would end up with.

"Ready to go?" Rose asked. "Ready," Lily and Violet said in unison. They turned away then Lily's hand in her own as Rose walked ahead of them, footsteps lighter then they had been in a long time. Violet thought about turning back once, but she was tired of living in the past, everything in it was done and over. Instead, she turned to her friends and smiled knowing the only thing they had was the future.

Arthur: Shadow of a God
By Richard Denham

King Arthur has fascinated the Western world for over a thousand years and yet we still know nothing more about him now than we did then. Layer upon layer of heroics and exploits has been piled upon him to the point where history, legend and myth have become hopelessly entangled.

In recent years, there has been a sort of scholarly consensus that 'the once and future king' was clearly some sort of Romano-British warlord, heroically stemming the tide of wave after wave of Saxon invaders after the end of Roman rule. But surprisingly, and no matter how much we enjoy this narrative, there is actually next-to-nothing solid to support this theory except the wishful thinking of understandably bitter contemporaries. The sources and scholarship used to support the 'real Arthur' are as much tentative guesswork and pushing 'evidence' to the extreme to fit in with this version as anything involving magic swords, wizards and dragons. Even Archaeology remains silent. Arthur is, and always has been, the square peg that refuses to fit neatly into the historians round hole.

Arthur: Shadow of a God gives a fascinating overview of Britain's lost hero and casts a light over an often-overlooked and somewhat inconvenient truth; Arthur was almost certainly not a man at all, but a god. He is linked inextricably to the world of Celtic folklore and Druidic traditions. Whereas tyrants like Nero and Caligula were men who fancied themselves gods; is it not possible that Arthur was a god we have turned into a man? Perhaps then there is a truth here. Arthur, 'The King under the Mountain'; sleeping until his return will never return, after all, because he doesn't need to. Arthur the god never left in the first place and remains as popular today as he ever was. His legend echoes in stories, films and games that are every bit as imaginative and fanciful as that which the minds of talented bards such as Taliesin and Aneirin came up with when the mists of the 'dark ages' still swirled over Britain – and perhaps that is a good thing after all, most at home in the imaginations of children and adults alike – being the Arthur his believers want him to be.

A Storm of Magic
By Ashley Laino

Being brought back from the dead is an impressive trick, even for magician Darien Burron. Now he must try and use his sleight of hand to swindle modern-day witch, Mirah, to sign her power away, or end up a tormented demon in the afterlife.

Meanwhile, sixteen-year-old Mirah is starting to lose control of her powers. After an incident at her aunt's Witchery store, Mirah is sent to a secret coven to learn to control her abilities. While away, Mirah meets up with a soft-spoken clairvoyant, a brazen storm witch, and the creator of dark magic itself. The young woman must learn to trust in herself before she loses herself entirely to the darkness that hunts her.

Weirder War Two
By Richard Denham & Michael Jecks

Did a Warner Bros. cartoon prophesize the use of the atom bomb? Did the Allies really plan to use stink bombs on the enemy? Why did the Nazis make their own version of Titanic and why were polar bear photographs appearing throughout Europe?

The Second World War was the bloodiest of all wars. Mass armies of men trudged, flew or rode from battlefields as far away as North Africa to central Europe, from India to Burma, from the Philippines to the borders of Japan. It saw the first aircraft carrier sea battle, and the indiscriminate use of terror against civilian populations in ways not seen since the Thirty Years War. Nuclear and incendiary bombs erased entire cities. V weapons brought new horror from the skies: the V1 with their hideous grumbling engines, the V2 with sudden, unexpected death. People were systematically starved: in Britain food had to be rationed because of the stranglehold of U-Boats, while in Holland the German blockage of food and fuel saw 30,000 die of starvation in the winter of 1944/5. It was a catastrophe for millions.

At a time of such enormous crisis, scientists sought ever more inventive weapons, or devices to help halt the war.

Civilians were involved as never before, with women taking up new trades, proving themselves as capable as their male predecessors whether in the factories or the fields.

The stories in this book are of courage, of ingenuity, of hilarity in some cases, or of great sadness, but they are all thought-provoking - and rather weird. So whether you are interested in the last Polish cavalry charge, the Blackout Ripper, Dada, or Ghandi's attempt to stop the bloodshed, welcome to the Weirder War Two!

Click Bait
By Gillian Philip

A funny joke's a funny joke. Eddie Doolan doesn't think twice about adapting it to fit a tragic local news story and posting it on social media.

It's less of a joke when his drunken post goes viral. It stops being funny altogether when Eddie ends up jobless, friendless and ostracised by the whole town of Langburn. This isn't how he wanted to achieve fame.

Under siege from the press, and facing charges not just for the joke but for a history of abusive behaviour on the internet, Eddie grows increasingly paranoid and desperate. The only people still speaking to him are Crow, a neglected kid who relies on Eddie for food and company, and Sid, the local gamekeeper's granddaughter. It's Sid who offers Eddie a refuge and an understanding ear.

But she also offers him an illegal shotgun - and as Eddie's life spirals downwards, and his efforts at redemption are thwarted at every turn, the gun starts to look like the answer to all his problems.

Burning Bridges
By Chris Bedell

They've always said that three's a crowd...

24-year-old Sasha didn't anticipate her identical twin Riley killing herself upon their reconciliation after years of estrangement. But Sasha senses an opportunity and assumes Riley's identity so she can escape her old life.

Playing Riley isn't without complications, though. Riley's had a strained relationship with her wife and stepson so Sasha must do whatever she can to make her newfound family love and accept her. If Sasha's arrangement ends, then she'll have nothing protecting her from her past. However, when one of Sasha's former clients tracks her down, Sasha must choose between her new life and the only person who cared about her.

But things are about to become even more complicated, as a third sister, Katrina, enters the scene...

Father of Storms
By Dean Jones

Imagine losing everything you loved as well as the future you'd wished for so long to come true.

Seth was born with the gift to manipulate energy, unfortunately his skills mark him as a target for one who wishes to control everything. So began a life running from those who would seek to command him, a life that spans over a thousand years waiting for the day when all will be once again as it was.

Captured in modern day London, Seth needs the help of his companions, the Mara, to show him who he is through dreams of his past, so he can save the family he has waited so long to have. A warrior bred for battle must fight once more but this time the battlefield is his mind. Can Seth win, or will he finally lose who he is and become the weapon of the man who started his nightmare all those years ago? *Father of Storms* is a story told through time, a tale of love and hope where there seems to be none and above all it is a reminder that if you believe, truly believe then even from the darkest places, good things come to those who wait.

www.blkdogpublishing.com